Sinister Creation

By

John Daniels

This Terrifying Novel
Is a Sequel to
'Wolves
The Next Generation'

This Book Is
Dedicated
To
All Those I Love
You Know Who You Are

Prelude to Disaster

How it all began:
A brilliant scientist discovers a method of isolating and strengthening gene cells in such a way to enhance many biological characteristics and behaviors in living creatures. This ingenious break-through took genetic engineering and gene-splicing to new heights. Unfortunately, the gene-enhancing process got out-of-hand resulting in a world-wide calamity.

Zoltan Proziver was a gifted scientist far ahead of his time in the field of genetics. While living in the wilds of Africa he devised a procedure for not only identifying immune cells in primates but isolating and manipulating those cells in such a way that he could strengthen the immune system in various species of monkeys. The result of exhausting and seemingly endless attempts at perfecting the procedure finally paid off with many cages at his compound housing the healthiest and most disease resistant group of primates ever tested. He was beside himself with pride of accomplishment; when revealed, his revolutionary findings would stun the scientific world. He was elated as he visualized how the offshoots of these first experiments would open up a new science that could rid the world of many maladies that affected both the animal kingdom and man himself. His mind was full of the many contributions and benefits to mankind this incredible breakthrough would provide when disaster struck. As a result of a political uprising, his compound was attacked, killing, or releasing his test animals and burning most of his records. He was devastated!

Because of the raging conflict erupting throughout the country, he was forced to leave. He ended up back in the United States where he was contracted by the government and sent to Fairbanks Alaska to head up a team of scientists to further develop his gene-splicing program with the goal of improving the immune system in wolves.

Within a short time of the program's launch, Zoltan's genius came through when he successfully perfected a method of clustering immune cells into incredibly strong 'super-cells'. The scientific community was astonished when they learned that the strong immunity of the small animals being tested became a permanent inheritance gene that passed on to future generations with no noticeable weakening or adverse side-effects.

His experiments to-date were performed on small animals under laboratory controls but now it was time for the next step; to impregnate female wolves (a species of animal susceptible to contacting several life-threatening diseases) with powerful immune enhancing gene cells. He was certain that this new miracle gene altering procedure would accomplish his immediate goal of boosting wolf's immune systems and result in a healthier wolf population. Strengthening immune systems in all creatures, including humans, would be one of the biggest breakthroughs in scientific and medical history. The benefits seemed endless to him; however, health issues were not his only objectives. Genes controlled every trait and characteristic in all living creatures, and during the extensive testing that the scientists performed at the Fairbanks Wildlife Center laboratory, Zoltan's dream of discovering how to isolate other cells became a reality. Numerous samples of unidentified cell clusters were collected and an intense effort to determine their gene functions was put in place. Once he determined their purpose in the complex miracle of life, he would be able to alter and influence them in ways yet beyond his comprehensions. He envisaged that much good would come from his discoveries; and all of that good was waiting for him to unearth.

Zoltan's world was shattered when he learned he had incurable cancer and had but a short time to live. During the days prior to the transport of wolves from Alaska to Yellowstone National Park, he became paranoid and disillusioned and literally went insane. With the unwitting help of an Innuit Eskimo that worked at the Wildlife Center, the muddled and very ill scientist administered an unknown quantity of unidentified altered gene clusters into one of the female wolves destined to be released in Yellowstone.

In the highlands of Yellowstone's pristine wilderness, three pairs of wolves littered in the spring. Two of the litters of young whelps were normal and when tested for the immune gene that was administered to the mothers, biologists found that the strong strain of genes had passed through to all the young wolves.

However, shortly after the wolves were released, a young male and female wandered off to a remote corner of the park where the Cody Wildlife team who monitored all animals in the National Park, lost track of them. A large litter was born to these two run-away wolves, a litter of all black whelps that grew into huge terrorizing monsters that wreaked havoc throughout the northern Rocky Mountain states, killing any living creature they encountered, and that included humans.

An extensive hunt was organized to track-down and kill these monstrous animals but three of the demon wolves survived the efforts to exterminate them and fled north to settle in the wilds of Canada.

It began with a trapper in the northern wilderness of Alberta. An excitement filled the old woodsman as he approached a set that held a lynx firmly clamped in the jaws of a size 4 Blake and Lamb trap. It was not an everyday occurrence to catch a lynx; in fact, it was quite rare. As he approached the snarling spitting animal, he swung the basket off of his shoulders and set it down in the snow. He then laid his trusty 30.30 Marlin on the pack and as he straightened up a movement caught his eye. In that same instant the lynx lunged with all its weight and power against the chain in such a fury that it seemed for sure it would break free. But it was all-futile because the trap was built to withstand much more force than the cat could possibly generate. Standing no more than thirty feet away from the trapper was an animal that sent a fear running through his body. He knew it was a wolf, but it was like no wolf he had ever seen before. It was so huge he could not believe what he was looking at. With a trembling hand he grabbed for the rifle but before he could bring it up for action the wolf made its move. The trapper was dead in an instant and in the next, the lynx was crushed between the jaws of another wolf that came in behind the first.

It began with the trapper who disappeared in the remote forests of the Canadian wilderness. It did not, however, end there. This was only the beginning of a horrifying pandemic that would terrorize the world.

One
Frank Wallace

Yellowstone National Park is one of nature's most magnificent geological creations. Its vast diverse land area consists of unique geographic characteristics that have made it one of the most visited parks in the country. Rugged and lofty mountains, some of which reach skyward to heights exceeding 11,000 feet, surround a broad plateau located in the heart of this national wonder. From the high mountains, wooded ridges and spurs radiate down from all sides, adding even more character and charm to this beautiful basin. Immense forest wilderness' stretch for miles in all directions reaching out into Montana, Idaho, and Wyoming. Mixed conifer forests consisting of fir, spruce and pine dominate this pristine wild land but there are also great expanses of aspen trees with leaves that tremble in a breeze and blaze the landscape with brilliant golden hues when the chill of autumn touches their tender leaves. Birch with whitish bark streaked with horizontal black slashes and willows that thrive along the rivers and lower marshy areas also add natures touch to this glorious land. This large plateau that averages eight thousand feet in elevation is graced with lakes and rivers making it even more alluring. Some of the rivers glide lazily through grassy meadows while others cut their way through the park creating canyons that range from modest in size to immense.

Yellowstone is the setting where Frank Wallace and his wife Sarah were in the final stages of completing a filmed documentary sponsored by the National Geographic Society. The theme of the four-part series (that was scheduled to be aired on the Society's television channel in the spring) was the reintroduction of wolves into the eco-system of Yellowstone National Park and the interaction and impact that these predators have with the Parks wildlife population. They were also developing an article for the National Geographic Society magazine that would appear in a future issue.

In the early stages of planning the two-year project, even though the Society wanted to use their own professional photographers for the project,

Frank had convinced them to allow him to have control of the filming. He had worked with the Society several times in the past when he was Director of the Wildlife Management Center in Fairbanks, Alaska and the success of those programs had a great deal to do with their agreement. The plan and schedule that Frank and the Society agreed to was that he, his wife Sarah, Ray Douglas, (an employee of the Wildlife Center in Cody, Wyoming who was the division's pilot and photographer) and a local Cody professional photographer by the name of Doug Clemons, would be responsible for the filming. However, before the project began, the NGS insisted that they all attend a crash course in learning the latest wildlife videoing techniques and the use of various new cameras and photography equipment they would be using.

It had been an active and often exhausting two years for the four photographers, but their efforts were rewarded with a great deal of out-standing footage. Most of the filming was centered on four wolf packs that were thriving in the park as they went about their everyday doings and the strong bonds they developed within their strict social structure. The photographers spent much of the spring and summer months, videoing two litters of pups as they grew from small whelps just out of their dens and followed the progress they made as they grew into young adults. To give the documentary a complete portrayal of the fauna and flora of Yellowstone National Park, the team provided the editors of the project at the National Geographic Society's film studio with many videos of elk, deer, bears, bison, antelope, coyote, and a variety of small game and birds. Their filming included many incredible panoramic views of the landscape that the Park so magnificently displayed during the four seasons of the year. One segment of the project was devoted to the work being done in Yellowstone by the Cody, Wyoming Wildlife Center. Enough videos had been taken to complete an in-depth account of the team's projects and the biologists involved in managing the health and well-being of wolves and other animals in the park. High on the wildlife filming team's list was capturing footage of wolves on the hunt. Several times during the two years of filming their cameras caught a wolf pack as it chased and brought down, elk, moose, and deer. The best of those films was taken from a high ridge overlooking an open park where Frank had videoed the wolf pack he was following as they attacked a moose. To make this piece of video even more spectacular, in the mayhem of the battle, one of the wolves was killed by the hooves of the panicky animal as it thrashed out to protect itself. The footage was outstanding and would be one of the highlights of the documentary.

The editors had sifted through hundreds of hours of videos to put together a story line that would hopefully meet with their viewer's approval and were quite pleased with how the work was coming together. But they would like to have one more sequence of a wolf pack pursuing elk in the deep snow, something with pizzazz, something that would blow the socks off the public when they saw it.

Two years of filming by two professional photography teams had come up with a few videos of wolf packs chasing down and killing elk but the team had to agree with the editors, they were lacking a spectacular encounter between these two animals. But if they hadn't been able to film a quality attack during the many months that they pursued the wolf packs of Yellowstone, the chances were pretty slim that they could pull it off in the next month or so before they had to call it quits.

Frank and Sarah did most of their filming with two of the northern-most packs of wolves in the park. Concentrating their efforts closer to Montana where they lived saved time in traveling to and from the wolves' stamping grounds. They drove to the high plateau of Yellowstone most of the time, weather permitting, but also had the use of a helicopter owned and operated by the Montana Department of Forestry. For much of the winter, snow machines were the mode of travel through the deep snow that covered the land as they followed the wolf packs. One thing that Frank was thankful for was that the heavy and bulky camera equipment of the past had been replaced with smaller compact units easy to carry and much easier to use.

Ray Douglas and Doug Clemons on the other hand centered most of their efforts on wolves whose territories were located in the southern and central part of the park. The Cody, Wyoming Wildlife Center that was responsible for the safety and well-being of all animals in Yellowstone, owned a helicopter that was used quite extensively by the biologists and their support people for the work they performed in the park. Only when circumstances permitted was the chopper available for the National Geographic's filming project.

It was late December with a high-pressure system hanging over the Rocky Mountain West providing some of the best weather the high country had seen in the past two months. In what Frank thought of as a last-ditch effort to get footage that his editors desired, and wanting to take advantage of the good weather, he convinced Johnny Burwick, the manager of the Cody Wildlife Center, to let Ray use the chopper for at least a week, or until the weather broke forcing the aircraft down.

As Ray and Doug spent every hour possible in the air hoping to encounter wolves attacking elk, Frank was in the hired helicopter hoping for the same result with the pack of wolves he was monitoring. At dawn of the third day of the fine weather that was hovering over the park, Ray revved up the engine of the chopper as Doug completed his task of checking the cameras and loading the equipment needed for the day's work. The sky was clear, and the forecast promised more of the same for several days as he lifted off and headed for the park.

Ray located the wolf pack he planned on watching this day and kept his craft far behind them as they loped along in single file down a frozen and snow-covered river bottom. He had followed wolves many times during the past two years but only twice during that time was he lucky enough to witness an elk kill in an ideal location for filming. Unfortunately, the footage of those two encounters was not as good as he or the society would have liked. Doug was the one to spot a small band of elk about a quarter of a mile ahead of the wolves. The seven animals in the wolf pack were traveling into the breeze, as their kind almost always do when on the hunt so their sensitive noses could pick up scent of prey. Ray's job was to keep the helicopter running as smooth as possible and oriented so Doug could keep the camera directed on the targets. Doug occasionally adjusted the camera's telephoto lens to assure the best possible focus as he videoed both the strung-out line of wolves as they trudged through the deep snow covering the river bottom and the dozen or so elk idly feeding far down the valley. From their distant vantage point suspended above a heavily timbered ridge about halfway between the two groups of animals, the two experienced wolfers were not surprised when they saw the wolves stop and test the air when they were still several hundred yards from the elk, because they had often witnessed these animal's incredible ability to detect pray at extremely long distances.

Ray skillfully maneuvered his aircraft, holding it in the air as steady as if it was sitting firmly on the ground as Doug's camera followed the wolves as they stalked their prey. The camera swung from the approaching wolves to zero in on the elk just as they first discovered they were about to be attacked and then zoomed back to get the charging wolves in the frame. The small band of elk did what elk always do when being attacked by wolves, they panicked and scattered, spraying clouds of snow as they fled. In the chase that ensued, the lead wolf soon singled out a large cow and a spectacular scene unfolded. Even though most of the river was frozen solid, there was an open patch of steaming water where a geyser pumped hot water into the flowing river. The frightened cow with a wolf hanging onto her flank ran into the water but her retreat for safety was in vain. The water was less than three feet deep and with one wolf's powerful jaws firmly imbedded high on a hind leg, another wolf leaped from the icy edge of the open water and landed on her back sinking its fangs into her neck causing her to panic even more. She lunged out of the water to the far shore of the snow-covered bank of the river where she was met by more of the menacing wolves. The powerful cow weighing upwards of 450 pounds ran headlong into a cluster of willows causing the two animals to release their hold on her. Freed from her attackers she burst out of the thicket and dashed out into the open snow. Her fate was sealed as the predatory instincts of the pack were roused with the smell of blood in the air. She was soon surrounded by seven vicious predators all lunging at her from different sides. Within minutes the big cow elk was down in the deep snow with the ravenous pack mauling her twitching body. The entire episode was filmed from a distance of about four hundred yards, but the hi-tech camera had caught one of the most spectacular wolf attacks ever filmed.

After inspecting the video through the camera's viewfinder, Ray pointed the chopper towards Cody and home. He called Frank who was circling high above a pack of wolves far to the north and informed him of the excellent quality footage they caught on camera. When Ray said it was the best he has ever seen, Frank could not wait to see it.

The past two years had been especially busy ones for Frank and Sarah Wallace. Not only did they have to dedicate more than half of their time to the film project, which at times was a difficult and exhausting ordeal, they also had a cattle ranch to run. Plans to increase his herd size to three hundred head in the coming spring required a great deal more work as well. Especially the additional fencing needed to contain the additional animals. Frank had entered into a limited partnership with Elmer Horton; a cattleman who had built his herd to well over two thousand head and who also owned a feedlot operation.

At eight o'clock in the morning of January 12th, as Frank and Sarah were having coffee at the kitchen table, the phone rang. Sarah answered it and the familiar voice of Eric Tuttle said, "Sarah, that you?"

Sarah, always one to have a quick and sassy and sometimes even a little racy word for some of her closest friends, said. "Hi Eric, I can only guess that calling this early means it's something important and you don't have time to talk about the affair that we never had."

Eric, with a slight laugh said, "There's nothing more I would like to talk about, but that old man of yours might not take kindly to it. And as we know, he is at least twice as strong as me and I don't take kindly to a bruising. But yes, it is important, is he there?" From the tone and urgency of his voice she knew that something was bothering her old friend from Alaska.

"Eric." Frank said.

"I've got some more bad news about these damn wolves. Three more people in northern Alberta were killed by what was reported to be two huge wolves. The local game warden with several back-up rifles followed the tracks with snow machines and when they caught up to them there was a hell-of-a battle. They killed the wolves, and it apparently took a lot of lead to put them down, but before they did, two of the hunters in the party were ripped apart making it a total of five deaths. From what I hear, the wolves were so big and so savage that the two men were killed instantly. I have the report of what happened and photos of the dead wolves."

"Oh no!" Frank groaned. "How many deaths is that now, must be a few dozen in the past year or two!"

"More than that I'm afraid. But that's not all. The Canadian government is in an up-roar. They are jumping all over this. Not only the killings but they also want to take a closer look into the unusually high number of missing people that have been reported over the past couple of years. They think it's likely that some might be linked to our wolves."

Frank groaned. "Damn Erick, what a mess."

"Our friends from Canada contacted me yesterday afternoon. They are putting together a task force to look into these killer wolves and the disappearances. The public is beginning to panic, and they want to do something before this gets out of hand. They want someone from our country who is closely involved with these mutant wolves on the team, and I immediately thought of you."

Frank, feeling he had just had an enormous weight lifted from his shoulders with the completion of the National Geographic project was looking forward to getting back to fulltime ranch life. He did not want to get involved with anything that could lead into a major catastrophe, and he felt that's exactly what this would become. He let Eric know his feelings in a flurry that was unlike him. Even though Sarah did not know what the conversation was about, she knew from the expression on her husband face and the profanity he used, that he was very disturbed.

"This will most likely become a can of worms." Frank complained. "We know those damn wolves are spread out across northern Canada and it will be all but impossible to find them, let alone kill them all."

"I'm sure you're right but no one knows as much about wolves and especially these devils as you do, and I feel strongly that you should be involved."

"Shit," Was Frank's response. "I'm retired and don't need this."

"I know," Eric sympathized. "The Minister of Natural Resources would like my input by next Monday. Will you think about it?" Eric asked.

Frank thought for a moment before responding and then reluctantly said. "Yes, I'll think about it. It's possible that there's not as many of Zoltan's nightmares out there as we think there are. But who am I kidding? If the way they reproduced a few years ago here in Wyoming is any indication, there's likely more of them than anyone realizes." He then added. "Send me the report and photos."

Frank stood looking at the phone as Sarah put her hand on his shoulder. In a sympathetic voice she said, "Not again!"

There was just enough coffee in the pot for each of them to have half a cup. After pouring the black brew and lightening Sarah's with cream, they sat at the table. "There are a lot of people who throw some of the blame on me for the disaster we had with Zoltan's damn project. And I agree with them. I was in charge and should have kept tighter controls on everything going on at the time."

"Don't go blaming yourself. Will Hogan and Zoltan were the cause of all the problems. Will was so self-centered and egotistical he had to throw his weight around and overrule the cautions you wanted to put in place. Then Zoltan went crazy and sabotaged the program by pouring dozens of unknown genes into those wolves. None of this would have happened if they listened to you. And besides, you were the one who killed all the monsters."

"But I didn't kill them all, did I? It's been almost five years since the first devils were born. God knows how many are out there now. And yes, I think they are devils, devils right out of Hell."

"Eric's right." Sarah said. "You are the best person to help with this mess."

"I know." Frank sighed.

When Frank's call was answered on Monday morning, he recognized the familiar voice and said, "Hi Mandy its Frank." Mandy was the secretary at the Fairbanks Wildlife Management Center and had served him faithfully when he was the director of the operation.

"Hello Frank, it's good to hear from you. You must be calling about the fiasco going on around here."

"Yes, but before I get into that, how have you been?"

After a few niceties between the two friends, Mandy said." Eric is motioning for me to switch you over to him, so here he is."

Before Eric could ask him if he reached a decision, Frank said. "Yes, I'll do it."

When Frank ended his conversation with Eric, Sarah handed him another cup of coffee and they sat quietly at the table looking out the windows of the sliding glass doors watching two of their horses as they roamed around the snow-covered fenced field behind the house. Frank's mind drifted back to Fairbanks and how simple life seemed in those days. The Wildlife Management Center in Fairbanks was, and still is, acclaimed to be one of the best equipped and most efficient wildlife laboratories in the world. The team of scientists, biologists, and game management people that he worked with and the things they accomplished brought back fond memories. But oh, how much had happened since then and how long ago it seemed.

As Frank Wallace sat contemplating his future involvement with the Canadian team he was about to join, and the uncertainties of how it would unravel, he thought back to the days when he headed up a group of hunters to track down and kill the monsters that left a trail of slaughter and carnage in their path. The hunters finally caught up to them and when the last shot was fired, he had hoped beyond hope that they had killed every last one of the demon monsters. But he had been wrong.

Two
Canadian Taskforce

Friday morning, four days after Frank talked with the Canadian Minister of Natural Resources and agreed to join the committee being established to address the wolf problem that was panicking many citizens of Alberta and British Columbia, he arrived at the headquarters of the Department of Fish and Wildlife in Edmonton.

Six people were in attendance and as soon as all were seated, the moderator addressed the group. "I've known Frank Wallace for several years, but I don't believe anyone else here has met him before so let me introduce him to you. Doctor Wallace's dossier is quite impressive. He is retired and what I hear was somewhat reluctant to leave his ranch in Montana and join us here. But we are fortunate to have him. Frank was the Director of the Alaska Division of Wildlife for many years. He also served as U. S. Director of Wildlife in Washington and prior to his retirement he was the Director of the U. S. Department Fish and Wildlife; the equal to my position here in Canada! He is also one of the top authorities on wolves in the world. Welcome to Canada Frank."

As Bryce Mann stood before the small group wearing khaki pants and a sweatshirt with an Ottawa Senator's logo on the front, he appeared to be anything but the high-ranking leader of a large government agency. He was average height and weight with brown hair, dark eyes, and nondescript features. He could easily be mistaken for a carpenter, or plumber, or any other kind of blue-collar worker. But Frank knew that the impression he might give to those who first met him was nothing like who this man really was. As Director of the Canadian Fish and Wildlife Service he reported to Timothy Aston, Minister of Natural Resources and was highly respected and regarded as a strong leader with exceptional organizational skills. Frank smiled as he thought how impressions can be so misleading.

"Frank, let me introduce you to Torrance LaBlank." When Torrance stood and nodded her head to him, Frank, who had briefly spoken to her before the meeting convened, nodded back. She looked to be in her fifties and carried herself with dignity and grace but at the same time she appeared to be tough, as though she could take on the world and never lose any dispute or battle that she might encounter. There was no doubt in Frank's mind that here was a no-nonsense woman. "Tory works for the Director of the Environmental Protection Agency and has been involved in many field operations throughout her career. I'm sure some of you know of the great impact she has had on our country's environment. One of the reasons that the Minister has asked Mrs. LaBlank to join us on this committee is because of her ability to get things done in a fast and thorough manner. She will be wearing several hats on this taskforce. We all know how important tourism is to the economy of our country. We count on people from all corners of the world to come here each year and hopefully spend lots of money. Anything that negatively affects our tourism trade is of utmost concern to our country's well-being and that's one of the reasons Tory is here. She will be in charge of public relations. Any communication between this committee and the outside world will go through her. We will expound on this later. I have worked with her on several occasions and have witnessed her doggedness and tenacity in tackling any problem that she has faced."

"Tony Bidwell." Tony, a tall slender man in his early fifties with piercing black eyes and a neatly trimmed graying beard, looked to be a serious man. He was the only man in the room who wore a suit. A suit, Frank though must have been custom made by a quality tailor. Addressing Tony, Bryce Mann said. "Tony and I have been friends for a long time. He is Director of our Canadian Forest Service and volunteered to be involved with this committee as soon as our government leaders made the decision to assemble it. You will find that he is also a doer who tackles projects head-on with a drive of getting things done." Tony made a slight salute to Frank by touching his hand to his forehead.

"Bill." Bryce said as an introduction to the next man. "Bill Stocton joins us from Prince George, British Columbia. He heads up the Fish and Wildlife operation there and will be our man in that part of the country. Bill works for me, and I must say that he knows more than a little about wolves and bears. Frank, you, and Bill will have a lot in common and should get along well. Welcome to our group Bill." Frank sized up this short powerful looking man as a real outdoorsman and looked forward to knowing him.

"Lastly, we have with us a local Edmonton man. George Benson heads up Alberta's Fish and Wildlife Service and we have worked together for quite some time. How long have you been doing this George?" Bryce asked.

"Nearing thirty years!"

"The kind of experience we need." Bryce said.

"Now that the niceties are taken care of, let's get started. We'll be going over the agenda that you have in front of you but before we do, let me ramble on a bit. As you know, we are gathered here in Edmonton because of these Demon Wolves. I assume that's what you must have called them when you were dealing with them Frank." Not waiting for a reply, he continued. "We are charged with a most difficult and possibly undoable task. There are an alarming and growing number of known deaths attributed to these wolves. And it's likely that some deaths that have been blamed on grizzlies might be attributed to these wolves as well. An increase in sightings of huge wolves is being reported at an ever-increasing rate leading us to believe that more attacks are imminent, and the numbers will escalate. Frightening thoughts! Adding to this calamity, we are faced with another issue. There have been far too many reports of missing people across northwestern Canada over the past couple of years and we now suspect that there might be a connection to at least some of those disappearances and these wolves. We have been concerned about these issues for some time but have dragged our feet in seriously addressing them. The latest attacks and the press coverage of them have finally set our government's behinds into gear and that's why we are here."

"This committee's job will be fact-finding with the mission of compiling information that will provide us options on determining ways to address this critical situation. George and Bill are assigned to take whatever actions that they and I feel appropriate to eliminate these wolves. We will have full support of every game and wildlife unit in the country at our disposal."

"There is no doubt that we have a great deal of brainpower between us in this room and I want to use every bit of it. The Prime Minister has assured us that he and every government department in our country are behind us in this matter. We literally have hundreds if not thousands of people in every branch of our government at our disposal. What I am trying to say is that this is big, and the powers 'that be' do not want a national public panic on our hands." Brice paused for a moment with a somewhat disturbed look on his face. "But I'm afraid that panic might be hard to prevent. Adding recent deaths that have been widely publicized over the past few weeks to those already attributed to these animals are becoming a great concern to many." He paused once again before adding, "And I fear that the worst is still ahead."

"You all know about five people being killed a week ago. On that occasion we were fortunate enough to kill the two wolves. George has their carcasses here for us to see. Frank has made arrangements for the bodies to be sent to the Fairbanks Wildlife Center later today, so let's head to the lab where you can see first-hand what we are dealing with."

Two enormous black wolf-like creatures laid-out on sheets of plastic presented a ghastly sight. Immense heads with somewhat short blunt snouts and powerful looking jaws made these beasts not only hideous looking but down-right frightening. The team was distressed to think that there were possibly hundreds of these monsters ravaging the population of the Canadian Rockies and how helpless a mere human would be against these incredibly powerful animals.

During the long day that the team convened in the cold and snowy city of Edmonton, Frank had time to fill the alert and astute group in on everything that happened related to the wolf program in Alaska and Yellowstone National Park years earlier. He emphasized the importance of using tapes of howling wolves to lure the mutant wolves in close enough for a kill and urged Bill and George to utilize this tactic whenever possible. It was a tiring and grinding day and when it had ended, each member of the group had been assigned a specific area that they 0would be responsible for.

Torrance LaBlank and Tony Bidwell were teamed up to investigate missing persons, sighting, attacks, and deaths that might be attributed to these monstrous wolves. A big job but as Bryce had said, they had unlimited support whenever they needed it. Torrance would liaison with both Bryce Mann and the Minister on all communications. Every statement or press release related to missing persons or the wolf problems would go through her. Every precaution possible would be taken to prevent a national panic, but as Bryce had stated earlier, that might be easier said than done.

These latest deaths had already begun to cause a public uproar and people in high places were starting to make a ruckus.

George Benson and Bill Stocton would be responsible for following up on sightings, attacks, and deaths with the objective to 'find and destroy'.

Frank, because he was the only person familiar with the demon wolves, plus the fact that he held a doctorate in biology with first-hand knowledge of the experiments performed at the Alaskan facility in Fairbank, was issued the task of working with the Fairbanks laboratory and Drechsler International in hopes of learning more about the mutant wolves. His goal would be to find any possible ways that the science that created these monsters could somehow help destroy them.

Bryce Mann would reign over the operation. He would assign and oversee all work done by the team and assist with any and all of their requirements.

"Our next meeting is scheduled one week from today at 10 am Edmonton time via phone and video linkups." Bryce said as he ended the meeting.

One week to the day, each member of the team was sitting at their computer wherever they happened to be, and once Bryce was assured that everyone was online, he started off by saying, "I have talked briefly with each of you and have a thumbnail account of what we have accomplished so far, but I'm anxious to hear the full story. Let's start with Tory and Tony. I have a map that I will now share with you." He touched a couple of keys on his computer and a map was displayed on each team member's monitor. "Go ahead."

"Tony and I have put in a lot of hours during the past week, and we have some pretty disturbing news," Torrance began. "We had a group of six people call many town and city officials in just about every municipal district in northern Alberta, Saskatchewan, and British Columbia, plus a few in the Yukon and the Northwest Territories; requesting reports of missing people. This first look into missing persons is quite concerning. We have pin-pointed every reported incident that we have discovered to-date. Refer to the map in front of you. Tony will talk more about the map shortly. So far, we have a list of ninety-six reported missing people over the past three years. As you can see, the area we have targeted covers a very large piece of real estate. Most of the missing people reports are from isolated areas. In many cases a long time had gone by before someone determined that they were in fact missing. It's normal for people who live in the big woods not to communicate with the outside world very often, so this is not surprising. It makes us wonder how many more people might be missing out there, people no one knows about yet. This is the first time that anyone has pulled this type of data together so there was no way of knowing before now how big a problem existed. Tony and I are very concerned about this… but let me turn this over to him, he has some issues he would like to share with you."

"Please look at the map." he said. "The graph above the map shows reported missing people by month over the past three years, including year-to-date this year." He paused long enough for the team to look at the graph. "The red marks on the map represent locations of these missing people. Two things stand out. First, note the steady climb of unaccounted for people every month. The trend indicates this problem is growing quite rapidly. Even though the numbers we are looking at are preliminary and will need more research to determine their validity, Torrance and I believe these figures are somewhat accurate. One thing these statistics might indicate, in theory at least, is that our wolves could be, (and in our thinking most likely are) responsible for at least some of this in-balance. We'll come back to that. Secondly you will notice that most of the dots are centered around northwestern Alberta and northeastern British Columbia with a few others scattered over a much wider area. We will be discussing this later as well and show how it interplays with wolf sightings and attacks. Torrance has another topic she wants to talk about."

"We have some very insightful information on wolf sightings. At first, they were not taken too seriously. Something like Big Foot sightings. Some people serious about what they saw or think they saw but nothing to substantiate it. But that all changed when proof of their existence surfaced. Three or four years ago there were only a few reports about large wolves being spotted here and there throughout the northern forests. Now there are many reported sightings. Bill and George have given us a direct line to every Fish and Game office in the areas we are targeting. We have contacted many already and will be contacting more as we dig deeper into this. Bryce, please bring up the next map."

The map that appeared on the team's monitors covered the same territory as the first one. "You will see four sets of colored dots on this map representing sightings, one for each of the last three years and January of this year."

A shiver ran up Frank's spine. There were too many sightings spread over a much larger area than he could have imagined.

Tony's distinct voice came through the phone system very clear. "Once again, we have two very unusual things to look at. First, wolf sightings are escalating at a very fast rate just as missing people reports are. Our study shows that there were very few sightings three years ago as indicated by the yellow dots. Note that two years ago there was an increase in sightings as shown by the green dots. Again, blue represents last year and red this past month. Last year there were four times more wolf sightings reported than the previous year. A huge increase. I'll now show a graph displaying sightings by month over the past three years. Sightings are progressively increasing at a faster and faster rate. Another thing to note is that when we overlay the wolf sighting map and the missing people map, the markers cover the same general areas."

"We are also tracking attacks and deaths." Tony said as another map appeared on the viewer's screens. "In all cases that we have listed, attacks have resulted in one or more deaths. Again, these reports are rapidly escalating, and their locations correspond with the concentration of sightings. This is a lot of information to digest but before you start with questions, Torrance will summarize and give you a few of our thoughts."

"If the information we have received from our inquiries is only half accurate," she began, "we have enough data to solidly link wolf sightings to missing people. Our findings show that wolf sightings and attacks as well as missing people are escalating quite rapidly. Tony and I have a theory that might explain some of these disturbing issues. We think a pair of wolves migrated from Yellowstone and settled somewhere in Northern British Columbia or Alberta. The map showing their general locations lead us to believe that their offspring began to settle close by and each year as their population grew, they spread further away. During the past year they extended further yet, as far as Alaska and across the border into the United States. And we also agree that the trend will continue, and if it does, the wolves will extend their range into more populated areas. We realize that we have only begun our efforts to gather information but what we have already learned is enough to scare the hell out of us."

Bryce cut in. "I agree Tory. I am sure it's scaring all of us. But to be honest, I didn't think this would end up as good news. I have an important call to make so let's take a fifteen-minute break."

During that short break, every person on the committee reacted to the morning's meeting in their own way. Frank for example, got out his calculator and began punching in numbers. Torrance was shaken! If this pending disaster developed as she now was sure it would, how could they ever calm the situation and prevent a national panic? The public would be inundated with newspaper, radio and television reports of more horrid attacks and deaths that she was sure would come. George, the sensible and pragmatic man that he was, thought about how he could come up with a plan to kill wolves. Bill wondered what he was doing on this committee and wished he was home with his family. Tony, always level-headed and logical, couldn't wait to gain more data and get a better handle on what they were faced with.

When all were back on-line, Bryce once again addressed his team. "Before we finish with Tory and Tony, let's hear from George. He has been a busy boy also."

George began by saying. "I'm sure you have heard by now that there were three more people killed by these huge monsters four days ago. The witnesses who saw the two animals as they departed the scene claim they looked the size of horses. We immediately sent out hunting parties but once again we got there too late. They gave it their best effort but were not able to find them in the heavy mountainous terrain." After a pause he added. "Our success rate in locating these animals after sightings, or in some cases attacks, has been very low. Case in point! We had another attack up near Rainbow Lake two days ago. When we got the report that a man had been killed by wolves, I contacted my local man up there who confirmed the death and said that neighbors had seen two huge wolves attack one of their neighbors. They were horrified because all that was left of their friend was blood and gore. There is no question that the wolves ate the body." As he hesitated, a sense of despair passed through the listeners. "There were two sets of huge wolf-like tracks leading into the forest, but the woods were so thick and dense that Tim and five other men on snow machines couldn't follow. I sent a helicopter there but after hours of flying over the mountains they came up empty. Not a pleasant story and not a good ending. What worries us is that we have had three attacks in a week, all resulting in people being killed. Bill and I have contacted every Wildlife Center in the western half of our country. We set up a communication system with each of them and will be notified as soon as anyone reports seeing a wolf, regardless of its size. Our plan is to have people at the site of every wolf sighting or attack as fast as possible. Knowing how dangerous they are and that we have already lost men who were hunting them, we will have at least four men on every investigation and more where possible. We are urging them to use large rifles and to shoot on sight. Hunting these animals present several problems. It takes our men some time to reach remote areas where many of these occurrences happen and we invariably arrive too late to encounter them. Most of our efforts to track the animals end in forests too heavy to penetrate; it's a big world out there and the dense mountains are all but impenetrable. You would agree if you flew over it. There are thousands of square miles of nothing but timber and mountains. Believe me when I say we are faced with a most difficult task. More than difficult in many cases; more like impossible. Like looking for a handful of needles in a hay field! But regardless, we will be giving it our all."

The deep brisk voice of Bill Stocton said. "We have the use of several helicopters but unfortunately none are very close to the areas we are most concerned with. Bryce is having a couple of machines relocated to better suit our needs and that should help. One will be in Meander River and the other in Fort Nelson where we can get to areas where many of the sightings have occurred, much faster. But after looking at the extended range that these wolves are covering, George and I agree that we need more air cover if we are going to do this job right."

Bryce nodded. "Nothing is off the table. Helicopters seem to be the best tool available for locating these monsters, so I'll look into getting us a few more."

"Tony… Christ did I really put a Tony and a Tory on the same team?" Bryce allowed a small chuckle during these troubling times. "I must be daft. Anyway, you've given us an idea how big a problem we have, now fill us in on how you are addressing the missing people dilemma."

"We have already implemented a plan to investigate every missing person that is reported as soon as possible. We have contacted authorities in all parts of our target area and by this time next week we will have enough people in place to investigate everyone on our list. We hope to complete this operation within the next two weeks. We can only hope that our results are favorable, and the missing people are located."

"Amen to that." Bryce said. But his thoughts were far from optimistic.

"The snow is deep in the mountains," Tony continued, "and that's where most of the missing people live. Many have no roads or live on un-maintained roads and that will make it hard to reach them. We'll be checking as many as we can with four-wheel drive vehicles and will be using people who can handle snow machines to get to as many outlying places as possible. For anyone we cannot get to by ground, we will be sharing helicopters with George and Bill. We're going to do everything we can to address this issue."

"Good start!" Bryce said. "Keep at it. Frank, you're up."

Frank had listened carefully to what the others had to say and responded by saying. "I'm sure all of us find these statistics to be shocking. I agree with Torrance and Tony; with the limited amount of investigation, you have done so far; it scares me to think of what will be uncovered as you dig deeper."

"When I first started hearing about sightings of large wolves in northern Canada I had thought and hoped there were only a few of them; but the evidence shows there are many of these damn evil devils out there and I am sure, as I know you all are, that they most assuredly have a direct connection to missing people. But the numbers don't add up for me. I've been studying the map and I am very puzzled. Wolves have rigid and well defined social and mating behaviors. They are animals that live in packs with a strict hierarchy order. In almost all cases, a dominant leader is the only animal to mate in a pack and he normally only mates with one female. Nothing in nature is set in stone and neither is this but it's very rare for this pattern to vary. A pair can mate in two consecutive years but more likely they mate every two or three years. This is one of nature's ways of controlling their population. There are usually four or five whelps to a litter, and they customarily remain with the parents for a couple of years or more before breaking away to start their own family. If the first pair of our wolves mated five years ago, under normal conditions there should be no more than thirty or possibly even fifty animals that we are dealing with. Wolves generally travel in packs of four to eight animals but if we assume here that for some reason there are only four wolves in each pack; that would mean there should be no more than a dozen wolf packs. Looking at the map, sightings are stretched far and wide over many miles, some hundreds of miles apart. No matter how I look at this, I think it would take more than forty wolf packs to be in as many places and spread as far apart as our findings show. And that does not account for some of the more isolated and singular sightings in even more remote locations. All of this mystifies me; the math just does not add up. And compounding this issue and adding to my dilemma, these are only the reported sightings. It's only logical to believe there are many more that have not been observed. I have little doubt that further investigation will reveal more sightings spread further afield just as Tony earlier suggested."

"I racked my brain trying to think of what could cause the seemingly impossible dispersal of these animals over vast areas in such a relatively short period of time. Assuming our data is right, I was left with some scary thoughts. It's possible the wolves we are dealing with do not follow the laws of wolf nature. Could they be having many more births to a litter than normal wolves? Are the males mating with all of the females in the pack? It seems that many of the sightings have been of two animals. This could indicate that the young leave the parents earlier than normal. Maybe the young mate sooner than normal wolves. Maybe this new generation of wolf does not travel in packs. Maybe, maybe, maybe… Some or all of these things could account for so many sightings in so many areas. As I said, I am puzzled but I will research this further and keep you informed."

"Unfortunately, I don't have much information about the wolf carcasses we have here in Fairbanks. There were delays in getting them here because of weather and our team has only had them for two days. I arrived here quite late last night and haven't had much of a chance to talk to anyone yet, but I will be reviewing what they have learned so far as soon as this meeting is over. The only information I do have for you is that the female was pregnant."

"I've scheduled meetings with the staff at Drechsler International in Los Angeles. They have some brilliant scientists there who I hope can assist us in at least learning more about these creatures. Again, its early times but I will keep you informed as we progress."

Bryce summed up the meeting: "Even though our results are not favorable, we are at least getting a clearer picture of what we're dealing with. We will talk again next week, same day and same time. Keep digging everyone! Before we adjourn, I must call Minister Aston. He is more than anxious to hear from us so please hang on."

The 'hang on' lasted for more than fifteen minutes. When Bryce finally was back with the team, he addressed them in a very serious voice. "Minister Aston is under extreme pressure. Our government is demanding immediate actions from us. They are not interested in the difficulties we are faced with; they only want results. They want a viable plan on how we can eradicate these cursed animals and they want it as fast as possible."

The task force had no way of knowing that during late winter and early spring, only about two and a half months from when this meeting took place, several thousand mutant whelps would emerge from dens throughout the northern half of North America. If these creatures continued to reproduce at the present rate, there would be many thousands more the following year.

Three
Genetics Gone Wrong

Eric Tuttle assigned Finn Sorenstam, the Alaska Wildlife Centers wolf biologist to examine the two wolf carcasses that Frank had sent from the Canadian Fish and Wildlife office in Edmonton. Finn had Harvey Flores, Carl Everly and Lisa Ingles supporting him as they dissected the animals that lay on the surgical table in the departments operating room. The team worked long hours for two days analyzing the animal's anatomical and genetic make-up and when Frank's phone meeting with the Canadian task-force ended, they were ready to review their findings with him.

Several changes to the staff at the Fairbanks Wildlife Management Center had taken place in the few years since Frank had managed the facility. Jeffrey Hurst had finally retired as did Ernest Klouse; and several others had moved on to other places. The operation under Eric Tuttle had grown not only in the number of people who worked there but also in the laboratory equipment required to keep up with new technologies.

The conference room was the same as Frank remembered it with the exception of a larger combined television and viewing screen mounted on the wall. Mandy had the urn steaming with hot brewed coffee before the meeting began and once all six people in attendance had served themselves with a cup, Eric began with introductions. "Not all of you have met Frank Wallace but you have certainly heard of him. Frank, this is Harvey Flores. Dr. Flores specializes in genetics and the biological makeup of living organisms as related to health, growth, and development of North American animals. With our number one objective being the health and well-being of Alaska's wildlife, he fits in very nicely. He supports every biologist here at the Wildlife Center and works very close with Finn and Drechsler studying the effects that Zoltan's enhanced immune system has on our wolf population."

"Carl Everly is our operations manage. He runs our research lab and is responsible for all animals brought into the compound for whatever reason. Similar to what Ernest Klouse did for us in your time here."

"Lisa Ingles is our intern from North Dakota State University where she's studying for her master's in genetics. Her theses' is based on Zoltan's method of strengthening the immune system in animals. She chose to intern here because this is where it began."

Once the introductions were made, Eric addressed Frank. "Sorry I wasn't able to see you when you arrived last night. We were all burning the midnight oil trying to pull together what we've learned so far about these incredible animals. We're still in the middle of our examinations but will share with you what we have so far. Finn." Eric said in way of turning the meeting over to him.

"We've learned some pretty wild things Frank; and will certainly learn more as we dig deeper into these anomalous creatures. Eric informed you earlier this morning that the female was pregnant. We'll get into that but let's start with Carl. I know you will be as astounded as we are when you see what we have here."

Frank thought Carl, a rather short rotund man with slightly protruding eyes, somewhat resembled Peter Lorre. But that thought ended when he spoke. His deep resonating voice exuded confidence and self-assurance as he displayed a picture on the big screen showing the two wolves laying on the large table in the centers' operating room. "You will have to excuse us for our un-kept appearance Mr. Wallace. We have been up all night trying to prepare at least a preliminary report on these two animals and must look a bit ragged."

"I certainly appreciate the effort you have all put into this. The results of your tests might help us find ways to deal with the crisis these aberrations are causing. And please call me Frank."

"Certainly… Frank!" Carl replied. "We have a substantial database of information relating to the biological make-up of the original mutant wolves that were born in Yellowstone and we are using that data as comparison to these animals. In the short time we have had these two animals here, we've been able to make a few genetic comparisons between them. DNA of these creatures are definitely of the same lineage as the animals tested several years ago. They have almost identical percentages of wolf and grizzly bear DNA as the first generation that you dealt with in Wyoming. Some of you have seen creatures like this before but for us newcomers, they are frightening; however, they represent a challenge in evaluating their genetic structure and we were anxious to put them under a more rigorous scrutiny. Three things that we discovered surprised us. I should say, astounded us! As huge and grotesque as the two wolves are, they are very young. In fact, they are less than a year old and surely nowhere near full grown yet. And possibly just as astonishing is that we are certain these animals are the fourth generation of the two original wolves that started this mutation. On top of that, the young female was pregnant with seven semi-advanced embryos; (five females and two males) making them the fifth generation."

Frank raised a hand to interject. "This is incredible. it's hard to believe these two animals are only young whelps. We know this new breed of wolf is huge, but to grow this much and reproduce in less than a year is inconceivable. As is the fact that they are fourth generation. That would mean that all of these animals must have reproduced in the first year of their life. This is against everything I know about wolves. How sure are you about this?"

Finn Sorenstam replied to Frank's question. "We're positive Frank. I know it doesn't sound possible, but facts don't lie."

"Wow!" Frank said with a worried look. "This would solve a puzzle that has been bothering me. But it isn't what I hoped for. I hate to even think how the multiplication factor could increase their numbers."

"I've worked out a formula showing those potential numbers. We'll go over the details with you later."

"Harvey and Lisa will discuss what we've learned so far about the animals' immune systems; some interesting findings." Finn said as the meeting continued.

Lisa Ingles was a big, over-weight girl. Her straight stringy auburn hair with bangs hanging down to her eyebrows made her look unkempt and somewhat scruffy. However, her dazzling hazel eyes highlighted the beauty of her face. Frank thought she would be a very attractive girl if she fashioned herself with a comely hairdo and used even a little makeup. "I have only played a minor role in assisting Harvey and Carl." She began." But as Erick said, we have some very interesting things to discuss. We have analyzed the immune genes in both of these animals and also the seven unborn babies. Even though they are not fully developed, we were able to get good samples of their DNA and cell structure for analysis. Harvey has displayed a graph showing levels of immune potencies taken from records of the mutant wolves several years ago. This is the first time anyone has compared this latest generation of animals to those records."

Harvey went over the chart in detail. The end result was that the strength of the immune systems in the two dead wolves and the fetus' averaged somewhat less than the recorded averages in the earlier animals. Immune cells found in the female had declined by approximately six percent and the male by eight percent. The fetus's immune systems recorded numbers averaging about three percent weaker than the mothers.

Frank immediately saw a bright spot in these figures but before he could analyze them in his mind, Harvey continued.

"Even though the results vary, these numbers suggest a slight but definite decrease in the strength of immune genes through time. However, we only examined a few animals and have very limited data so far. What makes these figures suspect is the fact that every evaluation made on normal wolves and other animal species that have been subjected to clustered immune cells, show the potency of the immune system to be stable with very little, or no deterioration whatsoever. We need to examine more of these animals to verify this anomaly, especially from different generations."

Frank thought about this as he poured himself another cup of coffee. When he sat back down, he commented on this latest report. "I agree, we need more animals and I'll have them sent here. We can only hope that the declines continue as your study suggests it might. Assuming there is a weakening in every generation of these animals, let's consider what might cause it. One apparent variable between these mutant creatures and normal wolves is that their biological organisms consist of a mixture of wolf and bear DNA. Could the blending of the two different DNA structures result in a gradual weakening of the entire immune system in this new strain of animal? Are the two different molecular structures working against each other in some way? These animals were also subjected to an unknown number of unidentified gene clusters. Could this mixture of 'thinister therum' as it was once called, be upsetting the pass-through of inheritance genes?"

Finn got out of his chair and raised both arms with outstretched fingers shaped as claws. Giving his impression of Frankenstein's monster, he gave out a loud menacing "Argh" as he staggered, stiff-legged toward Carl.

"You damn fool," Carl said, trying to keep a serious face, but failing. He began laughing with the rest of the group.

Frank couldn't help but look back to when he worked at the Wildlife Center and how his wolf biologist had always been able to lighten a serious situation with his flair for humor.

The group soon settled back to seriousness as Frank continued with his assessment of the team's findings. "If the female's immune system has fallen by six percent in four generations and her fetuses by another three percent, which might indicate the deterioration process is escalating at a faster rate with each new litter. Yes," he mused out-loud. "We need more animals. Eric, will you deal directly with Bryce Mann and his men?"

"I'll get right on it." Eric nodded.

"Good. That will take me out of the loop. There are many people hunting these beasts. I'm sure they'll have a steady supply for you."

Frank directed his next words to Dr. Flores. "Harvey, I think the variables you found in these animal's immune systems is of utmost importance." Frank's mind was looking ahead as he tried to analyze what this could mean. "Yes… weakening resistance… Sorry," he said. "I was thinking out loud. If the trend continues, eventually their resistance to fight off disease might be their downfall. Until we get more data, we can only hope that the deterioration is exponential (as it appears it might be) and affects all of these creatures. Wishful thinking maybe, but unfortunately, even if the immune systems of these monsters do diminish and eventually affects their health, and possibly even lead to their demise, the weakening process appears to be a slow progression and God knows what devastation they will cause in the meantime."

Frank thought for a few seconds before adding, "There might be some significance in the fact that the males' numbers dropped off more than the females. You should keep that in mind as you proceed."

Although the results of the experiments discussed during the mornings review were shocking, they revealed a great deal about these creatures. But not surprising to Frank, no immediate solutions in solving the dilemma they were faced with surfaced. So far, the team's findings only brought up more unanswered questions; however, they did open up several interesting areas worthy of further research. "I know I keep rambling on but just one last thing I would like to throw on the table for your consideration. It's apparent from what we have already learned that this new generation of wolf has a completely different mating and reproduction cycle than normal wolves and possibly this high rate of propagation is due to an evolutional foul-up caused by the blending of a variety of unknown altered genes. Or maybe for some totally different reason. But everything has cause and effect. I'm pretty sure we know at least some of the effects; I hope as you dig deeper into this you can uncover the causes."

"I told you Frank was a pretty damn good wildlife biologist." Eric said to the others in the room. "And I think we just got a taste of it."

Addressing Frank, he said. "You asked us to work with Drechsler on these animals and we agree. Finn and Harvey are working with them on other issues and in light of what we discussed today; especially in attempting to determine the effects of every altered gene introduced to these animals, we're looking at a great deal of time-consuming work and can use their help. I know Carlene Linser will be as anxious to join us in this study as we are. I'll contact her and see if she can get it approved at her end. Between the two of us we can hopefully get some fast results."

"Good." Frank said. "I'll be traveling to L.A. tomorrow. I'll discuss all of this with them."

The meeting ended just before one o'clock with the two biologists and the one soon to be, heading to their homes for some much-needed sleep. Frank, Eric, and Finn retired to Eric's office where Mandy supplied them with lunch of sandwiches from the nearby Subway. As they ate, they discussed the morning's events.

"You seem to have an impressive staff." Frank said.

"Yes, we have some pretty good people. Sometimes a little iffy about our wolf biologist though."

"Ouch!" Finn groaned.

Frank chuckled. Nothing seemed to have changed between his two friends. Then he became quite serious. "Some very disturbing results. We already have a major catastrophe; and from what we learned from these two animals I'm really scared about how this can turn into something much worse. If the birth rates are as prolific as we think they might be, I shudder to even think about how many of these god-forsaken beasts..." He cut himself off there and addressing Finn, he said. "Let's take a look at the numbers you came up with."

Finn handed him a spreadsheet showing a progressive set of numbers listed by year. "We know the wolves in Yellowstone had a large litter of mutant whelps and this pair would have had seven. I've made a few assumptions to come up with these numbers: (That it all started with a single pair. That every litter from the first to this latest one averages five pups and three are females. That every female gives birth in her first year and every year thereafter.) Simple math adds up to possibly a thousand animals. Even if the birth rate is less than what I used for this calculation, we are still dealing with a large number of these devil bastards. If the average birth rate is more than five and the ratio of female to male is more than what I used, then the totals will be much higher. What's really scary, is the multiplication factor. This next generation could result in several thousand more and what of future years? Any way we look at this, we are faced with a large number of killers out there and the likelihood of a staggering number in the future."

Frank had tried to estimate the potential number of animals that could be out there based on the data that the Canadian task force had presented and even though his guess was considerable, he still grimaced when Finn presented the magnitude of the problem that they were faced with. "None of this seems possible. Christ what a mess. If we can't find ways to stop them, and stop them fast, they just might become unstoppable."

"They probably already are." Erick said distressingly.

Everyone agreed that whatever the future held, it would not be good.

Drechsler International is a large corporation consisting of more than four thousand employees. They are one of the leading pharmaceutical, medical and biochemistry research companies in the world and continually lead the way in technological breakthroughs in their industry. Three years prior to Frank Wallace's meeting with them, Drechsler was awarded the project of following through where Zoltan Proziver had left off with his developments in the field of genetic engineering. Strengthening immune systems by clustering immune cells into what was now referred to as 'Super-Cells' was ingenious. The process was under strict Government guidelines and to-date the results achieved at Drechsler were very successful. The targeted areas for this new science were not only directed to sick or diseased wildlife but also to domestic animals. The treatment of animals was already resulting in healthier and more prolific offspring. The corporation's sphere of studies was not restricted to the immune system. Research had been expanded to include many other physical and mental traits and functions in both animals and humans. The Los Angeles division of Drechsler International consisted of four major departments, each managed by a Vice President. The conglomerate had research laboratories in several major cities throughout the world with its main headquarters located in Munich, Germany.

The evening that Frank Wallace arrived in L.A., he had dinner with Roland Swecker, one of Drechsler's Vice Presidents. During the cordial meal, Frank learned that Mr. Swecker had little to do with the day-to-day operations of the hundreds of projects that his staff of close to two hundred people were involved in. He was however well prepped on Frank's business there.

During the evening's conversation, Mr. Swecker filled his dinner guest in on how the word had come to him about the priority that would be placed on Frank's requests of his corporation. "A rare thing indeed, but I had a personal call from our CEO at corporate headquarters in Munich. This project of yours has some pretty powerful people behind it. The Prime Minister of Canada talked to our CEO resulting in an agreement to give your project top priority. I thought I would give you a cordial greeting and assure you in person of the full attention you will have during your stay with us and of our best efforts to satisfy any and all requests that you have. I have made arrangements for you to meet the key people involved in what we call our 'Super-Cell' project at eight o'clock in the morning." The dinner was excellent as was the California wine that Vice President Swecker ordered with the meal. After coffee, the two diners retired to comfortable chairs in the lounge and talked for nearly two hours as they sipped brandy. Frank found his companion quite interesting and learned at least a little about some of the work being performed by some of Drechsler's diverse companies throughout the world. By the time they said their goodnights, Frank, who seldom drank very much, felt a bit tipsy from the half bottle of wine and the three glasses of brandy that he had enjoyed that evening.

Six thirty the next morning came oh-too soon. Yesterday had been a tiring day. Delayed flights due to poor weather conditions followed by the long evening had caught up with him. And to make things worse, there remained a slight fussiness in his head from his wee bit of over-indulgence.

But a shower and shave took the cobwebs away and after his morning coffee, he was ready for the day.

The huge facility located in the valley was ultra-modern and without doubt the cleanest and brightest business Frank had ever set foot in. Once he had been cleared by security and issued a badge, he was directed to the meeting room where he was greeted by Michael Danvers, Hanns Korman and Carlene Linser, the three people who would be working with him during the two day's he planned to be there. After introductions Frank poured himself a cup of coffee, chose a pastry from the tray and sat down at the small conference table.

Michael Danvers, Director of Operations for one of the departments at the Los Angeles branch of Drechsler held a doctorates degree in biochemistry and a master's in business management, making him an ideal leader for the position he held. He began the meeting by addressing Frank. "We have been briefed on your visit and why you are here and told that we must provide you with any information you request about this project. We have been asked to support you in any way we can; and we will do so."

If Frank was a little set back by this curt, somewhat rude reception, he did not let it show. Instead, in a calm yet very professional tone he said. "I'm sorry for the short notice of my arrival but as I know you have been told, the matter that brings me here can be vital to the wellbeing of many people. I assure you that I will be as expeditious as possible and try to keep you from your very busy schedules no longer than necessary."

Michael Danvers nodded his head as if in agreement but before he could respond, Carlene Linser interjected. "Don't mind him Mr. Wallace. We had a little setback last evening with one of our experiments and he's been in a snitty mood ever since."

"Sorry!" Danvers muttered and then added in a somewhat concerned tone. "More than a little setback, we were pretty sure we were onto something and now we're back to square one." He once again addressed Frank, but his tone and demeanor remained the same. "We have also been instructed to give you a tour of the lab and experimental test center but before we do, let's discuss exactly what you want from us. The Fairbanks lab has already been in touch with Dr. Linser requesting our help in analyzing mutant wolves. Let's start there."

Frank explained everything the Fairbanks lab had discovered about the two mutant wolves and stressed the urgency of following up on those findings and the urgent need for Drechsler's expertise to aid them in determining the effects of every altered gene that these animals were subjected to. Dr Linser informed him that Finn Sorenstam was in the process of providing her with information and samples of the two specimens and that her department would begin work as soon as possible.

As the meeting progressed and it became evident to all that Frank Wallace was much more than a politician from Washington but in fact a brilliant scientist in his own right with the distinction of having the word Doctor appear before his name, Michael Danvers became at least somewhat more civil in their conversations.

The Super-Cell project at Drechsler consisted of two areas. One dealt with animals and the other with human beings. Carlene Linser was a woman in her fifties with a pleasant personality and a witty sense of humor. She headed up the Animal Research Center. Hanns Korman was recognized as one of the country's leading brain research specialists and one of the hats he wore at Drechsler was to oversee the Super-Cell program as related to humans. Dr. Korman, prior to taking the position at Drechsler was a renowned brain surgeon. He gave up his illustrious career to pursue his true desires which were in the field of human behavior. Both Dr. Linser and Dr. Korman reported to Michael Danvers.

Carlene held a doctorate in genetic engineering and because Frank's interest was in work being done with animals at Drechsler, he spent much of the two days of his stay in Los Angeles with her. Once the government had transferred all work related to Zoltan's break-through in genetics to Drechsler, the program, under the control of Mrs. Linser, flourished. As Frank studied the results of the progress made in recent years he was impressed. What started out to be the creation of an immune strengthening project in wolves had now developed into a considerable science. To date the scientists at Drechsler had identified hundreds of genes that effect many physical conditions, characteristics, and functions of living animals and as Frank found out, Hanns Korman was also making headway in the same areas with humans. The government had put many restrictions on how these classified cell clusters could be used for experimenting with live animals and even tighter controls with human experiments. Dr' Linser, even though she felt the heavy hand of the government impeding the work she was doing, and that much faster results could be made if the overall program was in the hands of the scientific community rather than politicians who knew little or nothing about the process, still made a great deal of progress.

Frank got along very well with Dr. Linser who was an open and friendly woman. But Korman on the other hand seemed to be somewhat aloof and stand-offish whenever the two men were together. Or, Frank surmised, it might only appear so because he was busy and preoccupied with his work. But regardless, in the brief time he had spent with the brain specialist, Frank determined that this man was truly a brilliant scientist. Certainly, one of the most exceptional he had ever met. Because Hanns seemed to have little time to spend with him, Frank was quite surprised when the brain specialist invited him to lunch.

As they sat at a table in a small diner not far from the Drechsler building, Hanns addressed his guest. "This place is probably nothing like you are used to, but they make the best BLT's and if you're game I would like to treat you to one."

Frank had to laugh. "I would be delighted."

When the waiter arrived, Hanns ordered the BLT and a large glass of milk for himself.

"I'll have the same," Frank told the waiter.

"I'm sorry I haven't had more time for you Dr. Wallace but I'm working on something very complex. Actually, it's quite unique and I keep thinking I'm getting close to a breakthrough, but every time I do, I seem to run into a stumbling block. Anyway, I know your interests here are to learn all you can about the wolves that are causing you what must be major headaches and you wouldn't have much time or interest in what we are doing in this area with humans."

"You're right about headaches. This wolf problem is escalating throughout Canada and spreading into the United States. It's a hell of a bad situation and the worst part of it is that it's going to get a lot worse. But you're wrong to think I don't have an interest in the work you are doing. In fact, I am very interested. When Zoltan Proziver first developed his procedure of clustering cells, I knew that someday the process would include human. But to tell the truth, it scares me. I try to look at the positive side and visualize the good that it could provide mankind by fighting off disease and improving health. The benefits seem endless. Yet I fear that man, being what we are, will abuse the science and cause problems that I don't even want to think about."

"Yes, and I'm sure you're right. But, man, being what we are, will certainly pursue this science regardless. We can only hope we will be smart enough to control it and keep the negative impacts that occur to a minimum."

The sandwiches and milk arrived and both men dug in. Frank had to agree. Wonderful homemade bread, fresh tasty tomatoes, crisp bacon, lettuce and what must be homemade mayo added up to a wonderful sandwich.

"Seeing you have an interest in the human side of our program, let me fill you in on a few of our projects. I have several areas I oversee here: one being the 'super-cell' project. I've divided my efforts in this program into two areas. The physical biology of humans, of which you will be familiar with because they mirror what Carlene is doing with her animal research. We have identified many human cells that govern traits, characteristics, and bodily functions just as she has, and continue to add to those findings. The problem we're facing is that we are very limited in using these incredible finings with Humans because of bureaucratic regulations. I can't tell you how frustrating this is. We are on the threshold of the greatest discoveries ever made and our hands are all but tied."

Frank had to agree to some extent. A scientist who thought he could provide benefits to mankind must certainly feel ill at ease with all of the restrictions he was faced with. On the other hand, he felt the process had to be kept under tight controls. There were too many unknowns of what, both short and long-term problems might occur by altering man's genetic makeup. Knowing how seriously Hanns felt; with a smile on his face, he interrupted by saying, "What do you really think about this Hanns?"

Hanns laughed. "Sorry about that. I get carried away sometimes. But even more interesting is the second area of study I'm involved in. The human brain. Think of what that entails. Every mental element of the cerebral brain. We have already identified cells that effect man's ability to reason, his psychological makeup, rationality, intellect, emotions and much more. No one knows how deep this science will delve into the core of our mental capabilities, but I believe it is almost boundless. Even though I feel as you do about the potential of ill-use of these incredible 'super-cells'; as a scientist I crave to dig deeper and deeper into them. Don't get me wrong, I know we have to creep before we walk but at the rate we're going, I won't see any real results in my lifetime, especially not anything related to the brain. That is, unless I can do something about it, and it's just possible I might. One of the main holdups in experimenting with humans is that our only method of transferring these genetic gene cells is through reproduction and no one is about to go there until the regulators feel there is no risk involved. One of the projects I'm working on now is to prove the manipulation of animal and human traits can be achieved not only through genetic reproduction but also by implanting super cells directly into targeted areas of living tissues. I am almost certain there is a way to introduce cells into living matter and have them react immediately. I've been experimenting with this for some time, but I'm not there yet. When I do get there, and, as I said, I am certain I will, I'm hopeful that restrictions we are now faced with will open up and we will begin to make significant gains."

Frank was amazed at what he had just heard. Cells planted in humans resulting in immediate reaction sounded absurd, yet so did Zoltan's clustering procedure. If some, or all of the 'super-cells' discovered could be introduced in animals and humans with instant results… Incredible. "You really think that is possible?"

"I'm sure of it. Well, almost sure. As I said, I haven't been able to perfect the process yet but I'm confident I will and when I do, Carlene…, Dr. Linser and I will test it on mice and other small animals. I shouldn't be telling you this and can only hope that you keep it to yourself. As I said, we are working in many areas, and this is just one of them."

"WOW!" Was Frank's reaction. "This would change everything. I can't even imagine the impact of such an incredible discovery."

"I know." Hanns said. "It's the only way to open up this science and gain the benefits that it can provide; otherwise, I see it laying stagnant for years."

Hanns was certain that the human brain was capable of unbelievable things and was determined to explore the seemingly endless possibilities that this clustering science promised. Another area he was most interested in and was secretly working on was prolonging life. This new science had already proven to impact many functions in animals and even a few in humans; why not extending the span of life. Hanns felt confident he could accomplish this by enriching cell regeneration. He wouldn't share this information with Dr. Wallace; he would share it with no one. His secret project was to discover The Fountain of Youth.

Four
Wolves

The gray wolf, also known as timber wolf, is one of the most fascinating animals in the world. One of their traits that make them so is their strict adherence to a rigid social behavior. This mammal known as *Canis Lupus,* has developed one of the highest levels of social orders in the animal kingdom. Their adherence to the strict laws that govern the 'pack' is all encompassing and includes individual actions and status as well as interactions of all members of the pack. So strong are these rigid rules of behavior that wolves that do not abide by them are often driven from the pack and on occasion even killed.

Wolves travel and live, in small groups that generally consist of several animals. These wolf-packs can be made up of as few as two or three animals but more likely groups of as many as a dozen are more common. However, packs of twenty or more have been recorded. Dominant male and/or female wolves known as alphas, rein over wolf packs. These ruling mates are devoted to each other and will usually remain together for life. In the wolf's world, the male is almost always the leader of his pack and without question he is lord and master over his disciples. (But this is not to say that a female cannot at times take over this role). The remainder of the pack is normally made up of the alpha's offspring that might consist of broods from more than one year and quite often a wolf or even a few from outside the family join the group.

There is a strict order of ranking within a wolf pack whose cooperative hierarchy is upheld through dominant and submissive behavior. The alpha male, and to a lesser degree the female, show dominance in all social activities and display an air of their leadership role through body language by standing tall and confident with their heads held high and their tails stiff. Their strengths as leaders are further demonstrated through authoritarian sounds, imposing facial expressions fand by making direct eye contact with their subordinates who show definite signs of being followers. The underlings often whimper and cower to the leaders in displays of meekness when in the presence of their masters and will even roll over onto their backs with their vulnerable belly exposed to show complete submissiveness.

Even though alpha pairs display a stern behavior to the other members of the pack, almost always a peaceful non-aggressive attitude within the group exists. Wolves are generally light-hearted and tolerable with one-another, displaying much tail wagging, face licking and friendly body contact, and even playful muzzle biting. These personal interactions and close encounters among wolves reinforce their social relationship and fortify the wellbeing of the pack.

The name 'gray wolf' is a misnomer to some degree because their coloration can vary greatly. The wolf's fur is long and thick and varies in color from almost all white to all-black, but for the most part is blended shades and mixtures of gray, brown, black, and white. Color seems to have no bearing on a wolf's status within a pack, but size can (at least to some degree) have a relationship to the wolf's standing within the hierarchy if for no other reason than larger animals are usually stronger and will dominate those of lessor stature. However, there are many wolf packs throughout the northern wilderness that are led by average sized alphas that completely dominate larger animals.

The wolf's high level of intelligence backed up with exceptionally keen senses, plus their strict adherence to social order within their ranks, provides them with the skill and discipline they need to be among the most efficient hunters of all carnivorous flesh-eating animals. Wolves, like many other predators throughout the world, will weed out old and weak prey before taking on a full-grown healthy adult animal. But wolves have to eat often and because they are relatively large animals, they eat sizable portions of meat at a sitting. Even though they do their part in maintaining healthy herds of the animals they prey on by culling out the weak, they do take healthy mature animals as well. If the wolf has one fault in the eyes of a concerned populous and of game biologists, it's the fact that they prey on the newborn and young animals within their territory.

In her profound wisdom, Mother Nature has devised intricate and sometimes odd means of controlling the numbers of her species to maintain a balance that works in this complex existence of life and death on earth. In the case of the wolf, as a means of controlling their birth rate she has instilled in a pack's social order the rule that only the alpha pair will mate. For the most part this rule is strictly followed, but as we all know, rules, even those established by Mother Nature, are occasionally broken. Most adult males and females within a pack, even though they get the urge, which can cause some discontent among the pack, abide by this unwritten law and abstain from mating. But when the urge is strong enough, some animals leave the confines of their brethren and travel in search of a mate of their own. When two wolves do meet up and mate, it is the making of a new pack. During the three weeks that a female is in heat, wolves go through a period of increased activity and howl more frequently than normal. A female wolf will generally be ready for breeding at two years of age. A few weeks prior to giving birth, the female, with the help of her mate, will either find a suitable existing den, possibly one she has used before, or dig a new one; generally, in a bank along a river or on the side of a hill where digging is not too difficult. Dens have been known to extend for many feet into the earth and can have more than one entrance. Within these dens the female gives birth to her litter, which usually numbers between four and six pups.

Babies are born with blue eyes that are blind and sealed behind shut lids and remain that way for about a week. Adult wolves have either yellow or brown eyes and after a couple of months the whelps' eyes will turn to one of those colors. Wolves cannot see in color like humans, but rather in shades of gray. Through those shades of gray, they see quite well because most of their hunting occurs at night and wolves are night stalkers of the highest order.

As the female remains close to her newborn litter the male and other members of the pack hunt and bring food to her. The whelps develop rather rapidly and within a short time the mother will leave them in the security of the den and begin to hunt for herself; although she does not stray too far from the den until the pups are larger. All of the animals in the pack are very protective of the new litter and defend them from any danger that might threaten. Occasionally pups are moved to other den locations in efforts to keep them out of harms-way.

Within six or eight weeks the pups are weaned and shortly thereafter, they abandon the security of their den to join the pack as they wander throughout their established territory. The young pups weigh about fifteen pounds at this stage and have already eaten partially digested meat from the adult wolves and are ready to take on the world. Like most young, they are inquisitive and anxious to explore the new world that they were born into. As they romp and play and seemingly pester their elders, they slowly develop personalities and soon establish, generally through strength and aggressiveness, a social standing among themselves. Some will be more dominating than others and rise to a higher level in the hierarchical progression within their clan while others who are less so, find themselves at the lower end of the ladder. But regardless of what standing the wolves evolve to, they almost always remain in a non-aggressive environment.

Another oddity within the life of the wolf pack is that the entire pack joins in to raise the young and there is no animosity or bitterness between any of the pack members throughout the upbringing. Other females in a pack, possibly because of their maternal instincts, treat the young wolves as though they were their own. In all, the well-defined family order that exists within the pack makes for a very agreeable existence.

One of the most important lessons that must be learned in the life of young wolves is how to hunt. They begin to learn the fundamentals of hunting at three month and by the time they reach six months they're able to hunt on their own and are on their way to mastering the predatory skills needed for survival in their harsh world.

The mortality rate of young wolves is normally fairly high. In almost all cases, some of the young wolves born to a pack will not survive. However, since the intervention of Zoltan Proziver's immune enhancing procedure, these statistics are improving.

There is no set rule as to how long a young wolf will remain in the pack they were born into. Most will remain with the parents for two or three years (some even longer) before an urge to wander becomes strong enough for them to take off on their own where they will hopefully find a mate and start a family of their own.

Each pack has a defined and marked territory that makes up their hunting grounds. These territories can be relatively small acreage where heavily populations of prey exist, to vast expanses of land that could cover many square miles in areas where food is scarce. But regardless of the size of their territory, the members of the pack treat the area as their own and mark it well by leaving their scent around its perimeter. Wolves mark their territory with urine or by activating glands that excrete distinct individual odors or signatures. They do this by scrapping their back feet on the ground, rubbing the glands against objects and by rolling on the ground. Wolves recognize the scent of their pack members and if outsiders happen to venture into their territory, they will be met with an unkindly greeting that generally results in conflict. However, rather than these conflicts resulting in fighting, they are more likely to be settled by the alpha males displaying their prowess through strong body language and dominate behavior. Nature being what it is, there's always the possibility of the unexpected and at times wolves will face one another in battle; and a violent affair it can be.

The largest wolf ever recorded weighed in at 175 pounds. A typical large adult wolf will stretch out to six feet in length and stand about three feet tall at the shoulders and easily weigh over one hundred pounds. At times one hundred pounds of wild fury backed up with powerful ripping claws and vicious slashing fangs imbedded in mighty jaws.

Wolves hunt small game on an individual basis but when they pursue big game, they team up and go in force; they have mastered the art of hunting as a team. A wolf's long legs enable it to reach incredible speeds. They've been clocked up to 50 miles per hour but more realistically they can pursue their prey at 30 to 35 miles an hour and can maintain that fast speed for several miles. Their prey cannot match the wolf's speed or endurance and are soon overtaken by the persistent pack. Once a wolf pack picks out a target, whether caribou or moose or any other large animal, it's unlikely the pursued animal will escape. To aid them in winter hunting, their large paws act as snowshoes. Supporting their weight on deep snow allowing them to travel much more freely than their hooved prey.

Wolves have an extremely keen sense of smell. A wolf pack in their steady hunting lope of about eight miles an hour can catch the scent of a moose or a caribou from a very long distance. When the pack homes-in on an odor that represents food, in more cases than not the animal is overtaken and killed. Wolf packs can take down large animals in direct bold attacks, but their normal approach is to wear it down by ripping at its hamstrings and rump until it falls.

Once game has been killed, the alphas are first to eat. When they have their fill, they then allow other members of the pack to step in to satisfy their hunger. At times wolves go for days without eating so when there is an ample supply of meat, they usually put away many pounds of it. And as with man, when animals overindulge in food, they get sluggish and tired and look for a place to sleep it off.

Nature has a way of reducing in-breeding and in the case of wolves she has handled this in two ways. From time to time a wolf from one pack is allowed by the alpha male of another to join their ranks. This happens with hundreds of small packs throughout the kingdom of the gray wolf and through time some of the wolves that have infiltrated a pack will mate with a local wolf, thus mixing the bloodlines. Secondly, many wolves, both male and female, when they reach the age of two years or older, will leave their pack to wander throughout the land searching for a mate. Invariably they will team up with another nomad from a distant pack and once again improve the strain.

The size of a wolf pack is determined by the abundance of food in the area and also by the male alpha. When a pack gets too large for the liking of the alpha, one or more of the lessor wolves will either leave on their own, or more likely be driven away. Young males and females that wander off to start their own pack can run into difficulties. Much of the territory that wolves cover is already staked out by existing packs, and they don't take kindly to intruders cutting in on their turf. Confrontations between these two factions usually results in the newcomers backing off just far enough to suit the original tenants. But in the end, there always seems to be just enough space for another group of wolves.

Gray wolves have a life span of approximately twelve years and for the most part an alpha pair will lead their pack for as long as they can keep producing litters. However, older alpha pairs have been known to have their throne taken from them by younger more aggressive animals. When this happens, the older wolf is either allowed to remain with the pack as a subordinate, run off, or killed outright by the new leader.

The death of a wolf can happen in many ways. As stated above, some wolves die by the paw and the fang of their own kind. Disease and para-sites take their share and in hard times, some will die of starvation. Others will succumb to wounds and injuries from hunting large prey. In the heat of frantic in-fighting with large animals, if a wolf makes a reckless move, it can pay the consequences with its life. Humans also takes the lives of many wolves by means of hunting and trapping. The quantity of animals taken by sportsmen are regulated by game management organizations that establish seasons and limits designed to maintain desirable populations in areas of large wolf concentrations. Others sadly fall victim to poisons and poachers. Yet, through all the perils that befall the wolf, it still survives throughout the northern wilderness and on a dark winter night his haunting howl will put the fear of God in the bravest of men.

*****

A new generation:

A young male wolf, leaving the place of his birth in the mountain forests of Yellowstone National Park, was driven by a force that he did not understand. A powerful pull led him and his two female mates that followed in his footsteps in a northerly direction. For many days, the gangly black animals' long gaited strides put mile after mile behind them as they passed, for the most part, unnoticed through Montana. The few people who did see them as they crossed highways or ambled across distant fields, thought the three animals were black bears: a sight not all that uncommon in the Rocky Mountain west. Their route led them through a mixture of mountainous terrain and open grassland, where an abundance of deer, antelope, elk, cattle, and horses satisfied their hunger. So strong was the urge to head north that the male wolf drove the two females on, traveling as much by night as they did during the day. Roads and busy highways were crossed, and ranches and populated areas were generally bypassed and when the occasional river bared their path, regardless of swift currents, the powerful animals easily swam to the far shore. They didn't stop for any length of time as they plodded on, only long enough to kill game or livestock along the way to satisfy their hunger.

Their first close encounter with a human took place when they passed the outskirts of a small town in southern Alberta. Here, directly in their path, they chanced on a man working in his back yard and attacked with no hesitation on their part. Killing and eating this human was no different than killing a deer or a moose; it was only meat that was there for the taking. Even though grizzly bears were seldom seen in the area where this horrible slaughter took place, local authorities were convinced that a rouge bear was responsible.

More than a month passed as the traveling band of three wolves pushed deeper and deeper into the vast forests that seemed to stretch endlessly in all directions. Finally, after more than a thousand-mile exhausting ordeal through some of the ruggedest mountains and heavily timbered forests in North America, the leader of these huge black creatures with their grotesque looking faces found a place that his instincts told him he was looking for. Above the northern borders of British Columbia and Alberta, approximately forty miles east of Trout Lake in the Northwest Territories, the three wolves ended their journey. The terrain was ideal for the wolves; heavy timber inter-spread with open patches of land made for excellent hunting. Deer, elk, and caribou were plentiful and even a few moose frequented the marshes and rivers, making it an excellent place for the two litters of whelps that would arrive in early spring to start their lives.

The winter was what might be considered normal in southern Northwest Territories. No more than three feet of snow covered the ground at any time and even though temperatures plummeted far below zero on many nights, days were relatively mild. When the two females gave birth in late March, the young parents were only one year old and weighed close to three hundred pounds with more growth ahead of them. At the end of a crevice that sloped for about six feet into a rocky outcropping one of the females dug out a cavity where she gave birth to nine whelps. Six of the baby wolves were female and three were males. Not long after these ravenous furry babies started worrying their mother's teats, the second female gave birth to eleven pups in the warm dry den that she created at the base of a hill. Again, the ratio of female to male was weighted with females. Of these twenty wolf pups born in this remote area of Canada, sixteen would grow, propagate, and disperse a breed of ferocious animals that would plague the population of North America with death and carnage.

Once the pups were weaned, the male and two mothers hunted every day to bring meat to the young whelps who constantly craved food. Their stomachs were like bottomless pits, pits that could never be filled. It didn't take long before the growing pups joined the hunt and tagged along behind their leaders. Once an animal was down, adults and young ravaged the meat in crazed recklessness.

Before the wolves that migrated from Yellowstone arrived and inhabited this area, a pack of seven wolves roamed the prime hunting range. For many generations' wolves had lived, hunted, and bred there. As wolves generally do, they treated the land and animals that inhabited the forests and meadows in their natural ways. Killing the weak and old being their normal habit helped to maintain healthy and abundant herds that in return provided them with ample food of which they seldom took more than needed to satisfy their hunger. In all, a very satisfying balancing of nature! But once these newcomers arrived, the pack of seven wolves was met with a savage attack that left three of them dead and the remaining four fleeing to safer havens. Likewise, the coyote population took a severe beating and vacated the huge area that these new wolves reigned over. There were few grizzly bears in the area, but an abundance of black bears was soon thinned out, leaving the area with but one dominating predator. Predators that Frank Wallace once called demons from Hell!

There was no discrimination with these animals when it came to hunting prey. Unlike timber wolves, singling out the old and sick never entered their minds. Any animal they came across was taken down and in fact often killed just for the sake of killing. So fast were these huge black wolves that no deer, elk, caribou, or antelope stood a chance in out running them. They charged in with all caution to the wind and ripped their prey to pieces.

This new genus of wolf inherited from the gray wolf an acute sense of smell, sight, and hearing. Unlike their predecessor, these beasts y do not form packs; only the alpha male and his mate or mates stay together. They drive their offspring away to fend for themselves within four months of their birth. The young break off into mating groups as soon as they leave the nest with each male taking one or more females with him, depending on the number of females available in the litter. The young wolves mate the first year of their lives and every year thereafter resulting in an incredibly fast growth of the species. When males reach full maturity, they will weigh close to four hundred pounds. As staggering as this is, possibly the biggest difference between normal wolves and these terrifying animals is that they have absolutely no fear of man. And where gray wolves are cursed with a high mortality rate due to diseases, Zoltan Proziver's extremely strong immune genes that were introduced into this new breed of wolf has made them one of the healthiest species of animals in the world.

Five
The Wolf Hunt

Frank took a long draught of his cold light amber beer. The subtle malt flavored brew went down smooth and with any luck would help ease the tension that had been building up in him. So much had taken place since Erick's call informing him about the severity of the wolf problems in Canada and his joining the team to address the situation that had rapidly grown into a nationwide crisis. Wolves were being killed, but despite formidable and challenging efforts to hunt them down, results were anything but good with little hope of improving unless they could come up with something… People were dying! He shuddered to think how many more would die as these manmade freaks of nature multiplied and spread destruction across the land. The thoughts that were swirling through his head were interrupted by Bryce's words. "Are you still with us Frank?"

Despite the awkwardness of being caught in a daze, he managed a smile. "Can't get the enormity of this heinous mess out of my head; I guess it's starting to get to me."

The morning meeting had been every bit as daunting and discouraging as Frank thought it would be. Several hours of reports; reports filled with data that the team continued to accumulate; reports that at the end of the day resulted in little help in solving the dilemma they were faced with. There were only a few bright spots (or rather just shades of gray in the darkness that shrouded the seemingly impossible task that lay ahead of the team) to give at least a little hope to the team. Torrance and Tony were doing well in determining the geographic areas the wolves had spread into and were tracking all reported attacks and sightings, giving the team a clearer picture of what they were challenged with. Unfortunately, the more data the team amassed, the more frightening and overwhelming the enormity of the situation became. Results of the hunts that Bill and George orchestrated proved without a doubt that these creatures responded to recorded howling of wolves. Several helicopters were employed in the hunts and more than a thousand people were on-call and ready to support them as needed. Ground hunting teams usually made up of several riflemen continued to investigate every attack and sighting. But despite these seemingly positive actions, the overall results were very disappointing. Only a few of the hunting groups encountered wolves. In almost all cases the animals were gone when the hunters arrived, and the heavily timbered forests made it difficult for hunters to follow. On rare occasions wolves were located and some were killed but the price was often high with the loss of human lives. For a while, the use of hounds proved to be somewhat helpful, but the wolves killed so many dogs that dog owners refused to use them any longer.

The horror of what they were facing weighed heavy on Frank's mind as he joined the on-going conversation. Bryce, George, Bill, and he had visited a local pub when the meeting adjourned. Tony and Torrance had afternoon flights and could not join them. Frank took another drink of beer and said, "I have to agree with what we discussed earlier. The problem has grown so big and so fast that our earlier plans to send out small hunting parties to every wolf scare is reported is not the solution. We're losing too many lives for the few wolves we kill. We have to address this on a much larger scale."

Bryce nodded. "Mr. Aston is in contact with me almost daily. He urges us to explore every possibility we can think of to eliminate this horrific threat to our country. He's still behind us, but reading between the lines, I feel if we cannot show him some positive results soon or present him with viable plans to resolve this crisis... Well, I for one don't want to go there, so let's put our heads together and come up with some new ideas."

"I've been toying with an idea." Frank offered. "Our best estimates suggest there could be more than a thousand wolves out there and as our maps indicate, they are spread throughout Canada including the Yukon and as far as the Arctic Circle and east to Hudson Bay in the Northwest Territories. These animals are increasing their range very rapidly, as we anticipated they would. And we think at least a thousand or two new births are occurring right about now. If their propagation continues at this rate, there could be a few thousand more next year; and after that Christ only knows. I know none of us wants to hear this, but we are all thinking that it's only a matter of time before they spread throughout the world. And when that happens, thousands of lives could be in jeopardy. Rather than reacting to sightings and attacks maybe we should go on the offensive and attack them. If we get enough teams made up of, say, six to ten hunters with tapes of 'wolf talk' and we saturate the western half of Canada with them, we should entice some of these animals to investigate. We've discussed using the military and I think it's time to bring them in. The question is, how large an offence can we use against them? If we go all-out with a massive attack using thousands of men making up hundreds of teams, we should get results. Nothing we can do will get them all, but I think this would at least thin them out."

George was the first to respond. "I like it. Saturate every know location with lots of firepower. And I do agree, we should address this mess on a large enough scale to get results. Yes", he repeated. "I like it."

Bill also agreed. "Frank is right. The results we're getting from our hit-and-miss operation are appalling. We have put hundreds of hours into these hunts and to date we've lost more hunters than the number of wolfs killed. Add to these numbers the hundreds of known and suspected deaths attributed to these beasts and it's obvious we are losing the battle and losing it badly. Frank's estimates of more than a thousand new-born this year and possibly several thousand more next year scares the hell out of me. I think Frank is right. Hit these bastards. What do you think Bryce?"

"I can't think of anything that would work better. It wouldn't be a problem getting the manpower to set this up, the Army is willing and able to support any plan we can get approval for. We could run a test program first to prove the program works. Target certain areas and send in several teams to see how it goes. We could have many more teams at the ready if results are favorable and implement a full-scale assault across the country. But hell, we know that these animals respond to tapes, we might consider doing away with the test run and go hell-bent on a nationwide blitz."

Thirty minutes later, with everyone in agreement, Bryce Mann contacted the Minister and discussed the team's recommendations with him. Mr. Aston communicated the task force team's proposal to the proper people and within a day the Canadian Government made their decision. Timothy Aston, Minister of Natural Resources, called Bryce Mann. "How fast can you get a test program in operation?"

"We assumed that would be your directions. I've contacted several National Guard units and have forty-five teams of eight men ready to enter our targeted areas tomorrow morning." Bryce informed the somewhat startled Minister.

"That's one thing I've always liked about you Mann, you never let grass grow under your feet. You have our blessing so go give it hell. We'll all be awaiting your report. We need some positive news and hopefully this will be it. If this works, you will have the thousands of men required to implement your full plan. The Army will be ready with as many men as you require when you need them. You'll have to provide tapes and instructions on how best to use them. Anyway, I know you have a lot to do so I'll just say, good hunting Bryce."

The test, or first step in what was to become an all-out attack on the population of mutant wolves throughout Canada, was a simple and easily organized endeavor. Target areas were defined, each having recent sightings and attacks. Teams would enter their designated area, set up calling stations and play the tapes. Each hour the teams would move to another location and repeat this procedure all day.

By nine o'clock the hunters began entering the forests and upon finding suitable places began using the wolf tapes. One team chose what they thought to be a good place and positioned themselves in a shallow semi-circle with a hill rising behind them and began to call. The loud clear howling of a wolf filled the still morning air reaching far into the wilderness, but nothing responded. They had finished calling with the tapes and were about to relocate for the third time, but it was nearing noon, so they decided to break for lunch. Backpacks were opened and lunches unwrapped, soda cans popped and the eight hunters, a little discouraged by lack of activity, discussed what they thought to be a lost cause; three hours of calling had produced nothing. The forests ranged for hundreds of miles in all directions and locating a few wolves in such an expanse of wilderness would be like finding needles in a haystack. But as they sat eating sandwiches and drinking sodas, one of the men saw a movement. By the time he recognized the black forms of wolves and yelled to the others, two huge animals were boring down on them. Chaos erupted as the men scrambled to their feet and reached for rifles. Tripping, falling, and screaming, the hunters panicked as they floundered to right themselves, firing blindly into the black demons that were overtaking them. One of the wolves picked up a hunter and tossed him through the air as if he was a toy. The wolf's brains were blown out as it turned for another attack. Men were shaking with terror during the attack, but through the chaos shots were being fired from several rifles and the second enormous wolf in the pack went down thrashing on the ground. Several more bullets penetrated its hide, killing it alongside its mate. Several smaller animals continued to show signs of aggression and three of them were killed before the remaining four disappeared into the forest. The hunters later described the outcome of this terrifying encounter with monster wolves, a miracle. They had been caught with their pants down so-to-speak and came out of it with no loss of life. The man that had been bitten and thrown was injured and required a hospital stay to recover from his wounds and two other men had less serious wounds incurred from the battle. As chaotic as this encounter with the killer wolves was, the hunt was considered a victory. Five wolves had been taken out.

Five days later, Bryce Mann reported to the Minister. Their conversation was direct and defined. "We believe the overall concept of the plan is sound." Bryce began. "One hunt was foiled by bad timing when the team let their guard down by taking a lunch break. If the men had been alert, they might not have got themselves into so much trouble. In other encounters the animals acted as we hoped they would by responding to the tapes. But unfortunately, three men died in the battles. I know that losing even one man is a tragedy, but we did kill fourteen wolves. Me and my team all agree we should launch a full-fledged assault against these wolves."

"Good work." Replied the Minister. "I think you've found at least a partial solution to this mess we're faced with. I'll get back to you as soon as I report this to the Cabinet and a decision is made."

When the word came that it was a go, it was like a two-edged sword to Bryce Mann. He knew men would be lost no matter how careful they were, and that dug into his soul. Even so, he knew that this was the right thing to do and was anxious to launch the attack.

The decision was made to use as many as three hundred teams consisting of more than three thousand men. It took a week before the launch was ready to proceed; maps, assignments, training sessions, directives, communications, schedules, and deployment of men to locations had to be worked out. When the day came, close to thirty-three hundred men with high-powered rifles took to the forests of Alberta and British Columbia.

While this was taking place, Frank Wallace, with the approval of the U. S. Fish and Wildlife Department, implemented a similar program in the United States. The Fish and Game Department teamed up with the Forestry Department and amassed close to four hundred marksmen to tackle the dozen or so known locations of the dreaded wolves in the lower forty-eight and Alaska.

Three weeks later:

Frank Wallace, along with the rest of the Canadian taskforce, was summoned to Ottawa for a meeting with government officials. When the meeting convened, Frank found himself among what appeared to be about fifty men and women representing several government departments.

Mr. Timothy Aston, Minister of Natural Resources presided over the meeting and after a brief outline of the agenda; he turned the meeting over to Bryce Mann.

"You all know the general state of the wolf problems we as a nation have been faced with. Mutant wolves have spread panic across much of our country and devastated and upset the lives of many of our citizens. You have all heard of the results from the major offensive we unleashed against this nefarious wolf population. Our aim today is to give you as complete an update as we can on how this dreadful malign began, how it grew and what is being done to destroy these animals."

"Mrs. LaBlank who most of you know and Mr. Bidwell, Director of Forestry, will begin by showing you the magnitude of what we are faced with."

Tony Bidwell touched the proper button on his computer displaying a map on the large screen showing the western half of Canada. Torrance LaBlank with her refined speaking voice began. "When Minister Aston formed this taskforce, we had very little information about these animals or the enormity of the problems we were going to be faced with. High on our list of priorities was to gain as much knowledge about these wolves as we could as fast as possible. Our quest for data was three-fold: we targeted wolf sightings, attacks, and missing persons. We immediately employed hundreds of people throughout western Canada to accumulate data that would give us an accurate picture of what we were faced with; what we discovered was not a pretty picture at all."

"Mr. Bidwell will discuss some of the effect of this wide-spread menace."

"As Mrs. LaBlank stated," He began. "We gleaned a great deal of information from many sources and will share with you some of our findings. The red dots on the map you are looking at show the location of the mutant wolf population we believed to have existed two years ago." With the touch of a button a second and third map appeared. "The second map shows last year's estimated numbers and the third represents our projected wolf population just prior to the recent hunt that took place." A murmur of conversations spread throughout the audience. Bryce stood and held up his hands for quiet. Even though the major concerns that the wolf troubles were creating was on the minds and lips of everyone in Canada, (and the rest of the world for that matter) Bryce knew that many of the high-ranking people present at this meeting never took the time to totally understand the true impact of this menacing nightmare.

Tony continued. "Map one is very sketchy at best. We had very little data at the time, but it did give us an idea of what we were facing when we assembled our taskforce. The numbers of sighting and occurrences related to these wolves are somewhat more accurate on map two and even more precise on map three. As you can see by the indicators on the maps, the problem has been growing at an alarming rate. Dr. Wallace will discuss this concern later." Torrance and Tony continued with their presentation for about fifteen minutes, touching on several key issues related to attacks and missing people. The numbers they displayed were shocking.

Bryce Mann once again took the podium. "The data that you were just given comes from the result of thousands of inputs from DNR offices, Game Wardens, Forest Service personnel, City and Provincial municipalities and the general public. Mr. Bidwell and Mrs. LaBlank have weeded through thousands of inputs to come up with as accurate a depiction as possible of this menacing problem. Many of the wolf sightings that are reported are of timber wolves, not our mutant monsters, and they had to be sorted out. As a side note, it appears that the gray wolf is taking a beating from this new generation of mutant wolves and their population is dwindling, as is the populace of other animals throughout the country, but we do not want to get into that right now."

"I'll now review the details and results of the first three weeks of our hunt that I am sure most of you have followed quite closely. Under the directions of George Benson and Bill Stocton, more than three thousand hunters, broken down into groups of eight to a dozen men, stormed the Canadian wilderness in areas where these wolves were known to be. I think the results of our first attempt to search and destroy these animals proved our research and reconnaissance was quite accurate. Our strategy for this massive hunt was simple. It has been proven that these creatures respond to the howling of normal wolves, so we sent several teams into areas where wolves were expected to be, set up calling stations and played tapes of howling wolves. If there was no response in an hour, the teams moved on to other locations. More than three hundred teams of hunters repeated this every day for the past three weeks and as I speak, are still doing so. To date we have encountered approximately three hundred and fifty packs of wolves and our marksmen killed close to two thousand animals. We found that in almost every encounter with these huge wolves, the packs were made up of a mating pair with litters of anywhere from four to as many as ten young. It's been rare to kill all members in a pack during an initial encounter, so we continue to send hunters into the areas again and again if needed in hopes of wiping out the entire family group. Unfortunately, these incredibly large wild beasts are aggressive and ruthless, resulting in unavoidable clashes with hunters. We are dealing with powerful and brutal animals and when a human is attacked, he has little chance against three or four hundred pounds of one of the most vicious animals in the world. We have sadly suffered thirty-seven deaths and many more hunters have been wounded in this trying battle we are fighting." Bryce Mann continued with his dissertation for another ten minutes and then took questions from the attendees; of which there were many.

When all had quieted down Bryce addressed the assemblage once again. "I want to introduce Dr. Frank Wallace. I doubt that he needs much of an introduction. He is well known in the world of wildlife as well as in Washington D.C.'s political arena. Dr. Wallace is unquestionably one of the most knowledgeable authorities on wolves in the world. The successful hunting methods that we have employed are of his design. He has some interesting information for us; Frank..." He motioned for him to take the podium.

It was not like Frank to be nervous under any circumstance, but he felt uneasy as he approached the dais. He could not get the overwhelming magnitude of the problems they had already faced out of his mind, nor the troubles that he was certain loomed ahead. Yes, his plan was working, at least to some degree, but too many lives were being lost in the process. Bryce's numbers of casualties hit the audience pretty hard but what he failed to report was that in the few weeks that the hunt had taken place, more than a hundred more innocent people living their lives in the wilderness, died at the claws and fangs of the monsters that invaded their world. He took a deep breath and felt the self-assurance that he had always possessed return. "As you all likely know, Minister Aston and the U.S. Secretary of State John Simms have joined resources to address this issue. The United States is working with Director Mann in a joint effort to rid both of our countries of the grave and devastating position these wolves have put us in. At the same time that we launched our sizable offensive here in Canada, the U.S. initiated a similar, but smaller operation. There are fewer animals south of the border, but our results are similar. We are killing wolves but are also losing lives in the battle."

"A little background would be appropriate at this time. We are dealing with five generations of wolves. Their breeding habits are unlike normal wolves. These animals' mate during the first year of their lives, and it appears that all females breed and produce litters of young every year; resulting in an unbelievably rapid growth rate. That's the reason we have so many wolves spread over such a vast area in such a short span of time. These wolves do not travel in packs. They pair up and when the young are a few months old they are cast away, pair up and start a life of their own. One of the reasons for the success we are getting as our hunters scour the wilderness is in the timing of these hunts. Litters are still with the parents, allowing hunters to take out many of the young when they encounter the adults."

"We have another unsettling issue that has emerged from the success of our hunt. We based our first estimate of the number of animals we were dealing with on the assumption that a single pair of wolves migrated into Canada five years ago. Now, because of the number of animals already killed and how many we believe are still out there, we think there must have been two or more females that accompanied a male into northern Canada five years ago. And if that is the case, we have many more animals than we originally thought."

Another uproar erupted before Frank could continue.

"We examined two of these animals several weeks ago at our Fairbanks lab and discovered that the exceptionally strong level of immune genes found in all of the original mutant wolves a few years ago had weakened somewhat in these two animals, and this weakening was passed on to the female's unborn fetuses. This was welcoming news because if the deterioration continues it could eventually result in a low enough resistance to hinder their health. Our hopes were high that this was inherent in all of these animals but since then we have examined several wolves form each of the five generations. Our scientists have confirmed that only about sixty percent of the animals tested show declines in their immune systems. We are baffled at this time as to why. Drechsler International has initiated an intense program to determine what this means and what impact it might have in the health of future generations. They are also looking at other biological functions that might be following a similar track of weakening with each litter. It's early times with these evaluations and we don't have any firm data as yet, so I don't want to get any hopes up. But our scientists foresee a possibility that if the immune systems continue to deteriorate, eventually the science that created these monstrous animals might also be the cause of at least some of their demise. Director Mann will keep Minister Aston advised of further developments."

A bevy of voices broke out once again from the concerned attendees and Bryce Mann stood to quiet them. "I know you all have questions and concerns but please be patient. We will have time for questions later."

"Minister Aston and Secretary Simms have agreed that in my summary we should share some of our concerns and plans with you. Our intense hunt has produced some positive results. The biggest being that by killing as many animals as we have, there will be thousands fewer of these vicious beasts born next spring. However, we should not get our hopes up too high. Yes, we killed a lot of animals, but there are many more out there. They have spread over much of the western half of Canada and into Alaska and are appearing in areas as far east as Hudson Bay. And if they get into Russia; the forests there are endless. We can put some hope in weakening immune systems, however, only a little more than half of the animals tested so far show declines. With the information we presently have, we feel that if failing health does have an impact on these creatures, it may take generations before anything positive comes from it. With all this said, our only recourse is to continue to hunt and destroy these creatures and we plan to do so. By next week we will add an additional thousand men to our existing team of hunters and send them further afield. The United States has approved the deployment of another thousand troops to aide us in this war. With as many as five thousand trained troops scouring our nation for these animals, we will do our best to wipe out as many as possible."

Frank Wallace ended the meeting with a sobering statement. "With the massive effort we are undertaking, I am sure we will eliminate many of these animals, but I am quite certain we will not exterminate them completely. Mankind has learned to live with lions and tigers and grizzly bears and crocodiles; and we have survived with poisonous snakes and a multitude of other deadly creatures. I am quite certain this new species of wolf is here to stay, and we will somehow have to find ways to live with them."

Bedlam broke loose in the meeting hall and the next day newspapers and media world-wide carried the story. A new generation of deadly man-eating wolves was spreading across North America with little hope of preventing them from inhabiting the rest of the world.

Six
The Fat Man

At the edge of a high rocky crag, the fat man sat and surveyed the Alaskan wilderness that spread for hundreds of miles before him. A wilderness so vast and so far-removed from civilization, that few humans ever set foot in it. Other than a small number of ambitious souls who backpacked into the remoteness of these seemingly endless mountains, and the occasional hunter and fisherman who dared to wander this far back, the land was left to the wildlife that called this harsh land their home. The fat man was one of these adventuresome wilderness hikers and fishermen.

The backpacker was a big man towering well over six feet and weighting a stone more than three hundred pounds. He was referred to by many of his friends as the fat man; however, despite his flaccid and soft exterior appearance, beneath this thin outer veneer his body was made up of solid muscle. Not only was he a very strong man but to the surprise of his peers, he was also athletic and quite agile for a man of his size. As a boy growing up in the Fairbanks area, he was active in intermural sports, but he had a deep love of the outdoors and involved himself as much as possible in hunting and fishing. Having done well in business, he was comfortably retired at the age of fifty-seven and spent much of his time pursuing his outdoor interests. For many years it was his custom to journey into the Alaskan wilderness on what he called his get-away survival trips that generally lasted for about eight to ten days. His wife Emma loved to fish as he did and often accompanied him on fishing outings, but these extended backpacking trips where grizzly bears roamed, was not for her. His two daughters, lovers of the outdoors as he and his wife were, both lived in the Seattle area and in June or July when the fat man ventured into the wilds of the Alaskan outback, Emma would fly to Seattle and stay with her daughters, doing her very best to spoil their five grandchildren.

He tried to keep the weight of his backpack to a minimum but by the time he swung it over his shoulders and headed into the wilds, it weighed in the neighborhood of ninety pounds. A weight he could easily handle even in the mountainous terrain that he often chose for his wilderness adventures. In addition to his oversized pack that contained the latest in camping equipment, clothing, rain gear and essential food, he carried fishing tackle and a lightweight twenty-gauge shotgun. Fish and small game always played an important part in providing food for his evening fires while on these adventures. And he never left home without his 44-magnum side arm strapped to his waist. He knew that his arsenal was inadequate in keeping an enraged grizzly at bay but to date, even though he had seen many bears throughout his life, he had never been confronted by one. Now with the threat of the mutant wolves terrorizing the northern half of North America, few people ventured into the wilds, especially on their own; however, as yet sightings and attacks were seldom reported in northern Alaska and the fat man was not willing to give up his annual wilderness adventures.

It was early into the fourth day of his trek into the wilds of the Alaskan outback when the fat man found himself siting on a rocky perch watching the sun brighten the far mountains, announcing the beginning of a new day. Directly below him a narrow meadow stretched for several hundred yards following the brushy banks of a lazy stream where three moose browsed on the willows that hugged its banks. From where he sat, he could see the water in the mountain creek coursing through the willows and hoped to catch a few trout or grayling in some of the inviting pools after he had breakfast. After about an hour of taking in the tranquil solitude and beauty of his surroundings he was thinking it time to go back to his makeshift campsite and make breakfast when something caught his eye. To his amazement an enormous animal appeared from the forest and sped across the clearing toward a startled moose. He immediately brought his binoculars to his eyes and watched as an incredible beast attacked the cow. She just about got her long legs into action when the attacker was on her. At first the fat man was mesmerized at what he was watching but as the big cow went down under the weight of the enormous bear, he remembered his camera.

It took the beast but a few seconds to kill the big gangly, long-leggy cow and only as it tossed the dead body around like a ragdoll did the fat man realize the true size and strength of the creature below him. As fast as his shaking hands could work, he adjusted the zoom on his telephoto lens and began taking snapshots as the incredible beast ripped and tore the innards from the carcass and began to feast on its kill. When at least a dozen photos had been captured on the memory card in the camera, the fat man once again looked through his binoculars and studied the hideous face of what he was sure was a monster from Hell. Powerful jaws tore hunks of meat from the five or six-hundred-pound moose with violent savagery. As he watched, the massive head of the animal suddenly lifted from its feeding and then it stood on its hind legs to search the open meadows around it. As the fat man grabbed his camera for a photo of the animal in a standing position, he spied a young moose some distance up the valley and assumed that was the cause of the beast's concern. But just after snapping the picture, the animal turned and looked up the vertical cliff in his direction. The fat man was terrified as he backed away from the cliff edge but in his haste, he inadvertently loosened a stone that tumbled down the rocky face of the precipice. He wasn't sure if the commotion of dislodging the stone would alert the beast, but he didn't want to hang around to find out. Thoughts of what that huge animal had done to a full-grown moose and what it could do to him filled his senses with fear. He haphazardly threw his gear together and in a panicky flurry he swung his pack over his shoulders and headed down the ridge.

It was a two-day hike to where he could get service on his cell phone to contact the authorities about the incredible animal he had come on. He made good time as he drove himself on, keeping a constant lookout over his shoulder in fear that the beast, whatever it was, was not pursuing him. As darkness settled in around him that night, he studied the pictures he had taken of the moose attack and a deep foreboding spread through him. Even though he knew that no animal ever lived that could even closely resemble this monstrosity, the pictures didn't lie. He got very little sleep that night as images of the beast would not leave his mind.

Eric Tuttle was working at his desk at the Fairbanks Wildlife Center thinking about calling it quits for the day when Mandy informed him that he had a call from Robbie Turner. *The fat man*, Eric mused as he reached for the phone. "Robbie, haven't heard from you in a long time, what's up?"

The voice on the other end of the line was somewhat excited and to Eric seemed out of breath. "I just got within cell range and do I have a story to tell you. I witnessed the most unbelievable thing. You'll think I'm a raving lunatic when I tell you, but I have pictures to prove it. I was up past Steamboat Mountain when I saw an incredibly big bear kill a cow moose. I mean a real monster. I mean something two or three times bigger than anything I've ever seen before. If a full-grown grizzly, weighs close to a thousand pound, I can't even imagine what this thing weighs. He killed a moose like he was swatting a fly. I'm telling you Eric this thing is unbelievable."

"Whoa," Eric cut in. Slow down and tell me what the hell you're talking about."

Ten minutes later when Eric hung up the phone, he sat at his desk and tried to digest what he just heard. He knew the fat man was a level-headed and sensible man and would be the last person to make up a story, especially a wild story like the one he just heard. Robbie had assured him that he was not drinking and that every word about this monster bear was true. So intense was he that he insisted that Eric wait for him at his office until he got there to show him the photographs. But it was nearing five PM and Robbie was five or six hours from Fairbanks, so Eric convinced the excited man to meet him the following morning in his office. Eric's thoughts were a whirr as the fat man's words kept repeating in his mind. "Two or three times bigger than a full-grown grizzly!" Whatever really happened or what he really saw would have to wait until the morning. Then a terrible thought passed through him. Could it possibly be?

When Eric arrived at the office at eight o'clock the following morning, he found a rumpled and whiskered giant of a man waiting in the reception area with a mug of coffee in his hand. Eric nodded to him, poured himself a cup and led his visitor to his office. The first thing the fat man did was laugh. "I must look like the lunatic I sounded like yesterday, and I must smell like shit. Didn't sleep much the past two nights and with this crazy bear on my mind I didn't even take time for a shower this morning. Just wait until you see the bugger. I still can't believe it. It must be some kind of mutant monster like these wolf's you guy's hatched here a few years ago."

Eric shuddered. It was the very thought that came to him the previous afternoon and was the reason that he got little if any sleep. "Maybe we should take a look at what you have before we speculate." Robbie handed him the memory card and Eric plugged it into his computer and brought up the first picture. There crouching over a moose was something the likes of which Eric had never seen or even could have imagined.

It was a bear more than twice the size of the moose that it was straddling. Several other pictures followed as the fat man rattled on about his unbelievable experience.

Upon blowing up the photos on his screen and studying close up views of the creature, Eric had little doubt that this monstrosity of an animal was somehow connected with the immune program that had gone wrong with wolves. The one thing that he knew as he and Robbie sat sipping their coffees was that this was no time to panic. He had to think this thru and keep it quiet until he had a better handle on what in hell was going on.

"Can you show me on the map where this happened?"

When Robbie located the place on the wall map, Erick entered the rough coordinates into his computer. He then let Robbie search the satellite view of the area on the computer and he soon locater the exact place.

"Do you think we can land a helicopter in that meadow?" Eric asked as he studied the map displayed on the computer screen.

"Yeah," The fat man replied. "You can land right near where the moose was killed. The meadow is pretty flat and plenty big enough. But I'm not sure it's a good idea. If that big bruit is still around it could raise hell with the chopper."

"I can get Scott ready in a few minutes and I'll have Finn come with us. We can be there in a couple of hours." Erick replied, ignoring the warning.

Finn Sorenstam never called Robbie Turner anything other than the fat man and was surprised to see him in Erick's office. Especially looking like something the cat dragged in. Erick, who was in no mood for introductions, got right to the point and showed Finn the photos as he briefly filled him in on what had taken place near Steamboat Mountain. Finn's first remark when he saw the pictures of the giant bear was. "Oh shit! This has to be more of Zoltan's work. Will it never end?"

Addressing Finn, Eric said. "We're going to fly up there in a few minutes. Get a few syringes ready and make them strong enough to down a rhino. And let's take two heavy rifles. No telling what we will be dealing with but if the need arises, I don't want to be under-gunned. Scott's getting the helicopter ready so let's hustle."

As soon as Erick and Finn had piled into the rear seats and Robbie Turner buckled himself up front beside the pilot, Scott revved up the motor and when the rotors whirred to the proper speed, the craft lifted off. Scott had entered the coordinates that Eric gave him into the GPS and put the aircraft on a northeast heading that would take them in a straight line to the meadow where a cow elk had been killed by some sort of strange creature.

As much as all of the men in the aircraft that speed over a heavily wooded wilderness for as far as the eye could see wanted to discuss the fat man's incredible photos of the giant bearlike animal that they were now on their way to hopefully locate, the noise in the whirlybird forced them to sit in relative silence.

Robbie Turner was watching the screen of the GPS and announced. "Just about there. The meadow is below that drop-off."

Scott swung the helicopter in a circle around the clearing so he and his passengers could view the surroundings. As he passed over the meadow a murder of crows took wing and the fat man called out. "There!" and pointed ahead. Scott immediately spotted the site and hovered above it as the four men looked down on a red splotch in the grass with pieces of hide and a few bones scattered about.

"I don't see the bear anywhere near, set her down". Eric said.

Scott located a relatively flat place about thirty yards from the kill site and eased the craft to a gentle landing. As the group of men waited for the rotors to stop before getting out, Finn loaded the two high powered air rifles with syringe darts that he had laced with a very strong dose of tranquilizer. Once they stepped out of the helicopter, he handed one to Eric, he would man the other himself. Scott and the fat man armed themselves with high-powered rifles and they all slowly eased away from the static machine that the Wildlife Center named 'bird', keeping a close lookout just in case the huge bear might appear. When they approached the red-stained patch of meadow where the moose had been killed, they found little left of the carcass. Part of the head, pieces of bone, and swatches of hide strewn about was all that remained of the large animal.

Eric told Scott and the fat man to keep the rifles ready and a sharp eye out while he and Finn examined the area. It was not unexpected to find as much blood spewed over the area from such a big animal but what surprised Eric was that just about every bit and morsel of the animal had been consumed. Hardly enough scraps left for the crows that continued to fuss about the area. "Finn," he said as he looked down at a huge paw print embedded in the soft soil.

Finn, always the one with a quick response to just about any situation, stood staring down at the incredibly lager bear track for several seconds before his mind caught up with the reality of what he was looking at. "Shit almighty. That's not possible." He blurted as he bent down to study the track closer.

Twenty minutes later the team stood in the meadow at the edge of the willows with the stream gurgling in the background. They had taken photos and dimensions of the many tracks they found in the area. It seemed inconceivable that any animal could have paws as large as the animal that left the largest of the tracks. Even the smaller tracks were larger than those of full-grown grizzlies. Eric had no sooner declared that they would fly around the area and see if they could spot the bear when a thought entered his mind. "Let's take a look at the photo of the bear standing on its hind legs."

They walked to the chopper where Eric opened his laptop and brought up the photo. "We might get an idea how tall this brute is if we can use the alders by the stream as a guideline. I know you took the photo from up on that cliff Robbie but see the tree directly behind the bear; if we measure it, we can come pretty close to figuring out how tall our friend is."

After determining where the bear had stood when the photo was taken, they measured the distance between that spot and the tree that was pictured directly behind it. Then, as best they could, they measured the height of the tree and also the height of the high cliff that Robbie had taken the photo from. Using a range finder, they determined distances between all points and were sure that with all this data they could estimate the height of the standing bear quite accurately once they returned to the Wildlife Center.

They spent more than an hour in the noisy helicopter searching the area in ever increasing circles in hope of spotting the animals but to no avail. In many areas the heavy forest blanketed the wilderness showing little view of the ground surface below, so they headed back towards Fairbanks.

Erick knew that Frank was back at his ranch in Montana. The massive wolf hunts in Canada and the U.S., involving several thousand men had begun several weeks earlier. After the first somewhat feeble attempt made by the U.S. in eliminating this terrorizing threat, the leaders in Washington agreed to address the situation on a much larger scale. There were now as many as two thousand hunters hounding the animals in Alaska and the northern tier of the lower forty-eight. Dozens of animals were killed in the earlier stages of this massive offence but as time passed and the number of wolfs diminished and thinned out, fewer and fewer were being taken. But even so, there was no letup in the efforts being made to eliminate them.

Erick's call to Frank was answered by Sarah who informed him that her better half was working with cattle somewhere on the ranch. Erick told her that it was extremely important for Frank to return his call as soon as possible. Sarah knew from the urgency in Erick's voice and his haste in ending the call that something was bothering him. She knew that Frank, being under a great deal of strain, was getting the best therapy possible by working with the cattle and was hesitant to interrupt him but felt that the urgency in Erick's request was reason enough, so she called his cell phone.

Finn and Erick were analyzing the photos and the measurements they took at the scene of the moose kill yet again when Frank's call came in thirty minutes later.

"What's so urgent?" Frank asked when Erick answered the phone.

"We have something here that you just won't believe. Can you get on a computer?"

Frank knew his old friend to be one of the most level-headed and in-control people he had ever known; but he recognized in Erick's voice something he had never heard before. Erick seemed to be in a state of discomfort and almost panic as he described what had transpired, beginning with the call from Robbie Turner up until the present time. When Frank heard the story and viewed the photos, the strongest feeling of foreboding that he had ever experienced fell over him. With all the devastation and chaos that the mutant wolves were causing, and the certainty in his mind that despite the herculean efforts being employed to eliminate these terrifying creatures, those efforts would never completely wipe them out, now another beast was raising its ugly head. It felt as though an enormous weight was being lowered on him and slowly crushing him! His mind was reeling as he listened to Erick explain what they had learned and deduced in the short time since they returned from the moose kill.

By now, Erick had calmed himself to the point that he at least sounded like the Erick of old and carefully outlined their findings. "Let me go through all the data that we have before we start to speculate. The pictures speak for themselves. Robbie only saw one animal but as you can see from the photos of the paw tracks, three bears were at the kill site. Obviously, the animal in the photo is enormous. Using grizzle bear statistics, the size of the largest print would indicate that this monster could weigh as much as three thousand pounds."

"Doesn't seem possible!" Frank muttered. "Christ Erick, that's three times heavier than the biggest of grizzlies."

"I know. But let me continue. From the measurements we took at the moose kill we think that this creature stands about six feet at the shoulders and standing upright it may be sixteen feet tall."

"Give me a minute Erick. I want to study these photos again."

Several minutes passed as Erick and Finn waited and when Frank came back on the line he said. "Can't be much doubt that somehow, but I don't have a clue how, this god-awful monster is another one of Zoltan's gifts to us. Remember when we were working on getting our wolves ready to be sent to Yellowstone and Zoltan went berserk and injected God only knows what into one of the females? At the time we had a sow grizzly at the compound. The only explanation I can think of is that Zoltan somehow injected that sow with some of the clusters that we took from her. Have you talked with Needaname? He was involved with Zoltan and might throw some light on this."

"I'll get on it right now." Finn said.

Frank was beside himself with grief and felt a strong sinking feeling overtaking him. He could hear Erick talking in the background of his whirling mind but didn't hear what he was saying. How could so many things go wrong from what started out to be such a wonderful contribution to the scientific world. Zoltan's discovery of a gene-splicing procedure that strengthens the immune system in animals seemed so right at the time, and in fact was proving more and more to be the greatest breakthrough ever made in fighting disease in many species of animals. So much good was coming from this incredible discovery and so many more benefits loomed on the horizon. Drechsler was making great strides experimenting with human immune cells with hopes of perfecting the procedure to the point where it would benefit mankind in fighting many human maladies. So much good and yet so much bad! Mutant wolves that have taken so many lives and would surely take many more; and now this monstrosity of a bear that could cause more mayhem! A numb nauseous sensation was overtaking him as his mind reeled. "I'll have to call you back," he said and hung up the phone.

Ten minutes later, after he had composed himself, Frank made the call to Erick. "Sorry", he said when Erick answered the phone. "I needed a few minutes to take this all in. I've been so tied up with this wolf problem that your news of the bear hit me pretty hard."

"I know what you mean. We're going nuts here."

Finn, who had just entered Erick's office couldn't wait and cut in. "You were right Frank, that damn fish-eating Eskimo knew all along that Zoltan injected the bear. All this time and he never said a thing. I can't tell you how pissed I got at him when I demanded to know why he didn't tell us, and he said that no one ever asked him about the bear. Shit!"

"I wonder how many more surprises we will get." Erick said. "Hope to hell there are no more animals that were tampered with."

Frank was ashamed that he had lost control. This was the first time anything like this had ever happened to him. But now, as he addressed his two colleagues, he focused on the issue in his normal professional manner. "Needless to tell you that we have to find out all we can about this monster. I'm looking at the photo of the bear standing on its hind legs. I can't even imagine what devastation an animal that big might cause."

The three wildlife biologists discussed the urgency of capturing or killing an animal so tests could be performed to see what they were dealing with... They would keep this to themselves until they knew more about this incredible monster that seemed more like a prehistoric beast than a man-created mutant bear.

Seven
A New Beast

Zoltan Proziver's mind had been in a confused state, filled with paranoia and mistrust, (thinking that those around him were trying to steal his discoveries and deny him the recognition of the new science of clustering cells he was perfecting) when he administered numerous genetic cells into a female bear being held at the Fairbanks Wildlife Center years earlier. But he had been cognizant enough to adjust the records so no one would realize that samples of both identified and unidentified genes had been removed from the inventory stored there. He randomly chose bear and wolf cell clusters and as chance would have it, many of the cells from the two species of animals melded together. The result in mixing this haphazard conglomeration of biological cell structures created a most bizarre creature, a monstrous bear-like animal with many unusual features and traits.

*****

A sow grizzly emerged from her den located on the side of a ridge overlooking a vast expanse of Alaskan wilderness and beheld the snow-covered land before her. Regardless of the gauntness that made her appear emaciated from her long hibernation, it was apparent that she was a big and powerful animal. She walked with a pronounced limp and a ghastly scar ran across her face making her look somewhat hideous and even menacing as she surveyed her domain. Since she had been released from the Fairbanks Wildlife Center three years earlier, she had grown to a formidable size and eventually found a male that had more things on his mind than a pretty face. During this past winter she had given birth to two male and two female cubs. It was extremely rare for bears to give birth to four babies but then, no other female had ever been infused with the unpredictable wonders of Zoltan Proziver's genius discovery. It wasn't long before the baby grizzlies emerged from the security of their den to view the world they were born into. As they stood next to the big sow with her sagging rolls of skin hanging from her frame, the cubs were beginning to show differences between them and their mother. They were much larger than normal cubs and an irritable meanness was evident in them as they ravaged their mother's teats.

In many ways this new strain of bear is very much like any other grizzly. They are solitary animals; males and females live apart until the mating urge brings them together for a short time during mid-summer. They hibernate in the coldest part of winter and females give birth in late winter. Their colors are similar, ranging from almost black to various shades of brown and even blondish and generally have a silvery tint to their outer fur. Their eyesight is relatively poor, but they have a very keen sense of smell. Other than requiring a great deal more food than ordinary bears, they eat what other bears eat. But regardless of how similar these bears may be to normal grizzlies, there are a few marked differences. The most prevalent being their size. Where the average weight of a full-grown male grizzly is around 600 to 800 pounds, a male of this new breed of bear will weigh up to 4,000 pounds; almost as heavy as a white rhinoceros. Their ugly facial features portray an abhorrent look of evil and their devastating claws and teeth, capable of taking down any animal alive, make them the most menacing creature in nature. Because of their immense size, one might think that they would be slow and lumbering, but in fact, they are quite fast and cover a great deal of ground in a relatively short time, allowing them to easily overtake whatever prey they pursue. And like the mutant wolves that roam the northern forests, they have no fear whatsoever of man.

The female was overburdened with her four offspring. From the very beginning they were unruly and wild and as they grew their disposition worsened; but being a mother, she did her best to tolerate them. However, by the end of July, she parted with her first-borns to let them fend for themselves. She would mate every two years after that and give birth to many more, young mutant offspring until her death years later.

Shortly after leaving their mother, the young bears separated into pairs. They stuffed themselves on berries and plants and killed any animal they might encounter to satisfy their seemingly endless hunger. By the time the cold temperatures and snows of winter roused their inherent urge to hibernate, they were laden with a fat supply that would easily carry them through the long months ahead.

Snow covered the land when the young bears emerged from the warmth of their winter lairs. As all bears are when they wake from hibernation, they were lean and hungry, and it didn't take them long to locate any one of a number of large animals that lived in their northern territory and feast on rich protein. With a never-ending supply of animals for them to hunt, they feed heavily and often, resulting in rapid growth.

It was sometime in July when the two young female's reproductive urges begun to awaken and when they became sexually receptive, the males became aroused, and they mated. Shortly after breeding, a natural instinct to separate resulted in the pairs parting. Forever after, each animal of this new species of bear would be loners. Nomads, roaming the vast wilderness on their own until females came in heat and males searched them out for another brief encounter.

Not long after breeding with his littermate, one of the males encountered two grizzles. A female in heat had attracted the attention of a large silver-tipped male that aggressively pursued her. With the scent of the female's sexuality hanging strongly in the air, the two males confronted each other. By now the mutant bear weighed over twelve hundred pound and easily overpowered the silvertip that went down from a devastating blow, breaking the animals back. Sinking his long teeth deeply into the thrashing bear's neck, it crushed its spinal cord and killed the wounded animal almost instantly. The female who watched this one-sided clash of monsters ceded to the huge bear who promptly mounted her, passing on his extraordinary genes to her forthcoming cubs. The second male experienced a similar encounter with a she-bear in heat and before the mating season ended three more females were impregnated with the seed of mutant bears. Thus, began a steady spread of Zoltan Proziver's '*Thinister Therum*' not only through the lineage of the original mutant bears born to the miss-figured crippled sow who had been injected with altered gene cells at the Fairbanks Wildlife Laboratory, but also through the normal grizzly bear population of Alaska. In time they would spread to the eastern and western coasts of Canada and Alaska and across the Bering Strait into Russia, becoming a treat to the entire northern hemisphere. These man-created creatures would become the dominate predator in the world.

One of the young mutant females had given birth to three cubs in the depths of her den during the frigid winter. Upon entering the outside world, the cubs played, romped, fought, and fed on their mother's milk just as ordinary babies do. However, within a short time their diet included meat that the still-growing female killed with relative ease. Growth was not only rapid for the three cubs as they followed their mother throughout the wild mountains of east-central Alaska, but also for the she-bear. Spring and early summer was uneventful for the bears as they roamed about their territory with nothing more to do than eat, sleep, and explore. She, like her mother before her, abandoned her cubs during the first year of their lives.

The second female birthed five baby cubs. Three were normal, if you could call these incredibly savage mutant beasts normal, but the other two came out of their mother's womb as grotesque mis-proportioned freaks of nature. The mother killed these aberrations shortly after their birth. Something had gone wrong in the genetic development of these two offspring; something that proved that the mixing of too many gene traits could result in instability and produce severe side-affects.

Upon leaving his winter lair in early spring of his second year, the first boar grizzly born to the scar-faced sow, roamed a vast area of the Alaskan interior. There was no problem in killing whatever meat he desired as no animal in the north could match his speed. A strike from his incredibly powerful paw would lay-low his prey and he would feast until sated, leaving what remains there might be for scavengers. By this time, the massive beast weighed more than three thousand pounds with still some growth ahead of him.

His first encounter with humans occurred in early June. Smoke from a chimney drifted to his sensitive nose and not knowing what it was, he went to investigate. An old somewhat rundown fishing cabin nestled in a cove on a remote section of the Yukon River was owned by a group of people from San Francisco. Their annual trip to the remote retreat was where they could 'rough it' for a couple of weeks, mainly to get away from their hectic executive jobs in the city. If one can call it roughing after being dropped off by a float plane with an abundance of food and drink and a locally hired cook and all-around gofer to take care of their every need. Playing cards, drinking bourbon and vodka, and doing a little fishing in the river made up their rustic outing.

It was getting on towards late afternoon of the third day of their stay and the four friends were playing cards. A blazing fire in an open fireplace warmed the room as the cook prepared the evening meal when a sudden noise brought all to attention.

The monstrous bear walked up to the building and upon hearing voices and smelling smells he had never smelled before, slapped his paw against the side of the building and then swatted it again with a much heavier blow.

The men inside upon hearing the second loud crash against the side of the cabin jumped to their feet and one of them grabbed the 30.30 rifle from the corner. They knew that whatever was out there was big, and grizzly was the first thought that ran through their minds. Opening the door with a ready rifle they peeked out but saw nothing. Easing out the door, the man with the rifle had only taken two steps when the bear appeared from around the corner of the cabin to his right. He swung the carbine around and fired as the mighty beast rushed him and with one swipe of its paw slashed the man across the chest, ripping him wide open. Bedlam erupted within the cabin as the terrified screaming men tried to close the door. But the wounded animal with blood oozing from his shoulder powered his way through the tight opening and entered the three-room log structure. The enormous beast quickly killed the three card players as the cook ran into a bedroom and slammed the door shut. The bear, seeing the man disappear into the room rushed forward and easily bowled the door and doorframe in.

The wound in the boar's shoulder was not serious and because of the incredibly strong immune genes that it had inherited from his mother, the lesion would heal quickly. The bear ate his fill, and then continued wandering on his northwesterly route, following the Yukon River. A few days later he came upon another cabin and killed its lone occupant. From there he headed inland to the area of his birth. In his travels he located his littermate about the time her reproductive urges began to stir, and they once again coupled. Two more cubs were born to this pair of monsters that winter.

These two cubs tagged along after their enormous mother filling up on the meat she provided. Due to their extremely vigorous growth genes, they increased in size rapidly and were soon joining in on the hunt.

A day in June, as the cubs rested in the early morning quiet of the forest, the female wandered down to a meadow that stretched for some distance along the edge of a stream. She saw three moose feeding in the alders and immediately rushed in and killed one; not realizing she was being spied upon by a human high on a ridge above her. She heard a noise and rose upright to investigate but saw nothing and went back to her kill where she was later joined by her cubs.

A few days later the bears came on a few woodland caribou feeding on a grassy hillside. They gave chase and brought one of the animals down. As they fed on the hot meat a plane flew by but not close enough to push them from their feast. Shortly after, a helicopter chased them down and killed the young male. The first mutant bear killed of the many that would populate Alaska and northern Canada within the next several years and eventually cross the Bering Strait into the vast environs of Siberia. In time they would spread throughout the entire northern hemisphere.

Two days after the team landed in the meadow where the giant bear-like monster killed the moose, Erick Tuttle called six men to his office at eight o'clock in the morning. As soon as they were seated, he got right to the point. "Gentlemen, as I informed to yesterday, you're going on a bear hunt. And I know you agree that it will be a bear hunt like no other. You know how big these animals are and I cannot stress the need for caution if you locate them. Scott, you, and Finn will be in the chopper. Timmy, you and Bud will be in one plane and Robbie will be riding shotgun with Harry in the other." Robbie Turner had pestered Eric, insisting that he be involved in the hunt to the point that he finally gave in. "You will cover every square foot of the areas shown on your maps. Each aircraft will have two rifles and I suggest everyone strap a grizzly thumper to your hip. You just never know when a heavy caliber handgun might come to your rescue. Robbie, you, and Bud keep your rifles ready. It's difficult shooting from an airplane but do your best. If anyone locates these animals let the others know. I want the chopper there as soon as possible. I can't tell you how important it is to get one of these bears in our lab. Finn developed a grid centered around the place where Robbie Turner came on these bears. All of you have flown over this type of terrain; mixed forest with enough open country where you can hopefully spot these animals. If they're in our target area I wouldn't want you to miss spotting them, so keep your eyes open." Twenty minutes later Scott was reeving up the helicopter with Finn sitting beside him as the four others were on the way to the airport where two planes awaited them.

The second day of flying over vast expanses of northern wilderness turned out to be one of those perfect sun-filled days with visibility at its best! About ten o'clock in the morning Timmy and Bud flew over a wide-open hillside that stretched for about a mile in length and spotted three bears. A sow with two cubs! There was no question once they saw the bears that they were the animals they were after. The bears were feeding over a kill and paid little attention to the plane. No sooner had Timmy and Bud got close enough to recognize the bears, the pilot veered his craft in a turn to the right keeping as far from them as possible. The last the two hunters saw of the bears as the plane drifted over the trees and out of sight, they were still at the kill site.

Scott was flying along a winding creek searching the broken terrain of trees and open grass meadows when the call came in. Timmy Crouch's excited voice was loud and clear. "We got three of them spotted. They're eating over a kill right out in the open and didn't seem to be bothered when we flew by. Damn, is that sow big! Get over here as fast as you can." He gave Scott the grid number and the general location and told him he would be flying in a wide circle around them. Less than five minutes later the whirling blades of the helicopter carried the crew of two over the clearing and sure enough, three bears appeared ahead. The larger animal looked almost as big as the helicopter they were in. Finn, tethered to the craft, leaned out with his rifle at the ready. Scott maneuvered the chopper toward the animals that to both of their surprise, remained steadfast over the dead animal of which there was little left. However, just as the helicopter came within range, the loud thumping noise of the craft spooked the animals. The large female with cubs following close behind dashed for cove at a speed that surprised both seasoned bear experts. Never had either seen anything run at the speed they were witnessing. Finn's finger touched the trigger the instant the cross-hares of his scope found the last animal's ribcage as it was about to disappear into the heavy forest. There was no question in his mind that he hit the animal. It had all happened in an instant; the three bears bolted, and the marksman fired the rifle sending 270 grains of lead into one of the cubs. Finn had lived with grizzlies most of his life and had witnessed their incredible speed many times; but these animals were much faster than any animal he had ever seen.

Scott circled the area several times looking for the big sow and her remaining cub as the two planes scoured the wilderness from higher levels, but no sign of them was found.

When the chopper settled down in a semi-flat place not far from where the bears had entered the trees, Scott turned off the engine. Finn, picturing the mother somewhere near and ready to attack if they entered the woods looking for the cub that he knew he killed, was not about to take any chances. He immediately called Erick. "You won't believe this boss, but we just nailed a little baby cub. Unfortunately, we didn't have a chance to take the big sow, but I put a .375 magnum in a cub as it was entering the woods. The little shit must weigh a thousand pounds. Maybe more! And if you think that's something you should have seen its mother."

As the two airplanes circled above, Finn and Erick discussed the next step: finding and getting the big cub out. Finn irradiated his feelings to his boss. "There is one of the most incredible bears you could ever imagine in those dark woods, and she has a pretty menacing looking cub with her. And even though I'm sure I killed the one I shot, there is a chance that it's wounded. We know how bears thought to be dead have reared up and killed people. I'll be damned if me and Scott will go in after them alone. This might sound dumb but with only two rifles for protection, it could be suicide!"

Erick was quite surprised by getting such fast results. He had envisioned a long tiring search. "Any place Tim and Harry can land in the area?"

"It seems to be pretty steep where we are but let me get them both on the line with us."

Harry was the one to say he thought they could both set-down in a flat meadow about a half mile below where the chopper now sat. Timmy agreed and within ten minutes the two planes sat idle at the lower end of the long open patch of land. Scott lifted his machine and landed near the planes where all six men crammed into his small craft.

"We stick together!" Finn insisted as the six men entered the thick forest. "If we run into these evil bastards, I want to fill them with as much lead as possible, so be ready and shoot fast and straight. And for God's sake don't panic."

None of the hunters wanted to be in these woods following a wounded bear cub whose mother was like something out of a prehistoric age, but non-thee-less, the six riflemen walked almost shoulder to shoulder as they followed a heavy blood trail leading them into the dense forest. With every step they took they envisioned the monster sow crashing out of a nearby thicket and hoped beyond hope that there was enough gun power to kill her before she got to any of them. A relief spread through them all when they found the cub. There it lay; one of the biggest bears any of the hunters had ever seen. There was still the threat of an attack but at least they wouldn't have to blindly push further into the heavy forest.

Finn Sorenstram, knowing that the mother of the dead cub might be nearby hurried the men as they dragged the animal out. With one man guarding with a ready rifle the other five, with rifles slung over their shoulders, dragged tugged and lifted the huge cub over deadfalls towards the clearing. Choosing paths with fewest obstructions helped but it was still a strenuous and tiring effort; but eventually the animal was skidded to the edge of the clearing.

When the bear was loaded into the helicopter, Finn contacted Erick again. His first words to the anxious Wildlife Manager who had waited impatiently for the call were, "He's loaded." Finn was still somewhat out-of-breath as he continued. "Dragging the dead weight of that strange looking beast was anything but easy. Getting it loaded into the chopper was even worse." Finn would later tell Eric that the fat man had the strength of two men, and he wasn't sure they would have got the huge bear out and loaded without him. "Wait till you see him; and to think he's only a cub. Scott is motioning me that he's ready to take off. The airplane boys are footing it back to their planes; we'll hover behind them until they take off just in case mother bear makes an appearance. We'll be back as soon as we can."

By seven thirty that night the bear was laying on the lab table at the Wildlife Center where a small group of people stood gaping at the gruesome looking animal. The overall appearance of the creature was that of a bear, yet there were several features that made it look more like a demon from Hell than any bear any of them had ever seen. The young male's powerful legs were tipped with huge claws, much thicker and longer than the largest of grizzly bears. But the most striking difference between it and a normal grizzly was its face. "Look at his ugly contorted face." Finn said.

"His teeth must be half again bigger than a full-grown grizzly's. Looks like a Hollywood horror movie's rendition of a werewolf." And no one disagreed.

As Carl Everly, Harvey Flores, and Finn Sorenstram (with Lisa Ingles more-or-less looking over their shoulders as she usually did), began what was to be a long and tedious examination of the strange creature's biological make-up, Erick placed a call to Frank Wallace and informed him of the latest developments and that he would call again the following morning with an update.

Frank was deeply involved in assisting Canada and the United States in the war being waged against the menacing wolves that were still wreaking havoc across the northern wilderness of North America. Thousands of Canadian hunters were spread across some of the heaviest forests in North America, searching out these monstrous wolves and even though the number of hunters were fewer in the United States, the hunting there was no less intense. Wolves continued to be killed but wolves were also killing hunters. From what he now knew about these damnable creatures, it would only be a matter of time before they migrated across the entire northern hemisphere, and possibly even into the southern half of the world. And now these bears....

When Erick's call came the next morning as promised, it turned out to be a long conversation. "We worked all night dissecting and testing this animal's biological structure and have come up with some interesting information." Erick began. "I got in touch with John Riggs last evening regardless of the late hour at his end. He's agreed to keep the existence of these bears from the public, at least until we know more about them. But the more people that get involved the more chance it will leak out. I'm sure it won't be long before we hear another uproar that will surely spread around the world. I'll be calling Mr. Riggs as soon as we hang up to inform him about these results and you can only imagine how that will go. I'm sure he'll contact you about it; that's why I wanted to fill you in first."

"Thanks Erick. I agree. This will leak out and panic will raise its ugly head again. I keep looking back to when this all began and wonder how it got so out-of-hand. Damn! Well, tell me what you've learned so far."

"It's hard to call the bear we have here in the lab a cub but that's exactly what he is. We have results of his DNA breakdown. Just like our new generation of wolves, I'm afraid his DNA indicates we have a new generation of bear. He's about eighty percent bear and twenty percent wolf; verifying once again that Zoltan's clustering process can combine living organisms of two species of animals."

"Scary as hell, but it makes me wonder if combining more than two species is possible. But I don't want to think about that." Frank said in somewhat of a worried voice.

"Here is something very interesting. The animal's immune structure is stronger than our wolves'. About forty percent stronger! This is, or was, a very healthy animal. If others of his kind are like this cub, they will certainly have an incredible resistance to disease and possibly incomparable healing powers to any animal on earth. We think he is only about four months old and already weighs almost nine hundred pounds."

"My God!" was Frank's response.

The two wildlife biologists talked for close to an hour discussing the findings that Erick's team had uncovered thus far in their examination of this hybrid bear. Both men feared the troubles that lay ahead.

Eight
Doctor Bradhurst

To describe Doctor Gordon Bradhurst in a single word, it would be genius. To describe him in two words, it would be malevolent genius. He has three Doctoral Degrees, one in Psychopathology, another in Neuroscience and a third in Biochemistry; three business and mathematic related Master-Degrees and is also well-read with strong expertise in many other human related fields. He speaks several languages, has exceptional speed-reading skills allowing him to skim through text almost as fast as he can turn pages and is gifted with a photographic mind. There is no question that Doctor Bradhurst is a learned and brilliant human being.

Gordon Bradhurst comes from a very wealthy family. His father, being a skilled and celebrated surgeon, and his mother a partner in a New York law firm, contributed heavily to the fortune left to them by Gordon's grandfather; a financial entrepreneur who amassed more than a billion dollars in business and on Wall Street.

Gordon grew up in the Bradhurst's estate located in the Hamptons on Long Island. The Bradhurst Mansion is a large architecturally capacious Victorian building where a governess, private tutors and a small staff of attendants cared for the boy throughout his infancy and adolescence. As often happens, career parents with commanding positions in life seldom have time to personally rear a family, so Gordon grew up under strong and unloving hands of hired help. On occasion the busy couple would venture from their penthouse in New York City to spend a day or a few at their home on Long Island and invariably when they did, they would throw gala parties. Influential people from the city plus several prominent local elitists would attend these festive events thus bolstering the social standings of the Bradhurst name. These rare appearances at the opulent estate, for the most part was the extent of Gordon's interaction with his parents; there for him on occasions but rarely taking any special interest in him. They both had their demanding careers that were even more important to them than their wealth that continued to grow in the coffers of many financial institutions, or their son. Most of the time that the two professionals took from their busy schedules was spent enjoying their exciting social lives or traveling. As for their child, they provided him with everything in life he could ever ask for and gave him the best education available. What he did with his life after that would be up to him.

The outcome of spending his infancy and young childhood with austere, no-nonsense, often heavy-handed governesses and a few efficient yet uncaring tutors and servants, and with little contact or love from his parents, resulted in the boy growing up with no love in his heart.

At the age of thirteen his parents enrolled him in one of the most highly rated private boy's school in the country. There existed in the academy a strong hierarchy among the students with two domineering boys at the top of the pecking-order. Tim Robins was strong, handsome, and athletic. He was also quite smart and hovered close to the top of his class in most of his academic classes. It is not surprising that with his charm and charismatic character he was popular and favored by his peers as well as the faculty. Tim Robins was the boy to watch. The boy who displayed strong leadership. The boy most likely to be going places. His sidekick, Josh Perkins was very much like Tim. Just a half step or so behind Tim in all the attributes that made him the school's student leader, Josh was still an impressive and compelling young boy. Even though he reveled in the attention and respect shown to them by other students, he was not always happy about playing second fiddle. It was always Tim who was looked-up to and praised. At times he felt like the stooge standing in the background. But, as he always told himself, being second in command and standing next to the ruler-of-the-roost was better than not being there at all.

Then along comes Gordon Bradhurst. His ability to learn was far beyond any of his classmates and he immediately rose to the top of the class thus gaining the respect of his teachers, and many of his classmates. Because he excelled academically and was starting to make a name for himself among the school's top students, Tim saw a challenge and threat to the leadership role he cherished in the school. He, with Josh at his side targeted Gordon with verbal abuse and told him how things were going to be - or he would face what they called, the consequences. When Gordon ignored the threats, the abuse promised by his antagonists was carried out, resulting in a physical beating, Gordon had had enough. Two days after the beating, Gordan had the opportunity to enter the room of Josh Perkins and collected the items he wanted.

The next morning Tim Robins was found brutally murdered in his room. During the uncontrolled chaos and confusion that ran rampant through the school, Gordon, unobserved by anyone, visited Josh's room once again carrying Josh's tennis tote bag.

An anonymous phone call to the school security guard reported seeing smeared blood stains on Joss Perkins door. This led the investigators to him. Blood smears appeared on the doorknob and door of the student. One of the tennis shoes found in the back of his closet had traces of the victim's blood on it, as was a blood-spattered polo-shirt found in his hamper. During the investigation, the detectives determined that a very-expensive Rolex watch belonging to the victim was missing. They found it hidden between the accused underwear in a bureau draw.

The weapon used in the attack was determined to be a tennis racket belonging to Josh. Even though the racket had been washed in an attempt to remove blood from it, forensics found all the evidence they needed.

Only Josh's fingerprints were on the handle of the racket. Blood had pooled around the body and the killer had stepped in it leaving perfect imprints of a tennis shoe. Traces of the bloody footsteps appeared in a line leading to the door before petering out. Blood on his shirt resulting from repeated blows to the victim head. The stolen watch. A rumor, circulated from an unknown source that Josh's apparent friendship with Tom was a ruse and he actually despised him. He wanted to be the 'top dog' and done away with him so he could take his place. This information naturally got back to the detectives and Josh Perkins' fate was sealed. He was arrested for the murder. Regardless of Josh's insistence of his innocence, the evidence was overwhelming and his feeble attempts to cover-up the crime assured the prosecution of a certain conviction.

It had been simple to rid himself of his two antagonists. Looking back on how his plan had unfurled, Gordon could see where he had taken too many chances. Yes, his plan was quite brilliant. Using latex gloves not only left no fingerprints but also prevented any of his DNA from appearing at the murder site. He was pleased with his idea of carrying one of Josh's shoes for planting evidence and especially for thinking of taking a damp facecloth in a plastic bag to sop-up blood that he smeared on Josh's door. Everything had worked out quite well but there were holes in his plans. Someone could have witnessed him make the two phone calls or seen him entering or leaving Josh's or Tim's room. Or applying blood to the door. Fortunately, no one had seen him wearing latex glove. If they had, it might have raised suspicions. Starting the rumor also had some risk to it. If the circumstances ever arose that he had to eliminate anyone else, he would be certain that no risks whatsoever could lead back to him. At the age of thirteen he vowed to himself that all of his plans throughout his life would be thought-out very carefully and executed with infallible precision.

This first taking of a human life left Gordon with an incredible feeling of awe and power. He had relished in a state of exuberance and ecstasy as he battered Tim Robin's head with the edge of the tennis racket. A thrill and excitement he had never before experienced rushed through his being. As it turned out, before finishing his scholastic years, Gordon Bradhurst 'eliminated' four more people who he felt either crossed him or just rubbed him wrong. And in each case, he lived up to his vow to 'do it right. One murder, two accidents and one suicide. All flawlessly planned and carried-out to perfection with no possible connection to him. Each of his 'executions' left him with that same rush of euphoria. A thrilling experience he would never get tired of experiencing.

After the death of Tim Robins and the arrest, conviction, and internment of Josh Perkins, Gordon, through subtle and shrewd ploys, began to mold relationships to suit his best interests. Even at his young age he had the ability to influence and manipulate those around him and he nurtured and cultivated his gift of understanding the psychology of people. Using people to do his bidding was just one of the talents that he nurtured and would benefit from throughout his life.

He learned at an incredible rate and retained everything that he gleaned in his fertile brain. When he entered the collegiate world, his academic capabilities soared, and he rose to the top of every class he entered. With the ability to induce students and even faculty members into thinking of him as a friend and colleague, he was able to use them to his advantage. Thus, he became both elusive and popular as he traveled the university circuit building up his academic degrees and accolades.

Doctor Bradhurst is a nondescript man of medium height and weight. He has a full head of thick brown hair with just a hint of gray beginning to appear at his temples. The dominating feature on his face is his dark piercing eyes. Eyes that at times appear to be able to look right through people and in fact they do. He has an uncanny ability to read people for whom and what they really are.

He is a renowned authority on brain diseases and disorders and acclaimed to be one of the most talented and celebrated brain surgeons in the country. Recognized as such, hospitals throughout the world contact him for assistance in complicated cases. He sits on the Board of more than a dozen hospitals as well as several major corporations; one of which is Drechsler International.

After his distinctive education at several prestigious universities in the country, Gordon Bradhurst began his medical career by treating the very wealthy. As his practice and reputation grew, affluent people from around the world suffering from mental disabilities and brain dysfunctions sought him out. His exceptional knowledge of the human brain, and successful brain operations soon earned him the status of being-considered one of the most famous doctors in his field.

Upon his father's death during his university years, he became the heir to a considerable fortune from his family's lucrative estate. Through shrewd investments, many legitimate, some shady at best and others down-right clandestine and illegal, he built his substantial holdings into an enormous fortune. His total worth is not known but it's suspected that his overall holdings are between fifteen and twenty billion dollars. All this at the age of thirty-nine!

To many in the medical world and the general public, Doctor Bradhurst is not only a brilliant doctor and brain surgeon but a caring and attentive human being. His patients, especially those who benefit from his treatments, love him. A pillar of society! A stalwart of the community! A man looked up to by his peers! But…! There is a dark side to this extraordinary genius who has so successfully thrown a shroud over his true personality. Hidden beneath the veneer that Dr. Bradhurst presents to the world he lives in, there lurks a very different man. His inner-being is nothing like the deceptive image that he so convincingly displays to that world. He feels no compassion whatsoever for his fellow man; he only uses them for personal gains and could care less about those he built his practice around. Because of his strong self-ego and the fact that he cannot share any love whatsoever with any other human being, he never married. He in-fact, despises just about everyone he has ever come in contact with.

In the wake of his surge to power, Dr. Bradhurst has left an untraceable path of death to those who stood in his way. A ruthless, brutal, cold blooded, and heartless human being. Malevolent genius truly does describe him.

Four years into his practice he decided to put a plan he had been nurturing to use. He would create a facility where he could work unhindered on projects that were considered unethical and even immoral by the medical society; a society that constantly tied his hands, hindering research that he so desperately wanted to pursue. He was determined to explore the incredible untapped powers that he was certain were buried in the depths of the human brain, and to do so he had to operate on human beings in such ways that were forbade by the scientific community. With unlimited financial means and a partner to help develop and operate a facility where he could work in private and unrestrained, he began the process of putting his dream into reality.

During his university years Gordon Bradhurst deceptively befriended a fellow student. Russel Hieber was near the top of all of his classes but what interested Dr. Bradhurst was that he specialized in the human brain. Russel came from a poor background and had to work his way through his education. Gordon knew that Russel would be the right man for the job; not only was he an excellent surgeon with an in-depth knowledge of the workings of the human brain he was somewhat of a radical with few scruples about bending the rules now and again, especially if it was to his benefit.

Once the doctor found and purchased two hundred acres of land in a secluded valley east of San Bernardino, California, a property that cost him millions, he contacted Russel who was working at UPMC in Pittsburg where he was making a name for himself as a skilled Neurosurgeon. With Gordon's incredible ability to read and manipulate people, it had not taken him long to convince this chosen specialist to join him in this new venture. He described his plans to build a hospital and experimental research laboratory and wanted Russel to manage the operation. The hospital would cater to two distinct types of patrons. To the outside world the hospital would operate as a legitimate, profit-making institution for the mentally ill, catering to wealthy and celebrated clients who could afford the exorbitant cost of staying at such a prestigious institute where they would receive the finest service and care available anywhere in the country. But the real reason behind Dr. Bradhurst's creation of the hospital would be to study and operate on human brains without interference from the outside medical world. A place where the two of them could delve into the inner workings of the mind like no others had ever done. Many clients for this end of the business would be mentally impaired but they would also house his institute with sane individuals, preferably people without families, some on the down-and-out or homeless, people who would not be missed if they disappeared; others…well who knows.

Getting Russel to sign the lengthy contract was relatively easy. Gordon would form a new corporation where he would be the owner and CEO and Russel would become a junior partner and manage the operation as president and COO. The salary offered to Russel was staggering. And when the billionaire added to this lucrative offer a signing-on bonus of three million dollars, the deal was sealed. Russel Hieber smiled as he shook hands with his new boss. Not only had he became instantly wealthy, wealthier than he ever dreamed, he was to head up a secret hospital where he and his friend (and now new employer) could experiment on actual human brains! He was elated!

Russel Hieber was a tall rangy man with a bony body structure, especially evident in his broad protruding shoulders. Crowned with a close-cropped head of blond hair and his fair complexion likened him to his German heritage. As ungainly as he might be, he was bestowed with beautiful and dexterous hands. If there was one thing lacking in Russel's capability as a physician, it was in his bed-side manner. In general, his relationship with patients had been cordial but at the same time, somewhat detached. As one long time patient one stated, 'Lighten up doc. You are too serious. I don't think I have ever seen you smile.' That pretty much sums up Dr. Hieber, 'serious to a fault.'

Russel's first assignment was to oversee the construction of the new Hospital/Institution designed to Dr. Bradhurst's specifications. The facility was to be constructed in two distinct sectors. The main part of the three-story building would be made up of the hospital proper where the legitimate patients would be cared for. Attached but separated from the main hospital was the West Wing, Gordon Bradhurst's private research center and surgery where experiments on patients could be performed in unrestricted fashions. With unlimited funds behind the construction of this state-of-the-art facility it was completed ahead of schedule and furnished with the latest and best equipment available. Once the facility was completed and filled with patients the aesthetically modern building nestled in a beautiful setting in the foothills of southern California was undoubtedly the finest mental hospital in the country.

Doctor Bradhurst and Russel Hieber were fastidious in choosing an operations manager for Hidden Valley Hospital and Sanatorium. They not only had to find someone with strong administrative and managerial skills but someone with a medical background willing to fit in with the sometime questionable ethics of the work that would be performed in the research laboratory. They found such a person in Rebeca Hamilton. She was a beautiful slightly graying woman of forty-seven years with a soothing yet authoritative voice. She exuded governance and leadership and would be ideal to manage the day-to-day operation of the hospital.

A gated drive leading to the Institution is manned at all times and to assure the privacy that the owner of this secluded sanctum demands, the property is enclosed with high-voltage fencing, making it an impenetrable fortress.

Employees working at this highly specialized mental institution are carefully screened and to assure their allegiance to the firm and the confidentiality of the work performed there, they are extremely well paid with excellent benefits. Doctors and nurses chosen to work in this secluded asylum are specialists in their field and when required, selected individuals are ready to aid and abet in the sometime questionable ethics of the work being performed in the West Wing. The restricted West Wing where only classified personnel are allowed! Where hushed-up research and rumored unethical operations are performed.

Doctor Bradhurst's agenda for the asylum are many-fold. The brain is made up of several sections, each containing countless numbers of cells, all contributing to workings of the miraculous human mind. Much is known about the various sections of the brain and what makes humans tick, yet to Doctor Bradhurst, science has only touched on the surface of what the brain's true potentials are capable of. His quest to delve into the inner cores of the brain and learn the mysteries that lie there is paramount to him. There are so many areas that he wants to explore...

He and Dr. Hieber planned to operate on as many patients as possible in as short a time as feasible to gain knowledge in each of his many targeted areas. One of the first regions of the brain he wanted to explore was related to human intelligence and knowledge. Science had long since discovered the location in the brain that governs the learning and retention levels of man's intellect but to-date little has been learned about how these areas function or what levels they were capable of achieving. The variable levels of intellect between humans had always fascinated him. He wanted to know why brainpower differed so greatly between humans. Man had tried to discern the levels of human intelligence by devising IQ tests. These measurements range from extremely low to genius. But how much of the human brain is used even by a genius? Could the brain's powers somehow extend beyond is considered genius, and if so to what level; and if so, what is holding it back? His own IQ is within the top one percent in the world, but what makes his IQ so much higher than ninety nine percent of the world's population? He would so much like to know the answers to these questions and promised himself that he would do everything in his power to do so.

*****

Present day, three years after the opening of Doctor Bradhurst's hospital and with several hundred operations behind him, the doctor and his team had acquired more knowledge about the functions and workings of the human brain than had ever been learned and recorded before.

The main hospital where celebrities and affluent clientele stay to recover from various stress and mental disorders can best be described as luxurious. The amenities are exceptional and the service impeccable resulting in a waiting list of people wanting to be admitted to what had become one of the most desirable rest-homes in the world. At any given time, the hospital houses as many as forty 'elite' patients resulting in a sizable income.

The number of patients committed to the experimental wing varies but averages about thirty. Some of these patients may suffer from various degrees of mental disorders but others are just ordinary people considered derelicts who end up at the asylum. Some even under duress, more prisoners than patients. One of Dr. Bradhurst's criteria in choosing candidates for his experiments is based on I.Q. levels. He insists on having a backlog of patients with a wide coverage of intellectual levels ranging from feebly low to as high as he can locate. Being involved with institutes and hospitals throughout the world, the doctor knows the right people in the right places and can acquire from various institutions as many (desirable) clients for his experimental purposes as he needs. This never-ending supply of patients who end up at the Bradhurst's Asylum are nothing more than guineapigs and succumb to seemingly endless experiments and surgeries performed by the two doctors and their staff.

Dr. Bradhurst had realized that many of the operations they would be performing once the hospital was completed would be complex with a risk of fatalities, so during construction he had a cremation incinerator installed.

A large percentage of patients the doctor chose for his experiments were beyond help and close to death and because of their untraceable backgrounds he had no qualms about operating on them as often as he felt he could get some use from them; and if they died in the process, so be it. Likewise, when selected patients, both insane and sane, were of no further use to him they were eliminated. The records of these hapless human beings were eradicated, and their bodies cremated, leaving no evidence of them ever having been there.

It took some time, but the genius of Dr. Bradhurst finally began to surface. By isolating cell groups within the segment of the brain that controls knowledge, he was able to open up a totally new approach to his research. With the most sophisticated equipment and most powerful computers ever devised and with the use of chemical, electrical, laser, and radioactive stimuli, he discovered the means to measure the output of energy of cells and to determine variables between those energy outputs, thus providing him with some of the data he was looking for. He was yet to determine why the variables occurred; why more cells or less was actually used in different individual's brains but he was confident that that information would soon be discovered and that from there he could start working on ways to stimulate and manipulate living cells. Modifying cell structures to his desires presented many possibilities for him to consider. He would be able to change personalities and strengthen or weaken just about any characteristic or trait. A rare smile crossed his face as he thought that he would soon be able to change and control every attribute of human behavior.

Small leaks from employees who work at Hidden Valley Hospital, and sketchy guesses from those in the medical field that have at least a little insight about the operation that Dr. Gordon Bradhurst maintains in San Bernardino have created somewhat of a mystery surrounding the isolated facility. The hospital was known to be a celebrated and highly respected rest home and mental institute for influential people yet because of the secrecy and speculated unknown activities going on at the Institution, rumors ran rampant. As one restaurant patron stated when talking about the asylum with several of her friends! "It might be nothing more than what it's claimed to be, a mental hospital, but why all that secrecy and those electric fences around the place; you could get electrocuted just touching it." Another diner added, "I wouldn't be surprised if they do all sorts of operations on crazy people up there." A third said, "I hear that people have mysteriously died up there." One of the other women laughed. "Nonsense, nobody would allow anything like that to go on nowadays." In reality, many of the rumors that were spread about the goings-on at Doctor Bradhurst's hospital were true, and in many cases much worse.

Nine
A Leap into History

Doctor Bradhurst had kept abreast of Zoltan Proziver's achievements in genetic engineering and followed the progress Drechsler International was making on the ingenious gene-splicing project. Once his own break-through (enabling him to transfer living cells from one human to another) was perfected, he used his considerable influence to become a Drechsler International board member. At the time of his initial inquiry into joining the board, the company had a full slate of directors with little chance of any of them stepping down in the foreseeable future. As we know, Doctor Bradhurst is a very opportunistic man allowing nothing or no one to stand in his way and as it happened, one of the directors mysteriously died, leaving an opening that allowed Dr. Bradhurst to become one of the candidates for the newly opened position. Prior to his interview at the company's headquarters In Munich, Germany, he studied every aspect of the corporation and by the time he faced the panel that would fill this unexpected, vacated position, he knew as much, and in some cases, even more about the company than the executives interrogating him. Revealing his knowledge of the company greatly impressed his interviewers. Speaking fluent German, he intelligently delved into the workings of all of the divisions that made up the huge conglomerate and discussed in some detail: products, markets, and marketing strategies that the company utilized. He even touched on what he knew about future business plans and objectives that was thought to be somewhat confidential. In closing, he outlined a se-ries of beneficial contributions he could afford to several of those divisions. There did not seem to be much that this incredibly intelligent man did not know about Drechsler. The panel was so impressed with Doctor Bradhurst that it was not surprising that when the interviews were completed, Doctor Gordon Bradhurst had earned himself a seat on the board. There had been only one reason that he pursued this position and that was because of the gene clustering program taking place in the corporations Los Angeles facil-ity. He could see how this process of manipulating the genetic framework of living organisms could benefit his own research and wanted to get close to the people involved in this fascinating new science.

His first action as a board member was to visit the Los Angeles Division of Drechsler International and introduce himself. He met Vice President Ronald Swecker in his office where the two men met for approximately half an hour, discussing the Los Angeles Division's role in the corporation, and touched briefly on the projects being worked on there. When the topic of the Super-Cell program came up, Dr. Bradhurst stated his interest and requested a meeting with Michael Danvers the divisions operations manager and also Hanns Korman, one of the company's leading research scientists who was responsible for the human aspects of what was referred to as the 'Super-Cell' program. The busy vice president was glad to direct his visitor to Mr. Danvers and get back to his work.

Michael Danvers was anything but pleased when Swecker notified him that Dr. Gordon Bradhurst, a newly appointed member of the Corporation's Board of Directors was being escorted to his office and wanted to meet with him and one of his scientists.

The Director of Operations sat behind his large desk in a fashionable office facing his visitor and Dr. Korman. 'Shit', he thought. 'Where can this be going, and why Korman'? He said in his normal blunt manner, "Well Dr. Bradhurst, what can we do for you?"

Gordon Bradhurst had planned for this meeting for some time. He employed a private detective agency to investigate the two men and they dug deep into the background of each, providing him with a complete portfolio of their character and lifestyle. He knew enough about their likes and dislikes; their financial situation and home life to create a psychological assessment of each, assuring him that they could and would get him what he wanted. He just had to approach them in a way that would appeal to the proposal he was about to make them.

Michael Danvers was in financial straits. Due to his relentless philandering his recent divorce had not favored him. His wife took him to the cleaners, leaving him somewhat high and financially dry. Mike, as he is called by just about everyone who knows him, had always lived the highlife of fine dining, classy automobiles and expensive mistresses that turned out to be his downfall. Yes, Dr. Bradhurst could solve all of Michael Danvers' problems.

Hanns Korman on the other hand presented a different problem for the shrewd psychologist. Hanns' problem was not financial but rather domestic. His two grown children and his three grandchildren were living in Chicago where he had lived and worked prior to accepting the position he now held with Drechsler International. His wife Marge yearned to better her social standing and vigorously pursued that aim despite her husband's lack of drive and his reluctance to join any societal affairs within the elite circles of Los Angeles; circles that would allow her to rub elbows with the higher classes. His lack of interest in anything to do with raising himself and her above the bland and placated life that she felt she was trapped in, created a strong resentment between them. Even so, she attended as many social functions as she could worm her way into in hopes that she would eventually be accepted; but it was not easy without an interesting and enthusiastic husband at her side. Hanns lived for his work and had little interest in anything else, especially attending parties and mixing with the boring and uninteresting people that his wife so eagerly strived to impress. His obsessive love of the science he had made his life's work had built a wall between them and she grew, to loath him. Simply stated, Margery Korman was a people person and Hanns was not; and they had grown apart because of it. Her way to ease the torment that she endured because of her husband's lack of social drive was spending money. If nothing else, whenever she was invited to any social gathering, she was dressed to the nines. Money had never been a big issue with Hanns, so he never admonished his wife for spending it as fast as he made it. He had a private account that she could not use, with enough to hold them over no matter how heavy she dug into their joint account. Hanns Korman was a workaholic! He loved his job and only had one grievance that Gordon Bradhurst had uncovered. He hated the bureaucracy in his field of study that hindered progress with his research programs. The laws and regulations that slowed down and even prevented him from progressing with his experiments as he would like to, frustrated him to no ends. This was one of the reasons he chose Dr. Korman to become part of his team. He felt the same about government's interference, in just about everything they involved themselves in. This would be the area that Dr. Bradhurst would target to bring the medical doctor turned research scientist into his fold. There were other reasons he wanted to pursue Dr. Korman and have him join his team. Not only was he a brilliant and renowned brain specialist but he was also the leading authority in the world on Zoltan Proziver's gene clustering process. Yes, Dr. Hanns Korman would fit in nicely with his plans. He would not only convince him to join his operation, but he would also resolve his marital problems.

Responding to Michael Danvers' question he said. "Being a new board member and living in Los Angeles, I thought I would stop by to review this division's programs. I have not had the pleasure of meeting you Mr. Danvers but I understand you run a very efficient and effective operation. Mr. Swecker speaks highly of you." Then addressing Hanns Korman, he said, "We have met a few times Dr. Korman, and I want to say that I have always been impressed with your work. I might add that I was surprised when you gave up your surgical career for the research position you now have here at Drechsler."

Hanns Korman reciprocated by saying, "I am pleased to have you here and I too have followed your accomplished career; and congratulations on your appointment to Drechsler's board. Why research over surgery? Simply put, operating on individuals certainly has its gratifications, but opening up new frontiers has a strong appeal to me.

Michael Danvers obviously perturbed by having this outsider interrupt his schedule put an end this display of praise and amity between the two men by clearing his throat. "Ahem, can we get on with it?"

"Yes; certainly! First let me tell you a little about myself. I wear several hats but for the sake of this meeting let us just say I am a Neurosurgeon. I am deeply involved in several studies involving the human brain and have a strong interest in what you refer to as your Super-Cell program. I have kept myself up to date on the process since Zoltan Proziver first discovered his clustering process and have a fairly good understanding of the entire procedure. I know of the results achieved to-date and what your corporations' plans are for the progression of this interesting science for the immediate future." This raised Danvers' brow. "I have kept abreast of the wolf project ever since the first animals were introduced into Yellowstone National Park and the dreadful devastation these animals are causing now. I also know that Dr. Frank Wallace was here last week discussing the work being done by Carlene Linser and her team related to his concerns." Dr. Bradhurst's tone of voice had indicated to his attentive audience that he was troubled by the deaths that these wolves were leaving in their wake but in fact he could have cared less. Death meant little to him, but he wanted to portray a positive picture of himself.

Mr. Danvers held up his hand resulting in a pause in the doctor's oration. "How do you know these things and how did you know that Frank Wallace was here?"

With a slight smile Dr. Bradhurst replied, "I do my research Dr. Danvers. Before applying for the board membership, I familiarized myself with not only this division but all of Drechsler's operations. I have involved myself with several people in certain positions throughout the organization and keep abreast of any and all information that might interest me."

He continued in his soft yet convincing voice. "I know how genes are recognized, how they are clustered into various strengths and how they have been introduced into selected animal species. I also know that you have extracted hundreds of cell clusters from humans and identified many of them. But enough about my knowledge about this Super-Cell program! The reason I wanted to talk to you is because I have a proposal that I am sure you will want to hear. Believe me; what I have to say will be to your *great advantage*." He emphasized the words 'great advantage'. "However, I prefer not to discuss it here. Would it be possible for the three of us to have dinner this evening? I assure you that what I have to discuss will be very *advantageous* to each of you." Again, he emphasized 'advantageous! The mystery behind this world-renowned brain surgeon aroused both men's curiosity and they accepted his invitation.

Gordon Bradhurst reserved a private dining room in one of the finest restaurants in Los Angeles for his meeting with Drechsler's Operations Manager and Dr. Hanns Korman who, like himself was a celebrated brain specialist. The meal was excellent as was the wine served with it. Dr. Bradhurst directed the dinner conversation to sundry and mundane topics; a feeling-out on his part, to get a better understanding of the two men's personalities. Michael was a man who held back and as Dr. Bradhurst saw it, was unlikely open up or bare his soul. He was stern, direct, and obviously a no-nonsense man. It was also obvious that he was anxious and not comfortable sitting here. He was a man who liked to be in control; to lead and to direct and felt somewhat uneasy in the position he found himself in. Hanns, not in the habit of dinning in such a high-class restaurant, enjoyed his meal and enjoyed the wine even more. But he too showed signs of concerns about why he was here and what this new board member had in mind.

When dinner was over and cocktails delivered to their table, Br, Bradhurst addressed his two diner guests. "Before I discuss why I asked you here, I want you to agree that before you jump up and leave, thinking I am a raving lunatic, hear me through. Please listen to everything I have to say. Will you agree to that?" Both men looked at him as though he was the lunatic he had referred to, but now their interest was aroused even more. They agreed.

Let me ask a question; could samples of Super-Cells be taken out of the Drechsler?"

Michael Danvers looked at him with a questioning leer. "What in hell are you talking about? Has headquarters sent you here to check our loyalty?"

"I can see how that would cross your mind, but no, I can assure you that I have a completely different reason for asking the question. Is it possible?"

"Certainly not; they are under tight security. There is no way that anyone could steal anything from our company."

"And you, Hanns, could it be done?"

Hanns Korman thought for a moment before answering. "No, I agree with Mike, it would be damn near impossible."

'Damn near impossible.' Gordon Bradhurst mused. "Then let me rephrase my question. If the incentive, was large enough, could it be done?"

"What are you talking about? What kind of incentive?" Michael asked.

When Hanns hesitated and now with Michael's question, Gordon Bradhurst knew he had them. "Before we go any further, let me say that for reasons that do not concern you, I have a need for some of the human cells you have discovered, and gentlemen, I will make it very worthwhile for anyone who helps me obtain them."

When Dr. Bradhurst paused to let this sink in, his two listeners stared at him with astonished expressions. Michael Danvers was the one to ask the really important question. "What do you mean when you say helping you with this would be beneficial to us?"

Dr. Bradhurst, realizing that Danvers was already hooked must now sell Hanns Korman. "Before I answer that I would like to talk with Mr. Korman. Michael, would you be so kind as to wait in the lounge for a few minutes?" The question was more a polite demand than a request so Michael Danvers with a look of disgust departed with his drink in hand.

Alone with Hanns Korman, Dr. Bradhurst said. "Let me tell you about one of many experiments I am involved with. You have undoubtedly heard about my hospital. We specialize in patients with brain related ailments, including neurodegenerative disorders and anything from mild to severe cases of insanity to total lunacy. I have a team of some of the finest brain specialists and neurosurgeons in the country working there under rather unfettered conditions. We bypass many of the rules and regulations that hinder progress in the name of safety and security. I think you will agree with me Hanns when I say our hands are often tied too firmly, preventing us from getting fast and vital results. Our time here on earth is short and I believe we should make the most of it. One of the areas I have been exploring is isolating and identifying brain cells. Sounds familiar, doesn't it? We have had some positive and quite interesting results. For example, I have identified cells that control man's learning and knowledge retention. I know you have been experimenting in this area as well and that you have achieved limited results with simple traits in animals using clustered cells. Unlike your Super-Cell project where clustered gene cells are hereditarily transferred to offspring, I have perfected a procedure of transferring brain cells from one human brain to another. Rather than waiting for each new generation for results, my discoveries allow us to get almost instant results. Hanns, I want to use cell clusters to further advance the results I have already achieved."

"In the short time we have been in operation we have discovered more about the workings of the human brain than all of the research done before us. Hanns, I know we think along similar lines when it comes to bureaucratic restrictions in our field. My team and I perform many brain-related experiments and we do so in what you might call hush-hush conditions. The reason I am talking to you is because I would like you to work with me in advancing our science. Before you say anything, I would like you to visit the facility and if you like what you see, I will have a proposition for you that I am sure will be to your liking." Hanns Korman's attention was aroused, and he could not hide his excitement. Dr. Bradhurst was offering him a job to work for him. He enjoyed his work as a research clinician specializing in neurology and the human brain at Drechsler but if he was given the opportunity to work at Dr. Bradhurst's hospital, well… yes, he most certainly would be most interested in visiting his operation and told him so. "Good," the doctor said. ". We can discuss this later, and please do not mention this to Mr. Danvers. I would rather he knew nothing of this discussion. Now, let me call him back."

When the three men were once again together, Dr. Bradhurst began to lay his cards on the table. "Gentlemen, I see this as a simple transaction. I want cell clusters and you have them. I am willing to pay heavily for them so let's discuss ways we can satisfy both of us. I have chosen you because I am sure that it will take the efforts of two strategically positioned people to retrieve the cell clusters that I want."

"Hanns, I believe you have access to all cell clusters related to humans. Is that correct?"

"Yes, but even though I have full responsibility over our storage laboratory I can't remove any sample without signing them out. All transactions are controlled by computer. I don't see any way of bypassing the system… unless."

"Yes!" Dr. Bradhurst interjected. "Unless the computer records could be altered; and that's where you would come in Mr. Danvers. If I am not mistaken, you are very well-versed in computer technology and because of your position you have the clearance to assess every company system. How difficult would it be to alter records related to Hanns' removal of samples?"

"It can't be done. It would be too risky. Any number of things could go wrong. Every computer transaction is automatically backed up instantly to a hard drive whenever anything is removed from the laboratory repository. At the end of every working day all daily transactions are backed up to a corporate hard drive making it impossible for Hanns to remove samples undetected. The whole idea is too risky. It can't be done."

"Can't be done? I don't believe that. Risky only if you are careless and don't cover every possible scenario that could lead to discovery."

Dr. Bradhurst leaned forward in his chair and said, "Here's what I think and propose. I feel certain that you Hanns can retrieve any and all of the samples I will require. Yes, there will be a computer record but getting them out of the facility is something I am sure you can manage. Mr. Danvers, despite your insistence that you cannot successfully accomplish this task, I am confident you can. I think you can manipulate the records so no one in the organization will ever know that samples have been removed. Is there a time delay between the time the transaction is made and when the data is backed-up?"

Michael Danvers' mind was working as he pondered the question and visualized the computer program controlling that action. "No, as I've said, it's almost instant. As I keep saying, none of this hair brained scheme is possible."

"Yet I say it is possible," insisted the doctor. "And Mr. Danvers, if you can pull this off, you will receive two million dollars."

Michael Danvers' first though was that this was some sort of a scam. What was this guy up to? Was he really offering him two million dollars to help steal a few samples of laboratory vials? Samples of biological cells being stockpiled with no approved programs to actually use them in human experiments! If this crackpot was telling the truth, two million dollars would solve all my problems. "What kind of assurance do I have that you will live up to the two million dollars?" He asked.

"I will open a Swiss account in your name and one million dollars will be wired there immediately. The money will be tax-free, and you will be able to transfer into your local accounts as you see fit. Just be smart about it and don't overdo spending. We wouldn't want the Treasury Department questioning you. The remainder will be wired to your account within one week of my receiving the samples. That will give me enough time to examine and verify their validity."

Michael saw those dollar signs flashing before his eyes and throwing all of his concerns aside agreed to this fool's proposal. Certainly, he could alter the compute program. He could effect a temporary change in the time between the signing out of the samples and the time it took to download the data to the hard drive. Yes, the transaction time was almost instant but almost to a computer was a long time. He could do it in such a way that no one would ever realize it had happened. Two million dollars… He couldn't conceal the exhilaration that rushed through him.

Dr. Bradhurst now addressed Hanns Korman. "Hanns, the same financial offer is extended to you."

The breath came out of Hanns Korman. Two million dollars! Wow! Like Danvers, he was astounded. He had just over three hundred thousand securely safe from Marge getting to it and another hundred thousand or so in their joint bank accounts. He thought that was a lot of money… but two million! The way Marge was spending it faster than he could earn it, he would never be able to add to what he had. Two million dollars! The first thing he would do was buy her off with the divorce she had threatened so often. His thoughts were interrupted as Dr. Bradhurst continued.

"There will be nothing in writing. Shall we seal our agreement with a handshake?"

"Good, now, how fast can you get me a complete list of all the cell clusters you have in inventory related to humans?"

"Hanns can run off a report Monday morning." Michael Danvers said. "It will be more natural for him to run the report than me."

"Excellent! Hanns, can you take Tuesday off and visit my hospital? We could go through your records and come up with a list of what I want."

"Only if my boss approves it," he said looking at Mr. Danvers.

"Of course," Danvers agreed.

"How long will it take to accomplish this withdrawal?" Bradhurst asked.

Michael Danvers, with nothing on his mind but money, said. "The sooner the better!"

"I'll be limited on how many I can move at a time." Hanns said. "But I agree with Mike. Let's get this over with. I think by the end of the workday next Friday would be a good time."

As Dr. Bradhurst rose from his seat in preparation of leaving, Michael Danvers asked for a private word with him. Once Hanns Korman left, Danvers said in his normal brusque and autoreactive voice, "I think that because of my position being at a much higher level than Korman's and the fact that I have a great deal more to lose than him if anything goes wrong with this… withdrawal, I should be compensated at a higher level than him."

This did not surprise Dr. Bradhurst. He knew that Michael Danvers was self-important and would think he could push the envelope, so to speak. "What did you have in mind?" He asked.

"I think that because you are putting me in a very precarious position with a high level of risk and the fact that you are a very wealthy man, another million dollars would be appropriate."

"I see," Dr. Bradhurst replied in a calm and reassuring voice. "That sounds reasonable. I will deposit one million into your bank account Monday and will transfer an additional two million when the transaction is complete."

Michael Danvers was so pleased with himself for pushing the issue for an addition million dollars that he did a little dance and sang 'I'm in the money' as he approached his car that the valet brought to him.

Dr. Bradhurst smiled as he was chauffeured home. He would have his biological clusters and he would certainly pay Mr. Danvers for his services.

Ten
Thinning Out the Chafe

As planned, Hanns Korman met Dr. Bradhurst at his hospital at ten am Tuesday morning. Their meeting lasted for about two hours in which time the two scientists evaluated the long list of biological cell samples inventoried at Drechsler International. Dr. Bradhurst seemed very pleased with the list of close to two hundred samples that he settled on. Once this was done, addressing his visitor he said, "I'll leave it up to you and Mr. Danvers to work out how you want to accomplish this. I needn't remind you of being careful but non-the-less, cover your tracks."

"I have my part worked out already. I didn't realize how many samples you would require; the environmentally controlled case I will use to get them out of the building isn't large enough for all that you are requiring so I'll have to do this in two steps. Mr. Danvers is complaining about the difficulties he'll have overriding the computer and keeps harping on the fact that all the risks are on him. I can hear him complaining even more when he learns how many samples are involved and that it will have to be done in two stages."

"Yes, Mr. Danvers does seem to be somewhat neurotic about this. It makes me wonder if it is only a facade to…" Be broke off his thoughts; not wanting Hanns to know what he was thinking. Mr. Danvers was definitely becoming a problem. "But regardless," he continued. "I have no doubts you will succeed." Pushing a button on his deck phone he waited until a man's voice answered. "Russel, please join us for lunch in my office, I'll have sandwiches sent in from the kitchen." 122

Within a minute a tall serious looking man entered the room. "I want to introduce you to my partner Dr. Russel Hieber who runs this institution. Russel, please meet Dr. Hanns Korman. As we've discussed, Dr. Korman heads up one of the science labs at Drechsler. He is considering joining our operation. I think he will make a strong contribution to our staff. After lunch show him our operation. I trust him completely so give him a full tour and leave nothing out."

"So, you are thinking of joining us," Russel said once they left Dr. Bradhurst's office.

"Doctor Bradhurst informs me that your work here is pretty much unhindered by governmental regulations and that interests me very much."

Russel laughed. "Yes, you might say that. Gordon has undoubtedly informed you that our main objective is to learn as much as possible in the shortest period of time about the workings of the human brain. Something you should know right up front is that many of the patients we have here are beyond help and are subject to any and all experiments that Gordon and I agree to. You might think that some of the operations we perform are questionable and insensitive, but our mission is to get results and you will soon see how successful we are in getting those results. Many of our patients are all but dead already and we consider them at least somewhat expendable. If we lose an occasional person on the operating table, we have just hastened the inevitable."

Hanns Korman was somewhat taken back. He knew that humans were being used for research and experiments at this modern facility but had never thought that they were being sacrificed.

"I'll start by showing you our operating laboratory." Russel Hieber said.

It was early afternoon when the two men completed the tour. "Please get yourself a coffee or anything else you might want and wait in the cafeteria for a few minutes while I talk with Gordon." Russel Hieber said. "We will be with you shortly."

Once Russel entered Dr. Bradhurst's office and sat down he said, "He'll do!"

"How did he react when he learned about operating on patients?"

"Seemed a little concerned at first but the more he learned about the progress we've made, the more excited he became. He told me that he would very much like to work here. His knowledge of clustering cells and his outstanding qualifications as a brain specialist makes him the perfect choice."

"Agreed! Let's bring him in."

Hanns was impressed with the hospital and the incredible progress being made in understanding the workings of the brain and could not hide his enthusiasm. Dr. Bradhurst said, "I knew you would be impressed but please sit down. We have a good deal to talk about."

"Dr. Hieber and I think you will fit in nicely here and we would like to make you an official offer if you are prepared to work here."

Even though he was concerned about the apparent lack of human compassion for many of the patients who had been referred to as expendable, Hanns told himself the incredible results they were achieving were unparalleled anywhere in the world and the sacrifices were in the name of science. He assured his two interviewers that he certainly was interested.

"Good! First let's discuss your compensation. Your salary will be twice what you are presently making at Drechsler, and we have a very attractive benefit package." Hanns was speechless as Dr. Bradhurst continued. "Russel and I have big plans for you Hanns. You realize the importance of incorporating the gene clustering science into our studies and we do not want the supply to end with what you will be getting for us from Drechsler. So, let me ask you, can you create the process here in this laboratory?"

Without hesitation Hanns Korman said. "Certainly; if I had the equipment and resources, I could easily set up an operation similar to what I use at Drechsler."

"Wonderful; equipment and resources will be no problem. Russel will work with you on your needs. You will be on our payroll starting Monday however I want you to remain at Drechsler for at least another month. In that time, I am sure that Russel will have everything you need set up in or laboratory."

"I have researched you quite thoroughly," Gordon Bradhurst said to Hanns. "I know of your marital problems, and we wouldn't want that to interfere with your work here."

Hanns was a little embarrassed and quite surprised that his personal life was looked into, but not wanting this to be an issue between them he addressed the concern. "Yes, things are not well at home but thanks to you, now that I have enough money, I can afford to divorce her."

Gordon heard him but could foresee once his wife learned that he had money she might become a constant problem and if there was one thing that Doctor Gordon Bradhurst could not tolerate, it was problems. "That sounds like a good solution," he said even though he was sure it wasn't. "But as we discussed earlier, do not tell her anything about our arrangements until I think the time is right."

Monday afternoon Michael Danvers was once again paid a visit by Dr. Bradhurst. The meeting was short and cordial as the documents showing a Swiss account in the name of Michael W. Danvers in the amount of one million dollars were finalized. He was so elated and giddy that he only lightly scanned through the three-page legal agreement that was carefully prepared by Gordon Bradhurst and his attorney. All he really cared about was the Swiss account number in his name.

"The funds will be in your account by tomorrow morning, however as indicated in the agreement, there will be a delay of seven days before the account is activated. After that you will be able to withdraw from. But when you do, I once again urge you to use it wisely so as not to draw too much attention to yourself."

The feeling of euphoria that had rushed through Michael's mind when he knew for certain that Dr. Bradhurst had lived up to his proposal and in fact had come through with the money, sent a strong surge of power and boldness through him. After all, he was a high-ranking executive in one of the world's largest corporations and the man he was dealing with was only a local doctor; albeit a very rich and well-known doctor but non-the-less, just a doctor. He realized that the deal he had agreed to, was a once in a life-time opportunity and felt he had to make the most of it. Could he demand more from this man who was so desperate to acquire samples that were under his care? Demanding more money had easily worked before, could it work again? He would give it a try. "You realize," he said in his authoritative voice, "that I will have to go through this very risky undertaking twice. That doubles the danger and increases my chance of being discovered. This extremely difficult and dangerous task will be putting my reputation and career at stake, and I think that these additional risks should be considered. Financially that is. You are a very wealthy man, and I don't see how an addition sum that might be considered a bonus would put much of a dent in your bank accounts."

Without hesitation Dr. Bradhurst agreed. "Certainly; I should have thought of that. We didn't realize when we made our agreement that the samples I want, could not be retrieved at one time. If an additional million dollars meets with your approval, we can consider it a done deal."

The surge of power that Michael was experiencing grew ever stronger as he saw how easily he had turned three million dollars into four.

When the doctor had departed, he once again found himself humming that catchy toon, 'I'm in the money'.

Hanns Korman had no difficulties in getting the samples out of Drechsler's laboratory. He signed out as many units that would fit in his satchel one evening and because of his position at the firm, he just walked through security as he did every evening. In the meantime, Michael Danvers pushed a few buttons on his computer at precisely the right time and the files showed no withdrawals. The removal of the second batch of biological specimens was also pulled off with no mishaps.

Only when Hanns had delivered the second batch of specimens to the Bradhurst hospital and he and his team of scientists were assured that they survived the short time they were in transit, did Dr. Bradhurst take a sigh of relief. He had chosen well in selecting Hanns Korman and Michael Danvers and they provided him with what he wanted. It was only a matter of playing to individual desires. With Hanns it was by simply providing him with a work environment so much to his liking that he could not pass up the offer. Danvers was even simpler. He just had to dangle money before his eyes to feed his greed. Yes, he had chosen well and now it was time to reward his two collaborators. As it turned out, Hanns was just the man he wanted to join his team. After a short time, he would turn in his resignation at Drechsler and work at his research center where he could help in perfecting the process of obtaining and identifying specific brain cell clusters. He would also be useful in implanting clusters into living people's brains. His excitement to get started in this new science was overwhelming but first he had a couple of things that must be addressed.

He placed a private call to a special number that he used on rare occasions. A man answered, identifying himself as Sid. Not needing an introduction, Doctor Bradhurst got right to the point. "I have two jobs for you…" He hesitated and then continued. "No, only one job; I want to personally handle the other myself." Very little information was ever required when dealing with the man on the line. He was a reliable professional and had never failed him. The doctor gave his listener the name of Margery Korman and her address. He concluded by saying. "An accident at home would be appropriate when she is alone."

"Consider it done," was the only reply, ending their brief conversation.

As per Dr. Bradhurst's strong request, Hanns Korman had not yet told Marge of his involvement with Dr. Bradhurst or about his new-found wealth. Once he got the money, he would buy her off with a divorce and finally be rid of her constant bickering and pestering every morning and evening about anything and everything. They had not had a decent word for one-another in months. Even though he had made a strong name for himself in the scientific community, she thought of him as a failure in helping her achieve the status she craved in Los Angeles high society. Hanns' home-life was misery. He dreaded every minute he had to spend with her. But as anxious as he was to end his marriage, he would hold off in addressing the issue until, in Dr. Bradhurst's words, the time was right.

Marge Korman and her husband shared their usual cold shoulders for each other during breakfast, but she was not as abusive as normal because she had somehow managed to worm her way into a shopping date with two women she looked up to in the societal community. Looking forward to an exciting day of shopping and socializing, she pretty much ignored her husband this morning until he left for work. She still had about two hours before meeting her companions for a late breakfast and then off to Macy's. She was in her bedroom selecting the perfect dress for the occasion when the entire house blew up in an enormous explosion.

Within a few minutes the entire neighborhood was swarming with people looking on in horror. The beautiful home that had stood on the corner lot was reduced to a pile of smoldering debris. It took the authorities two days to determine that the cause of the explosion that took the life of Margery Korman was due to a faulty valve in the gas line located in the basement. Dr. Bradhurst smiled when he heard of the blast. Sid was an exceptional man, and he made a note to reward him with an extra bonus.

Hanns Korman could not believe what had happened. Sure, he did not like his wife and at times felt as though he could kill her, but that was only meaningless thoughts in his head. Now that she was gone, he felt remorse for her loss. Deep down he never really wanted any harm to come to her, he just wanted her out of his life. He was not as close to his children and grandchildren as Marge was. They all loved her and would be devastated by her loss but somehow, as in all tragedies, they would all get through this terrible misfortune.

Doctor Bradhurst could see that his newest pawn in the games he played with life and death was somewhat shaken with the death of his wife. "Hanns," he said. "It was a terrible accident but there are accidents happening all around us all the time. You must put this tragedy behind you. Don't dwell on the past but look forward to what you can accomplish in the future. You are a gifted doctor and scientist with a wonderful opportunity to contribute greatly to advances in your field. Hanns: trust in me and together we can accomplish unbelievable things. You and I are two of the greatest scientists in our field and I foresee nothing but greatness in our future. I have always though that the best remedy for grief was work, so the best thing you can do right now is to jump into your work harder than ever." Play him, Dr. Bradhurst mused to himself. Get him thinking he is not only important to me as a scientist but also as a colleague and friend.

Michael Danvers was undoubtedly the happiest he had ever been. Sure, he had made big money throughout his career, but bad luck had always befallen him. Gambling was one of his most enjoyable distractions and at times he had fared quite well and prospered in the rewards that he realized. But then that black cloud that so often hovered over his head would once again rain despair upon him with poor luck at the tables and bury him in debt. Prior to meeting Dr. Bradhurst he had never been in such desperate straits. His gambling debts were enormous, and he was being pressured and even threatened to pay-up. And the courts were on his case about delinquent alimony for his two wives. And now, like a gift from heaven, along comes Dr. Bradhurst to solve all of his problems.

"Mr. Danvers." Dr. Bradhurst said once he reached him on the telephone. "We should meet so I can thank you in person for the exceptional job you did and also to discuss the transferring of the funds you have earned to your account. Would it be convenient for you to meet me at my hospital this evening, shall we say eight o'clock? I have an excellent bottle of brandy that I have been saving for a special occasion and what better time to celebrate than now."

With no hesitation Michael Danvers agreed. In two days the first million would be released to him and he would pay off his debts and feel free once again. He had been dreaming of how this chance encounter with Dr. Bradhurst was going to change his life. The first thing he would do was quit his miserable job. Working for someone else would be something of the past. His prospects were seemingly endless; a villa in Monte-Carlo, a chalet in the Alps, and who knows what else. The world would be his to do whatever he pleased.

"Wonderful," Dr. Bradhurst said. "I will be looking forward to seeing you." Sitting in his office in Los Angeles, Gordon smiled. He had some exciting plans for Mr. Danvers. As soon as he hung up the phone, he called his hospital and asked the receptionist for Dr. Hieber. "Russel," he said when his partner answered the phone, "I have a meeting with Mr. Danvers at the hospital tonight at eight and will require your presence."

"Certainly," Dr. Hieber said. "I have been looking forward meeting him."

Michael Danvers was euphoric when he arrived at the hospital. For the past few days, a strong sense of well-being and power all but overwhelmed him. And now he was about to become the recipient of a fortune. Dr. Bradhurst personally greeted him at the main entrance. "So glad you could make it this evening Mr. Danvers. Please join me in my office. I have that bottle of brandy waiting."

"I've been looking forward to it since you invited me. I have always enjoyed a good brandy."

"I'm sure you will approve of this one."

Once they were seated in luxuriously comfortable chairs with tumblers in their hands, Dr. Bradhurst got right to the point. "I was very pleased with the results of our little exploit. I was sure you could pull it off but tell me, how sure are you that the disappearance of so many samples will not be missed?"

Michael Danvers laughed. "I am positive. I manipulated the system so no one will ever discover that anything has ever been removed. Besides, no one would ever have a reason to suspect anything." To doubly assure Dr. Bradhurst, he added. "I assure you that our little secret is one hundred percent safe."

"I am very glad to hear that," the doctor said. "Now, let's have another glass of brandy."

"I would love to. It certainly is as good as you said it would be."

Dr. Bradhurst went to the bar and poured another portion of golden amber liquor into their glasses. With his back to his visitor, he put a measured dose of clear liquid into his guest's drink and gave it a gentle stir. As he handed his guest the glass, he said, "Michael, I foresee you playing an important role in my future research here."

After taking a sip of the delicate and wonderfully flavored brandy, Michael, not quite understanding Dr. Bradhurst's meaning, asked. "What do you mean?"

"Well, I was thinking that you are a very highly intelligent man and I believe there could be much more you could contribute to the work we are doing here. I have taken the liberty of looking up your background and noticed that your IQ level is rated among the top fifteen percent in the world. Yes, you are a very intelligent man."

Michael, sipping his brandy smiled with that feeling of pride that had been with him throughout the day. Here, a brilliant and extremely successful doctor was praising him with what appeared to be the possibility of making even more money. He was anxious to see where this was leading.

"For the past few years," the doctor continued, "I have been working with many people here at the hospital, but none have ever had an IQ quite as high as yours. You are exactly the type of person that I have been looking for."

A slight fuzziness was beginning to pass before Michael Danvers' eyes and as he listened to the doctor's voice, he became mesmerized. He placed the empty glass on the table and seemed to drift into a state of lassitude and soon became totally immobile. He could hear every word that his host was saying but was helpless in any attempt to move.

"We are quite pleased with the advances we have made here. We have discovered how to transfer brain tissues from one human to another. By splicing cells to areas of the brain that govern various functions and traits we are able to improve mental abilities in some of the recipients. I am most anxious to experiment on your brain Mr. Danvers. Just think of the speed in which we can progress now that we have gene clusters that you have so willingly provided. We will soon be testing those clusters in some of our, shall I say less important patients. And when I am sure that we have achieved adequate results, I will impregnate your brain with selective cells." Michael Danvers was hearing every word in perfect clarity but was unable to speak or react in any way to the horrors that he was hearing. He had just been on the threshold of a new and wonderful life and now he was being told that he was going to be a guineapig in this mad doctor's nightmare of a lunatic asylum. He wanted to scream and fight his way out of this horror but was helpless to do either.

"Once we perfect the use of these super-cells, I hope to be able to strengthen certain areas of your brain. I foresee you being instrumental in helping me discover why human brains range from feeble-minded to highly intellectual levels. Just think about it, Mr. Danvers, we can hopefully increase your present intellect and IQ. Wouldn't it be nice to increase your brain power? You might become a genius."

Dr. Bradhurst punched a button on his desk and said, "Russel would you please join us."

As Dr. Russel Hieber entered the office Gordon said in way of introduction, "Russel, I would like you to meet Michael Danvers. Mr. Danvers will be our guest here for some time; I should say for the rest of his life."

"I'm so very glad that you will be staying with us Mr. Danvers. Gordon has told me a great deal about you and the important role you will be playing here at our institution."

"I'm afraid our distinguished guest is not able to talk or move at the present, but I assure you that he can hear quite well," Dr. Bradhurst said. "I will leave him in your capable hands. And as we discussed, keep him in the private room on the third floor. I want him isolated from most of our staff and it is especially important that our new doctor does not know of his presence here. I'm sure you can manage that."

"Be assured we will take very good care of our guest. I have asked Bill to assist me in transferring him to his new quarters. I'll have him come in right away." Bill Thomlenson was one of their trusted employees and could be counted on for his discretion in all matters; even with the occasional use of the crematoria oven to dispose of corpses that did not survive the operating table.

Once he was alone in his office Gordon poured himself another small drink. Yes, he thought, this is a very fine brandy. His attorney would cancel Michael Danvers' million-dollar account the following day. The over-eager Director of Drechsler International's biological operations had failed to read all of the fine print in the agreement before signing it. If he had, he would have noticed that the law firm of Swarchel and Brennon had the right to nullify the transaction within one week of the account becoming activated. He would also call Sid to find and destroy Michael Danvers' copy of the agreement they had signed. He would make sure that there was no connection between them. He sighed as he sipped the last of his brandy, all was going well.

Hanns began the training process for selected members of the staff of doctors and scientists assigned to the experimental lab in understanding the principals of gene clustering. They would soon begin the procedure of matching unidentified genes cells to actual bodily functions and traits. Once he was full time, they would begin the complex process of obtaining brain clusters from patients.

Gordon Bradhurst had no doubt whatsoever that he would soon out-distance Drechsler in this new science and become the leading authority in the field. He had no stringent industry and government regulations to adhere to as Drechsler did; there would be nothing whatsoever to hold him back and he would push on with the most aggressive and expeditious program he had ever been involved with. He was certain that every function of the human brain could be improved upon by strengthening cells that controlled those functions. But above all, the ultimate reason for obtaining Zoltan Proziver's clustering process was for personal reasons. He wanted to tap into the unused portions of the brain involving the intellect of mankind and when he felt he had mastered the science to the point of his satisfaction, he would have his team implant selected cell clusters into his own brain.

Eleven
Michael Danvers

Hanns Korman had gone through a very disturbing and tiring time after the death of his wife. His children wanted their mother to be buried near to them in the Chicago area, so the body was transported to a funeral parlor in Glenview. The funeral went as most funerals do; friends and relatives gathered for the church service and the reception that followed; all conveying sympathy and trying to comfort the bereaved.

His children were deeply saddened by the loss of their mother and consolatory toward their father. They had known things were not always congenial between their parents but didn't know how far the two had separated in the past couple of year. Once again, they urged him to return to Chicago to be nearer them, but to no avail.

He had always been at his best when engulfed in his work, something Marge could never understand. Now that he was back in Los Angeles, he was anxious to begin working at the Bradhurst Institute, however, due to his wife's death and the sudden disappearance of Michael Danvers, Dr. Bradhurst thought it prudent to wait a while longer before he gave notice.

It was six weeks after the theft of the clustered gene cells that Dr. Korman finally severed his employment with Drechsler International and reported to Russel Hieber at the Bradhurst Hospital. He was elated that the time had finally come, and he began working full time with an experienced team of specialists in a laboratory even more advanced than the one he left at Drechsler. He couldn't have been more jubilant about the new and exciting life he was involving himself in.

Michael Danvers' disappearance had been a shock to everyone at the company. It seemed inconceivable that he should just vanish like he did. When he didn't report to work, the company tried to contact him but failing to do so, notified the authorities with their concern. The police, finding his home empty of all clothing and personal items assumed he had moved from his present address. However, company officials had insisted that Mr. Danvers would never just up and leave his job without notifying them and continued to pressure the police. Inquiries were made in trying to determine his whereabouts, but to-date there had been no sign of him. When it became public knowledge that Michael Danvers was deeply in debt, Hanns had his own idea about his disappearance. He thought that once he got all that money and owing a great deal to bookies and creditors, he must have fled with his fortune to parts unknown, leaving those he owed in the lurch.

During the past few weeks Dr. Bradhurst and his team had not stood idle. Hanns had spent what time he could, teaching the team assigned to this project the fundamentals of the clustering process and the basics of matching gene clusters to actual human traits, but without Hanns there to lead them, little progress had been made.

Gordon Bradhurst was restless and anxious to start experimenting with this new science; he had biologic specimens, patients, and an experienced staff of doctors and surgeons. He couldn't wait any longer so no sooner had Hanns Korman reported to the hospital on a permanent bases, he called a meeting in the conference room with Russel Hieber, Hanns and three of his leading surgeons, all of whom would be performing operations as Dr. Bradhurst's plans unfolded. "I am ready to begin testing these clustered cells," he began in his usual confident and imposing voice. "The subject we have chosen for the first operation is Mrs. Parkins. She is forty-six years old and is in extremely poor physical condition. She has been in and out of hospitals and institutions most of her life. Her immune system is almost non-existent making her susceptible to a wide variety of diseases and ailments. It's a wonder that she is alive. I selected her for several reasons. One being her weak immune system. Secondly, she has semi-severe psychosis that is progressively worsening. She is in the middle stages of dementia and struggles with her memory. Her mental disorder is at the stage where she still retains some of her faculties but as I have stated, they are declining quite rapidly and she's slowly slipping away from reality. Unfortunately, there is some organic damage to her brain, but some of the brain cells are healthy enough for us to work with. We will be targeting those living cells and implanting clustered super cells that we are quite certain will merge with the healthy cells. The strong, healthy cells we will be implanting in her will hopefully strengthen her immune system and improve her health, but more important, I am optimistic that the cells we will be infusing in her brain will curb at least some of the deterioration she if experiencing and possibly even cure some of her mental problems. She is an ideal subject.

I will personally perform this first operation with the aid of Dr. Hieber and Dr. Korman. However, I want each of you to pay close attention to this procedure because you will all be involved in performing similar operations."

"Many cerebral and mental functions of the human brain are of great interest to me. I believe we can improve our learning ability, knowledge retention, level of intellectual aptitude and memory. We will be concentrating on as many biological and psychological makeups as possible, however, I have targeted two area that will be our first priorities. Man's varying levels of intellect is of great interest to me so we will be investigating the portion of the brain related to cognition. The second affects the portion of the brain that determines our memory capability. Dr. Hieber and I have compiled a list of areas we plan to explore. He will cover these areas in detail later. We will also be directing our efforts towards the field of medicine. The work you will be involved in will hopefully lead to cures for diseases and maladies that plague our society. I foresee no limits to the benefits the science we are about to embark on can make to mankind."

"Gentlemen, I want results and I want them fast. I plan to implant clustered cells into several patients every week and will be driving you all very hard, so be prepared to put in as much of an effort as it takes to give me what I want. Are there any questions? Yes… Dr. Mills."

"Will we have enough patients to meet the demands of the numerous operations you are planning?"

"Good question. We will use patients more than once when feasible; but let me assure you that I will be bringing new patients in at a rate that will meet our needs."

"Is there anything else?… If not, Dr. Hieber will bring our support team in and prep them on our plans." Gordon then left the room.

Russel Hieber made a call and said over the phone, "We're ready for you."

Six more scientists and doctors specializing in various fields related to neurological brain functions, cognitive psychology and human behavior entered the room. They were accompanied by a computer specialist. Addressing the group, Russel said. "You have all been involved with operations we've been performing on certain patients and witnessed many of the positive results we have achieved. But now, we are about to venture into a totally new science that I am certain will have favorable effects on many of our patient's mental disorders. We are on the threshold of discovering ways of improving mental capacities and curing illnesses and diseases that affect millions, and I have very important jobs for all of you to help achieve this goal. Tomorrow we will begin a series of operations on patients using this new procedure. Some of you will assist in the operating room and others will be assigned various other tasks. We want to determine if and how patients are affected by these procedures, and to what degree."

"We have a rigorous schedule of operations ahead of us and reaching our goals will require your utmost efforts and expertise. Gentlemen, Dr. Bradhurst and I foresee nothing but great things ahead of us and I'm looking forward to working with you."

It was obvious that the attentive group was enthusiastic about the upcoming program of which they would play important roles in.

"Dr. Korman is with us on full-time bases now. Dr. Korman," he said in way of letting him take the floor.

Hanns Korman was excited to be addressing the group. The promises of discoveries in the field he had put so much effort into during the past few years was about to burst wide open. His work would now be unrestrained with an aggressive agenda that he was sure would reveal fast and rewarding results. He could not have been happier. "By now you are all somewhat familiar with what we refer to as 'Super-Cells'. We will begin immediately to extract clusters of cells from our patients. The operation seldom has any severe side-effects but at times complications do arise. Our job will be to get proficient and skillful in obtaining these cells to keep any mishaps to a minimum. I have already began teaching the procedure to several of you and in a relatively short time I am sure we will add substantially to our present supply of biological samples. Determining what functions, the yet unidentified cell clusters affect, is a very intricate and laborious undertaking, but it is doable. Dr. Hieber, Mr. Drury, our computer expert and I are working with experts in the computer industry to develop computer technologies that will allow us to achieve faster, and more accurate data related to the intended functions of these cells. It is our hope to have super computers that will give us almost instant recognition of every cluster we extract. In the meantime, we have the means to identify every cell structure that makes our bodies function and every action that our brain commands, both physically and psychologically. It just takes an extreme effort to match cells to traits. As Dr. Hieber and Dr. Bradhurst have said, the good we will be providing to mankind is immeasurable. Gentlemen, you are all brilliant doctors and scientists so let's use our own brains to accomplish the imaginable and make this a better world to live in."

Four weeks later, Russel Hieber and Dr. Bradhurst were reviewing the whirlwind of activities that had taken place at the research center during the past month. "Thirty-two operations. Not bad for our first month!" Russel said. "Proving the process worked on our first attempt was of most significance. Finding that many cell clusters melded with like cells in Mrs. Parkins' brain, as they did in patients immediately following her operation, gave us confidence in the procedure. Statistics are pretty good. More than half of the cell clusters we implanted were accepted and this will improve as we learn and gain experience. Unfortunately, six died on the tables, or shortly after their operations. Installing the incinerator was a good idea. We've been firing it up quite often lately and we will be using it again soon. Two more patients who did not fare well after their operations are in bad shape and unlikely to survive. I will be helping them along shortly to make room for new patients. We knew there would be a learning curve and even though it might be a little more severe than we first thought; all-in-all, the results we are achieving make it quite acceptable, don't you agree?"

Dr. Bradhurst did. "Let's review Mrs. Parkins results and then we'll tackle the others."

Her first implant not only showed an immediate improvement in her long-term memory, but also her memory capabilities continued to strengthen as time passed, indicating the newly formed cell structures were continuing to develop into healthy cells. What remained to be discovered was how much longer this increase in her memory would last or how much stronger it might get. Even though the procedure slowed a slight slowdown in the deterioration of Mrs. Parkins dementia, her condition continued to slide. A second operation strengthening the targeted cells was performed on the patient. Ongoing tests were not only revealing further improvements in Mrs. Parkins memory, but she was showing marked improvements in her overall mental capabilities. Dr. Bradhurst was elated. He had proven that he could strengthen the brains intellectual powers and was anxious to perfect the process to the point he could safely boost his own brain to new levels.

Once they completed their review of the other patients that had been operated on, Gordon summed up their findings. "Many patients are showing positive gains in areas we targeted. Exactly what I had hoped for. There is no doubt about it, Russel; we are on the right track. I think it's time to consider my friend Mr. Danvers. I plan to give him clusters much stronger than we have used on any previous patient. I want to find out what happens when a human brain expands its capabilities beyond that of any human that has ever lived. Let's see how far we can push the limits with him."

Michael Danvers had been isolated in a secured room for the past several weeks. He had been subdued with just enough medication to make him listless and lethargic. Most of his time each day was spent staring somewhat lifelessly into space with not enough coherence or will to do anything but wonder where he was and what he was doing there.

When his medication was withheld for two days, his mind began to clear, and he fully understood the horror of what was happening to him. Orderlies that came for him paid no attention to his pleading as he fought the strapping that held him to his bed. He was moved to a sterile-looking room where Dr. Bradhurst and several other men wearing white robes awaited him. Terror filled his entire being as Dr. Bradhurst addressed him.

"I am so glad to see you Mr. Danvers. I hope your stay with us has been pleasant. I can't tell you how pleased I was with your contributions in helping us get where we are today. The samples from Drechsler have been invaluable. Now it's time for you to help us once again. We are about to introduce a number of clustered brain cells into your temporal lobe that if successful will make you a much more intelligent person than you already are. But I don't want you to worry; you will have a highly skilled group of surgeons assisting with the operation and I am sure everything will go well."

Michael Danvers was scared beyond reason as he screamed and pleaded before he was anesthetized into unconsciousness.

When Michael Danvers was brought out of his induced sleep, he was greeted by Dr. Bradhurst and Dr. Hieber. "Good morning Mr. Danvers." Dr. Bradhurst said. "You will be pleased to know that the operation was quite successful. Our post-operative evaluations show that many of the clustered cells we implanted have effectively joined your existing brain cells. In a few days we will be testing to see if my theory of being able to stimulate and strengthen certain cells has increased your mental powers."

Michael calmly looked at the doctor and said, "Why?"

Dr. Bradhurst smiled. "Mr. Danvers, I admire a great deal about you. You are intelligent, direct, self-centered, and greedy, and I am sure can be quite ruthless at times. All attributes that I regard in the highest esteem. But to answer your question as to 'why', it boils down to trust. I had no qualms about the greed you displayed in our dealings, but I could see you as a loose cannon so to speak. You would become careless in your spending and raise questions about where your newly acquired wealth came from and that could lead to me. So, you see, 'why' is because I am covering myself. And besides, I am fascinated with your highly intellectual brain and want very much to exploit it. If this first experiment proves successful, I will have more in store for you. I think of you as my 'brain-child' and look forward to a long and prolific future together."

Two mornings later when Michael Danvers awoke, he felt sharper and more cognizant of his surroundings than he had ever been before. Everything seemed so clear. Every word from the orderlies, nurses and doctors who attended him was firmly imbedded in his mind as was every word that Dr. Bradhurst and Dr. Hieber had said during their first visit. His mind was more fertile and receptive than he could have ever imagined. Even in the limited time he had spent with Dr. Bradhurst and the semi-conscious state he was in, he had been able to put together enough bits and pieces of information to get a clear understanding of Dr. Bradhurst's true agenda. Yes… he knew the ultimate plan of the doctor's was to perfect the brain enhancing process and use it on himself. And he also realized how expendable he was. Since the operation, he had acquired incredible mental abilities. His mind was bursting with knowledge that he never realized he had. It seemed that many things he had learned but had drifted from his mind had miraculously resurfaced. He knew that with this newly gained intelligence he could outmatch wits with Bradhurst, but he also knew that he was in a very precarious situation. Being confined, restrained, and drugged most of the time, would make it difficult to compete with the brilliant doctor who had all advantages going for him. Then a plan materialized in his mind, and he knew what he would do. He would not let anyone realize the magnitude of the strength he had gained from these new brain cells. He would carefully hold back just enough with the tests that were scheduled for this morning to show improvements. Enough improvements to make Bradhurst strengthen his brain even more, just as the good doctor had planned to do. He knew a great deal about the human brain and believed, like many other scientists that the brain was capable of much more than even the most intellectual people in the world could glean from it. He would be the first to find out just how far he could go and would manipulate the process with no one the wiser. His quest in life would be to beat Dr. Bradhurst at his own game. In the meantime, he would get to know the people who attended him better.

"Incredible!" Russel Hieber said. Results of the testing and evaluation of Michael Danvers mind boiled down to that one-word. "Incredible!" "Nearly all of the tests we performed have shown improvements in his mental capacities. And his I.Q. has increased and is now in the top six percent in the world."

As Dr. Bradhurst's studied the test results he stated, "I cannot wait to strengthen his mental capacities even more."

Gordon smiled as he looked down at Michael Danvers. It was three days after the patient's second surgical procedure and all indications were that the operation was successful. "The medical team did well." Dr. Bradhurst said. "You seem to have recovered from the operation very quickly." As the doctor looked down at the shackled patient he said. "You look well. Actually, you look better than well. There seems to be a calmness and air of peace and tranquility about you. How are you feeling?"

Michael Danvers had come through the operation with no adverse side-affects. In the past three days as he recuperated, he realized that the last operation had raised his brainpower to incredible levels. He now had total recall of nearly everything he had ever learned throughout his life. He realized that the brain did in fact retain everything that entered it and this new science that Zoltan Proziver developed some years earlier had advanced his brain to a level not reached by any other human being. He found that he had the ability to second-guess what the attendants, nurses and doctors who cared for him were about to say and his new powers also gave him the ability to communicate with their minds. His thoughts were interrupted by the doctor repeating his question.

"I am doing very well thank you. In fact, I am doing wonderful and I'm ready for the examinations to begin. I am quite anxious to see how this latest infusion of cells worked."

"I'm glad to hear that; but I must admit I am quite curious as to your new demeanor. You have always been somewhat hostile, yet now you appear to be composed, and even serene."

"I've had time to think and realize what a wonderful thing you are doing. Exploring the unknown powers of the human brain has to be one of the most exciting endeavors I can imagine. The contributions you can make to mankind seem endless and the more I think about it, the more I feel privileged to be part of it. After the first operation my mental proficiencies improved, and I am sure that they have reached a higher level with this last operation. You should know that my memory has improved also. Dr. Bradhurst, I have all the faith in the world that you can and will let me become a permanent part of your team and let me help you meet all of your dreams and expectations about improving our minds." Michael Danvers knew that the doctor's plan was to kill him once he learned what he wanted from these experiments. He spoke in a soft, convincing voice for another five minutes, conveying to his listener the many benefits of keeping him alive and what they could achieve together.

As Danvers prattled on, Dr. Bradhurst's mind began to fall into a hypnotic trance. Every word that he heard entered his mind as a positive and logical message and seemed to be firmly implanted in his brain.

Michael Danvers was pleased when he finished his brain washing session, knowing that he had planted seeds strongly in his adversary's mind and when the opportunity presented itself again, he would strengthen the hold that he now had on him.

Doctor Bradhurst seemed to have forgotten the questions he had planned to ask his patient. He said in parting, "We will begin tests right away."

When the examinations were complete, Michael Danvers lay in his bed planning the next steps he would take in dealing with the doctor.

Bradhurst had been in somewhat of a dither since his meeting with Danvers. He was sitting in his office in Los Angeles with Russel Hieber who he summoned there to discuss the outcome of the tests made on the patient. He had a very strong reason for distancing himself from the hospital and Michael Danvers.

Russel exclaimed, "Great improvements in every area of mental capacity. I.Q. jumped to the top three percent in the world. Hasn't reached your level yet but we are surely gaining on it."

"I wonder?" Dr. Bradhurst said. "Yes, I wonder!" After a long pause he continued. "I haven't mentioned this to you but now that I've had time to think about it, I believe our friend Mr. Danvers is playing with us. When I talked with him, he somehow convinced me that he was on my side and made me believe everything he said. I haven't been able to get those thoughts out of my mind until now. I'm sure that in the few minutes I was with him he somehow hypnotized or brainwashed me. If he could cloud my mind so easily, what other powers might he have?"

Russel was visibly shaken and spoke in a loud voice. "My God, could he have gotten to anyone else who is attending him? If he could influence you, it would be easy to persuade anyone with a weaker constitution to listen to him."

Dr. Bradhurst, in full control of his wits once again, thought for a minute and then said, "Here's what we will do. Reassign every person who has had interactions with him since his first operation. I don't want any contact between them again. Assign new personnel to watch over our patient and instill in them that under no circumstance should they be with the patient alone, and even then, never stay with him for more than a few minutes. And Russel, don't go near him. I don't want him getting to you like he did with me." The doctor paused and thought for a minute or two. "I want a completely soundproof room with cameras installed. Make this a priority. We'll move him there as soon as it can be completed. Until then let's keep a close eye on him."

"This is getting complicated and is scaring me." Russel confessed. "Maybe we should just kill him."

"We will, but first I want to learn a little more about his true capabilities."

Gordon thought for a minute before he continued. "I'm afraid if he already has an inroad to my mind, he might be able to tap into it again and at an even stronger level, so I will be most careful in the future. I want that room completed before I see him again. Somehow, I have a feeling that our Mr. Danvers has much stronger powers than he's owning up to and we will be taking every precaution we can to control him." He paused again as his mind thought through another possibility. "Have a schedule of people and times made of everyone who has been in contact with him and review the sign-in log to his room. Let's see if anyone has been spending more time with him than they should have. While you get these things going, I want to talk to Dr. Shuman."

Dr. Shuman was a prominent psychiatrist and among his specialisms was performing I.Q. tests. Once he was on the line, Bradhurst got right to the point. "Is it possible that the tests you performed on Michael Danvers could have been manipulated by him in any way?"

"No, I don't believe so. Why do you ask?"

"I think it's possible he may have manipulated the tests to produce a lower I.Q. than he actually has." Bradhurst said.

"Well, certainly that would be possible but why would he want to do that?"

"Regardless of why, tell me more about Mr. Danvers test."

"Well, as per your request we performed a very thorough examination. We carefully evaluated each of his responses and found no inconsistencies in his answers. I personally felt that he was forthright and truthful throughout the exam and doubt very much that he adversely influenced it in any way. Besides, he is extremely intelligent with a very high I.Q. If he did hold back on this exam, his I.Q. would even be higher than we recorded and would place him up there with the most brilliant men in the world. No, Dr. Bradhurst, I think you are barking up the wrong tree."

A disturbing thought passed through Gordon Bradhurst's mind. "Thank you. You have told me what I needed to know," but before Dr. Bradhurst hung up, he asked another question. "Could you drop by the hospital the day after tomorrow for a few minutes? There is something very important I need to discuss with you."

"Let me see," Dr. Sherman said as he scanned his appointment book. "I have an appointment in the morning, but I am free in the afternoon."

"That would be fine. Thank you, Dr. Sherman. And could you bring your assistant who helped with Mr. Danvers' tests?"

There was a pause at the other end of the phone before Dr. Sherman replied. "Yes, that can be arranged, but why."

"I'll fill you in when you get here. As always Dr. Sherman, I appreciate your assistance. I'll see you Thursday. Shall we say, two o'clock?"

Twelve
Hanns Korman

Thursday morning nine hospital employees who had had contact with Michael Danvers after his operations, waited in the conference room for close to an hour before Dr. Bradhurst and Dr. Hieber (accompanied by a third man who none of the attendees knew) finally entered the room. During that time there was a great deal of speculation as to why they had been summoned and why they were kept waiting so long.

Dr. Bradhurst arrived at his hospital at ten o'clock that morning, giving Russel time to accumulate the information he required. He limited his movements to his office and the small conference room located on the first floor of the West Wing; keeping as far away from Michael Danvers as possible. Not knowing the extent of the brainpowers that his newly created prodigy might possess; he was not about to take chances by being anywhere near him.

The previous afternoon, after ending his call with Dr. Sherman, he placed a call to a psychologist who he could trust implicitly. The esteemed specialist agreed to meet him at the hospital at ten thirty the following morning.

Upon digesting the information Russel had gathered, Dr. Bradhurst outlined the steps he planned to take. When Dr. Cummings arrived, Gordon informed him of his plans and the assistance he wanted from him.

Dr. Cummings accompanied Gordon Bradhurst and Russel Hieber as they entered the conference room to address the nine employees. "I am sorry for the delay," Dr. Bradhurst began. "Gentleman, I would like a word with each of you individually. I have asked Dr. Cummings to join us. Mr. Jacobs, I would like to begin with you. Please come with me. In the meantime, the rest of you remain here with Dr. Hieber."

It had not taken long to examine the mandatory sign-in log to Michael Danvers' room. Only one person had spent more time with him than required for his duties and that was nurse Carl Jacobs. Everyone else who entered the room stayed a minimal of time but non-the-less they would all be questioned.

The two proficient psychologists were certain that if anyone had been brainwashed or influenced in any way by Michael Danvers, they would quickly determine it. Carl Jacobs appeared calm and at ease as he sat across from the two men who confronted him. The more the skilled psychologists talked with Nurse Jacobs, the more his calm, smug demeanor transformed into an expression of fear. He began to stutter and slur his answers to the seemingly innocent yet probing questions. He was becoming visibly shaken and when he was asked if Mr. Danvers had given him any special instructions, he nervously responded, "No… Yes… No." and without warning he burst from his chair and ran headlong toward the window overlooking the beautifully landscaped lawn bordering the front of the building. Before either doctor could react, the confused and stupefied man threw himself into the window with incredible force. The heavy shatter-proof glass absorbed the impact and Carl Jacobs body bounced off the window with a sickening thud. He sprawled to the floor unconscious. His unconscious body was taken to a private room where he was strapped to a bed. They would continue to work with him to determine, if possible; to what extent his mind had been affected. It was obvious that for the man to try to commit suicide he must have been deeply under a very powerful spell.

When the last person had gone through extremely stringent psychological examinations, the two doctors reviewed the results. One other attendant proved to be under some sort of control of Michael Danvers. He was also restrained and would go under more stringent examinations.

"I have two more people I want you to look at with me this afternoon." Dr. Bradhurst informed Dr. Cummings. "Dr. Sherman and his aide spent a great deal of time with Danvers during I.Q. tests, and I want to take a very close look at them."

"I'll be glad to, but how are you going to convince Dr. Sherman to be analyzed by another psychologist?"

"I'll convince him."

While he waited for Dr. Sherman and his aide to arrive, he met with Russel. "As soon as we get through questioning the nurse and aide again, (this time while they are under the influence of sodium pentothal) regardless of what we find out, I want them to disappear."

"I'll take care of it." Russel assured his mentor and friend.

"Danvers was with Sherman for quite some time, and even though he seemed fine when we talked at the time of the tests and also on our phone call, I have some very strong concerns about our I.Q. specialist and his assistant. Cummings and I will be seeing them shortly to verify or disprove my suspicions."

"Michael Danvers…?" Gordon said in a question rather than a statement. "What to make of you? I want desperately to know your capabilities, but can I take the chance?"

Even though Gordon had not directed his uttering to him, Russel non-the-less responded. "I don't like it, Gordon. You think you can control him by keeping him sedated but what if you can't? We can learn what you need from other patients."

"I respect your concerns, but I suspect Danvers is holding back. It's possible he's much more intelligent than he's letting us believe, and if he is, I want to know more about his mental powers."

Russel was not convinced and stressed his trepidations about Michael Danvers' potential dangers to them. "I still don't like it. What if we can't control him? What if he has enough mental capabilities to take command of our minds?"

"Let's see what I can learn from Dr. Sherman. In the meantime, let's hurry the construction of the soundproof room. I'll feel more comfortable dealing with him when he's behind an impenetrable barrier."

When Dr. Sherman and his assistant arrived, they were shown into the conference room by Dr. Bradhurst. The pleasant speaking doctor offered his two guests a drink of his special brandy of which he would take no refusal. After all, it was one of the finest brandies in the world. Unlike the solution served to Michel Danvers, this drink was laced with a very strong dose of truth serum. An hour later when Dr. Cummings had left, Gordon summoned Russel to the conference room. "I was right," he informed his colleague. "Our I.Q. specialist is under a very strong spell. It's so deep-seated into his mind that it was difficult to explore. But we learned enough. I gave them mild sedatives and as you can see, they are sleeping peacefully. Only Dr. Sherman has been affected by Danvers, but I want to eliminate both of them." He said this as he reached for the phone. When he recognized the voice on the other end of the line, he said, "I have an urgent job for you."

Sid Ramone informed him that he was readably available.

"Please come to my hospital right away. I have two subjects that I want you to meet. An incident with an auto in the city might be appropriate. I have their car here so if you decide to go that way, you will need a second driver. I'll give you details when you arrive."

"We can be there in less than an hour."

Dr. Bradhurst was pleased with the progress being made in learning more and more about many brain functions and how they could be manipulated in various ways. They already had strengthened several mental capabilities in patients. Tests on patients suffering from any number of mental disorders were showing healthier and more vibrant brains. Dr. Bradhurst's belief that he could improve not only ailments of the brain but also increase man's intellect and brainpower, was becoming a reality. There were adverse side-effects resulting from the delicate operations, but those problems were becoming rarer as the team of surgeons improved on their techniques and skills. He was convinced that in a short time he would be able to alter every physical and psychological condition of the human body.

Hanns was disturbed about how hard Dr. Bradhurst was pushing experiments on patients. There was no control of the many procedures taking place on the operation tables. Dr. Bradhurst's only concern was getting results as fast as possible. Just operate, take a quick look at the results, and operate again. What deeply bothered Hanns was the number of deaths taking place. Dr. Bradhurst and Dr. Hieber had been up front with him during his interview, explaining how in the name of science and progress, some patients might not survive from the delicate and complicated operations performed on them. At the time, because of the way it had been explained it to him, he assumed that only a few patients who were very close to the end of their lives would fall into this category. But that was not always the case. It was true, that when he first arrived at the institute most operations that he participated in were performed on patients with maladies ranging from acute neurosis to various brain disorders including psychosis; patients who truly were at the end of their tether. However, lately, patients were being placed on the operating tables who showed no signs of having any mental disorders.

Then it happened. A man died during one of his operations. A man who was receiving brain cell implants for the third time died under his knife. A man who suffered nothing more than a nervous breakdown and from all indications was on the road to recovery. Why had this man been chosen and why had three successive operations been performed on his brain in such a short time? Because of Dr' Hieber's insistence, that's why. This man should not have died; and in Hanns Korman's mind neither should many of the others who had succumbed from brain surgeries performed on them. He felt that he had always been a fair and ethical man. He was certainly not an excessive extremist or for that matter a fanatical moralist in dealing with his fellow human beings. Like anyone else he had his likes and dislikes of people he had worked with or known throughout his life, but he never despised anyone enough to wish them real harm. Questions about the unethical and even immoral activities going on at the hospital began to plague him more and more; and what bothered him the most was that he was part of it.

Hanns had developed a close relationship with Rebeca Hamilton. They had been having lunch together from time to time and the day after his unpleasant experience of losing the patient, they met in the company's cafeteria. Rebeca managed the hospital and sanatorium. Other than a select staff of doctors and specialists who reported directly to Dr. Hieber for research work being performed in the West Wing, all other employees fell under her supervision. Her responsibilities were many and varied. They included hiring, training, and firing personnel and overseeing a team of doctors, nurses, and support people to assure the hospital was run at the highest levels of efficiency and professionalism. Office administration, records, purchasing… everything related to running a business fell under her capable hands and being the strong administrator she was, the hospital ran very smoothly.

Hanns and Rebeca had hit it off from the very beginning. They were two very different types of individuals, almost at opposite ends of the spectrum. He was quiet, reserved and somewhat of an introvert while she was verbal, outspoken and anything but shy and withdrawn. Yet as the old saying goes, opposites do sometimes attract and in this case, it was true, because they had become quite close.

When they were seated with trays of food in front of them, Hanns opened the conversation. "I felt pretty bad about losing Jim Price. I got to know him a little and that makes it worse."

"I know," Rebeca replied.

"I stated my concern to Dr. Hieber before the first operation as to why a man in such good condition as Mr. Price was selected. I knew the basic reason was to compare results from sound healthy brains that were infused with specific supercells to those of inferior and diseased brains, but it did not set well with me nor convince me that we were doing the right thing. He noted my concerns and tried to assure me that there would be no danger to the patient, so I didn't push it. It disturbed me when a second operation was performed but I said nothing. However, I brought up the issue again when a third operation was scheduled for him, an operation I was to perform. I was calmly put off and again I didn't press it. The man's heart could not stand the strain of so many intrusions to his body in such a short period of time and he died under my hand. Knowing the risks involved with that third operation and not speaking up loud enough to stop it… I feel responsible for his death." Hanns said this with a tear in his eye. "I'm not sure what to do."

"I wouldn't do anything or say anything." She could see how much this was bothering him and spoke in a quiet and soothing voice. "I know how you must feel but it's not your fault; patients die during operations all the time so put it behind you. Let me tell you something Hanns." She said this as she reached out and touched his hand. "One thing I have learned since I've been here is to just do your job and don't ask too many questions. This is a private hospital with very private agendas, and if we want to stay here, we have to accept what might be going on behind closed doors."

Hanns knew she was right. Making any kind of unfavorable waves would certainly not put him in good standings with either Dr. Bradhurst or Dr. Hieber and he certainly did not want to do that. "But I'm one of those behind the closed doors. It's just hard for me to ignore the fact that so many people are dying here. Too many people Rebeca! Too many operations too fast! We just plow blindly into one operation after another, and patients are dying because of this impatience. Dr. Bradhurst is on a drive for results and will not let anything slow him down. Human life seems to mean nothing to him or to Russel and that scares me."

Rebeca looked at him with concern. "If you're going to survive here, you have to toughen up. Think about the incredible advances that are being made and the important part you are playing in them."

"You sound like Dr. Bradhurst," Hanns cut in.

Rebeca laughed.

At that moment Hanns knew that Rebeca had become more to him than just a friend.

"I needed someone to talk to about this. Thank you, Rebeca! I will certainly take your advice." The work he was doing here was the most exciting and gratifying that he had ever been involved with and he was determined to stay regardless of what he considered heinous and immoral evils taking place. If he left, nothing would change. The work would continue without him. Then a frightening thought put a fear into him. Could he leave? Would Dr. Bradhurst let him go, and if he didn't what would happen to him? No, he would not attempt to leave, at least not yet. He would continue to work diligently on the clustering program and do his best to introduce positive gains in making a healthier world for mankind to live in. He changed the subject by asking. "What do you know about the patient on the third floor?"

She looked at him for a moment. "Where did you hear about that?"

"Just rumors, but enough to know it's true. I just don't know why it's been kept from me. I thought I was part of Dr. Bradhurst's inner circle but now I wonder."

"I don't know very much either. I do know there's been a patient there for quite some time but don't know who he is or why he's there. There's a mystery about the whole thing."

"I'll ask Russel about it."

"You might think about that. If Dr. Bradhurst doesn't want you to know about this, he must have a reason and I wouldn't go there. Like I said, I wouldn't ask too many questions. Remember what happened to the curious cat."

Hanns could see that his luncheon companion was serious about not wanting to make waves. "Yes, you're right." But his curiosity was aroused, and he would prudently learn what he could about the mysterious patient.

For the past few weeks Hanns had been busier than he had ever been in his life. He was burning the midnight oils almost every night and was getting closer and closer to solving many intricate problems that constantly arose surrounding his secret pet project that he called, The 'Fountain of Longevity'. 'Finally!' he exclaimed to himself late one night. His countless attempts at combining select cells and varying their strengths had finally paid off. On paper his theory had become a reality. Mathematics and scientific data did not lie. Life could be extended. He was elated to think he had created magical cells that would prolong life. The fountain of youth… He had no idea as yet as to how long the amalgamation of rejuvenating cells would increase a lifespan but knew that it would only be a matter of time now that the basic formula had been discovered. His mind was full of wonder and questions. Would future generations of man live to be older than they now did and if so, how much older? What would this mean to world populations? What? What? What? For the first time since he began experimenting on this theory of longevity, Hanns became frightened. Had he delved beyond the laws of nature? Would he dare to implant these cells into a human being to prove the process works? With his mind full of unknown outcomes that might derive from this breakthrough, he decided to keep his discovery secret; at least for the time being. He would continue his work and see how much more he could learn before discussing it with Bradhurst and Hieber.

In the cafeteria the morning after meeting with Rebeca, Hanns poured a cup of coffee and joined a male nurse who was enjoying a large breakfast. "Good morning, Hanns." Gary Huston said in greeting.

"Morning Gary! How goes it?" Knowing Gary was a longtime employee at the institution, Hanns' decided to feel him out to see if he knew anything about the mysterious man on the third floor. "Haven't seen you lately. What have you been up to?"

"Same ol, same ol. Been taking care of patients." Gary paused and then added. "But I got a new assignment yesterday. I start this morning."

He seemed to be reluctant to add to that, so Hanns took a chance by asking: "Not with our special visitor on the third floor by any chance?"

Gary was sworn to secrecy about the third-floor patient. Under no circumstances was he to divulge anything to anyone about this special inmate. His job and his future depended on it. But knowing Dr. Korman was a prominent doctor in the research laboratory and considered the top surgeon under Dr. Hieber, he assumed that he was involved with the patient in question. "Yes. I'll be looking after him. You sure have some pretty strict rules and the tightest security I've ever heard of. Even armed guards."

"I'm sure it does seem extreme." Dr. Korman said. "But he does need special attention."

"Yeah, that's what we were told, but Christ, it's weird. Have to have at least two of us when we're with him and we can't stay in the room for more than a couple of minutes. And a guard is always with us. And to make it even weirder, we have to have a lie detector test every night. Now what the hell is that all about? None of it makes any sense." Then he smiled and added. "But hey, the pay's good so why complain."

Hanns was quite taken with this information. What would cause Dr. Bradhurst to take such severe precautions? Why all the secrecy. "Well, we have our reasons so take good care of him." Then in a casual tone he stated in a question, "I must be getting old, I forgot our patient's last name?"

Gary smiled and said, "Danvers."

When Hanns heard the name Danvers, it shocked him. No, it couldn't be. Taking a chance, he said "Of course, Michael."

"Yeah," Gary said as he finished his scrambled eggs.

Hanns' mind was full of questions but before he could ask another, Gary stood up and said, "Got to go; It's almost eight and I can't be late for my shift."

A myriad of puzzling thoughts engulfed Hanns' brain. It seemed inconceivable that Michael Danvers was secretly held in an isolated room here at the hospital. And what could the tight security and the odd rules that his attendants had to abide by mean? And how was it possible that this could have been kept from him?

He had a restless night. His mind kept examining possibilities of why Michael Danvers was here. How long had he been here? Could it have been since he first disappeared? He was pretty sure that must be the case, but why? He concluded that Dr. Hieber and Dr. Bradhurst must have operated on him and if they did, what cell clusters did they use. Could Michael's brain have developed to a level strong enough to require full-time guards? And lie detectors; was it possible he could cloud people's minds and even read their thoughts? Knowing what he did about the clustered cell science he had lived with for the past few years he could not discount any possibility. The longer he lay awake the more determined he became that he would find the answers. Sleep finally came and when he awoke in the morning, he knew what he was going to do. He was going to approach Dr. Hieber about Michael Danvers.

He had a nine o'clock operation scheduled that Friday morning and even without a good night's sleep (something he needed and cherished as a surgeon) his hands were steady and the operation was a success. Another patient whose brain had successfully accepted three different cell clusters, each impregnated into targeted brain cells, would in due course be subjected to a series of tests to determine the effects of the operation. It was shortly after eleven o'clock when he phoned Dr. Hieber.

"How did the operation go?" Russel asked.

"As expected, all went well. I have something I would like to discuss with you, could we meet?"

"Yes, certainly. You sound serious Hanns, is it something important?"

"To me it is."

"Might I know the matter you want to discuss?"

"It's about Michael Danvers." Hanns said. "I have learned that he is here at the hospital, and I want to talk to you about him."

There was a pause before Dr. Hieber responded. "Yes, of course. Gordon is here this morning. I think we should include him if that is okay with you."

When Hanns agreed, Russel told him he would call him back. A few minutes later the phone rang and Dr. Hieber said, "how about lunch in my office shall we say at one o'clock?"

"Yes. Thank you. That would be fine." Hanns said.

He recalled as he waited for the meeting that he would be having lunch with Carlene Linser on Saturday. She said she had something she would like to discuss with him, thus the luncheon date,

No sooner had Dr. Bradhurst and Russel Hieber greeted Hanns, Reuben sandwiches and hot tea arrived. They sat at a small round table placed in the corner of the office for just such meetings. Hanns, addressing Dr. Bradhurst opened the conversation. "I haven't seen you for a couple of weeks. I hope your business in New York went well."

"Nice of you to ask," the doctor replied. "It went very well. I was negotiating with the Manhattan Psychiatric Center for the transfer of patients to our facility here. They agreed to give us eleven patients. All derelicts with various mental conditions! They will be arriving a few at a time beginning next week."

"We're always in need of more subjects for our research!" Hanns affirmed.

Hanns had thought carefully as to how he would approach the topic of Michael Danvers. He was calm and focused when he began. "Eventually everything going on in a small company like this has a way of oozing through the cracks. I have learned from more than one source that Michael Danvers is in a private room and has been here for some time."

If either of his colleagues were surprised by this, they showed no emotion whatsoever. They said nothing and waited for Hanns to continue.

"Naturally, I am curious about why he is here and also why I have not been informed."

Russel and Gordon Bradhurst had known the day would come when Hanns would have to be informed about Danvers. "I would think the reason for keeping you out of the loop is obvious." Gordon said. "You and he worked together and were friends I believe."

Hanns interjected with a slight smile. "No, Michael and I were anything but friends. He was the worst man I ever worked for, and I not only didn't like him I despised him."

"I am surprised to hear that. I thought otherwise." Gordon said.

"He was my boss, so I treated him as such and did my best to hide my dislike for him." Hanns replied. "I had mixed emotions when he disappeared. I was glad to be rid of him but on the other hand I hated the thought that he was probably basking on a beach somewhere exotic, living the life of Riley. He doesn't deserve that. Because he owed so much money to so many people, I thought when he got the two million dollars; he fled to avoid paying his debts. But now I see he has been here."

"If we knew your feelings about him, we would have included you in the plans we had for him." Russel Hieber said. "How much do you know?"

"I know very little, but I have some ideas as to why he's here and what you are doing with him." Hanns said. "Being isolated and under guard tells me that you have been experimenting with his brain and that you most likely have achieved some unusual results." He stopped here waiting for a response. It was Dr. Bradhurst who spoke. "You are right about Mr. Danvers being here since his disappearance. I am sorry that you had to learn of this the way you did. It was my intent to personally inform you, but I seem to have put off the timing too long. I seem to have misread you, something I rarely do."

"Let me address your concerns." Gordon continued. "When I first met with the two of you, I immediately knew that you were exactly the type of person we wanted working with us here; and you have proven me right. I don't normally give out praise Hanns, at least honest praise, but you have fit in well with us and we are more than pleased with the work you are doing here."

"Thank you. That means a great deal to me." Hanns said this in as honest and humble a voice as he could muster up.

Gordon Bradhurst could care less about Hanns Korman or his feelings; the doctor/scientist had something of value to offer with his knowledge of the clustering process plus his ability as a surgeon and it would serve Bradhurst well if he thought he was a welcome member of his team. He would give him what information he thought necessary to let him feel that he was important. "Michael Danvers presented another issue. He is totally unreliable, and I am certain he would have caused us problems; and problems are something I will not tolerate. By bringing him here, I could keep a tight rein on him. Once the procedure of clustered cell implantations began to show positive results, I chose Mr. Danvers as, shall I say my personal guineapig? He is a very intelligent man with a high I.Q.; just what I was looking for. I wanted to see how far we could raise his intellect level and thus increase his I.Q. However, before we began experimenting on him, I wanted to be certain of what we were doing. That's when I brought Mr. Price into the picture. Russel has informed me of your concerns about him and I will try to explain my motives for including him in our program. We have proven that our procedure improves the mental capabilities of many of our patients. But of the caliber of people available to us, none have extreme levels of intelligence and the gains we are making are minimal, I wanted to experiment on someone with a much higher level of intellect than any of our previous patients. Mr. Price, fit that need very nicely. He was very intelligent and somewhat unattached. And as you will recall because you questioned it at the time, we used much stronger doses of cell structures with him. When the first operation proved successful and his mental aptitude tests showed marked increases, I knew I was on track to where I wanted to be. Much higher results than any we had achieved as of that date I might add. His ability to acquire knowledge, retain it and recall it, increased dramatically and his memory developed to a quite astonishing level. We know the human brain retains a good portion of everything that ever enters it. The problem we have always been faced with is that much of this information is tucked away in some far corner of our brains and is seldom, if ever, brought to the surface. Some people have poor memories while others have what we consider excellent memory capabilities just as everyone has varying degrees if intelligence. Mr. Price was an ideal candidate to delve deeper into where this science might take us. It was unforeseeable and unfortunate that during the third operation he suffered a heart attack. However, I was satisfied with the results we had gained from our experiments with him and decided to waste no time and prepared Mr. Danvers for surgery. Calculating the strength of cell clusters used on Mr. Price and the results we achieved, I increased the potency of Danvers' dosage by about thirty percent. Risky I know, but I was ready to take that risk. The operation went well but when we tested his mental capabilities, even though the results were quite extraordinary, I expected more. Upon discussions with him and our exam specialists, we concluded that he most likely manipulated the test to hide from us the true effect of the operation. That being the case, I surmised him having a hidden agenda; a reason to disguise his newly acquired brain power."

"If this is true, why would he do such a thing?" Hanns asked.

"To deceive us. Our Mr. Danvers has developed incredible powers. I personally felt the prowess of his mental capabilities. When I was with him, he clouded my mind and influenced me to believe everything he said. It took a couple of days for the effects to wear-off but as soon as it did, I put tight restrictions in place in hopes of preventing him from getting to anyone else. Unfortunately, he had already gained control of at least two of the people attending him. We have taken care of that situation, but I am not completely certain that there were not more people affected so I am placing very stringent procedures for all dealings with him."

"Suffice to say Hanns; we have developed his brain to unprecedented levels, but I don't want to stop there. I want to see how far this science will take us."

Hanns definitely wanted to be a part of what they were doing with Michael Danvers. "I want very much to be included in the work you are doing with him." Hanns mustered up as sincere voice that he could, and it came out almost as a plea.

"We will be interviewing Mr. Danvers within a few days. Plan to join us?"

Thirteen
Brainchild

Heavily sedated, the patient was wheeled into the newly constructed triple ply soundproof glass enclosure. When the attendants left the room, they stopped to look through the window at the immobile man strapped securely to the bed. In an instant, Michaels Danvers brain connected with one of the men and knew what he was thinking. 'So,' he mused to himself. 'They thought they could block my powers out with a pane of glass.'

Three men appeared and stood behind the glass. Dr. Bradhurst, Dr. Hieber, and yes, even Hanns Korman. 'So, he is involved as well.'

Dr. Bradhurst peered down on the safeguarded man who had two intravenous tubes protruding from his arm. One led to a hanging bottle of anesthetic, the other to a glass container of Potassium Cyanide. Dr. Bradhurst felt pretty certain the enclosure would prevent Michael Danvers from penetrating it with whatever powers he might possess; but he did not want to take any chances. Dr. Bradhurst and Dr. Hieber each held remote controls that would instantly inject the patient's body with enough deadly cyanide to kill an elephant.

During the last operation he had added very strong cell clusters into Michael's brain and if they bonded as well as the first cells had, there was no telling what he might be capable of. If Michael could penetrate the thick class barrier and prevent them from activating the remotes, he would have to rely on his own mental ability to prevent his mind from succumbing to any brainwashing that the demon he had created could influence on him. If this happened it would be extremely difficult to keep negative thoughts out of his head and even more difficult to keep his mind a total blank when in close proximity to Danvers, but he would have to. He would have to convince his own magnificent mind to control his thoughts. He spent several hours prior to this meeting brainwashing himself to accomplish this. He felt he had; but was his willpower strong enough to fend-off Michael Danvers' penetrating powers? He could only hope that it was.

"Well Mr. Danvers, I see you are awake. How are you feeling?"

After a pause of nearly a minute, a pause giving him time to connect to each of their minds, he replied. "I feel quite good. I don't know yet what effect the last operation has had on me but like you Dr, Bradhurst, I am anxious to know."

By all apparent indications, Michael Danvers seemed to have transformed into a meek and well-mannered person. He made no apparent attempt what-so-ever to influence any of the men on the far side of the thick glass barrier, leaving Dr. Bradhurst to believe the wall he created was sufficient to block out the man's telekinetic powers. But even so, he continued to force his mind to retract into a void where he could control his every thought and hopefully prevent Michael Danvers from inflicting any influence on him, if in fact he could. He felt certain that his 'brain-child' possessed incredible capabilities and vowed to put himself in this mind-controlled state until Michael Danvers was put to death.

Michael Danvers continued to talk in a tranquil and composed manner. Always positive and reassuring; talking about becoming part of the team to help understand the magnitude of the power that he now possessed and how they could use that understanding for the better of mankind. While doing this he was gaining control over the minds of his three visitors. To all apparent appearance he was a model patient. Then suddenly, his demeanor completely changed. "It's time for us to discuss my situation." He said in an authoritative voice. "My powers have been enhanced greatly and I would like to openly share them with you."

Dr. Bradhurst tried with all of his power to hide his true feelings about what he just heard. Fighting to prevent any emotion or thought to inter his mind, he addressed his adversary in what he prayed was an honest and accepting voice. "I have always hoped you would open up to me so we could accurately evaluate the results of these experiments. I am so pleased that you are now willing."

Michael Danvers smiled. "I believe you. But before you say anything else let me tell you that a simple pane of glass has no effect on blocking me out. I can read your thoughts, so don't try to deceive me. From shortly after my first operation, I have known your ulterior motive for these experiments and your plans for me; but I assure you that I can prevent you from carrying them out. But let's not dwell on that."

Bradhurst immediately forced his mind to emit a message that he hoped his antagonist would pick up on. A message that he no longer wanted to get rid of him but wanted to work with him. The expression on Michael Danvers' face assured him that the message had been received.

"What an incredible gift you have given me Dr. Bradhurst. You have outdone yourself by boosting my mental abilities to levels you cannot even comprehend. I know my mind controlling powers have worried you ever since the unfortunate situation with Mr. Jacobs. I had the luxury of working with him long enough to totally control his mind and you can see the results. But now, after you have fulfilled my wishes by raising my powers even further, I have the ability to control countless minds and can perform this amazing feat almost instantly. I easily placed your two collaborators firmly under my powers. They stand there totally helpless, not able to move a mussel. But you have a much stronger will than they do. It took me a little longer to break through the barrier you are trying to place between us, but don't try to fool yourself. You are very strong Gordon, but you are no match for me."

"Hanns, you are the easiest to read. Because you have a soft spot in your heart for mankind, you had difficulties accepting the amoral methods in which the hospital is managed, but now you are (somewhat reluctantly) committed to Dr. Bradhurst and his agenda. You have been a bad boy haven't you. You made a discovery that you are hiding from Gordon and Russel." Hanns was powerless to respond.

"And Dr. Hieber; what a devious soul you are! You get great pleasure in firing up the crematory oven, don't you? You would have made an excellent Nazi." The skilled surgeon, like Hanns, was in a state of immobility.

His eyes shifted to Gordon Bradhurst. "Something has changed with you. You seem to have done an about-face with your thinking about me... I wonder? Anyway gentlemen, you are completely under my power and will do exactly as I say."

The extreme pressure Gordon was forcing on his mind to resist Michael Danvers' attempts to read his thoughts and control his mind was working, at least to some extent and he resolved himself to continue to block his mind for as long as he could. However, he felt somewhat helpless and knew he was under some type of hypnotic power, no matter how weak it might be.

"One of the many areas I am able to tap into is mind control. Dr. Bradhurst and Dr. Hieber, when you first approached the glass partition separating us, I made it impossible for either of you to activate the devices you are holding, Cyanide is such an unpleasant thing don't you agree? Please put the remotes down. Russel, having no will whatsoever of disobeying the command he was given, did as he was told. "Thank you. Now that wasn't difficult, was it?"

Dr. Bradhurst knew that part of his mental capacity was strongly influenced by Michael Danvers, but he also realized he had some self-control of his own. He tried with all of his will to push the plunger that would end the life of the monster before him, but his brainchild overpowered him with a surge of energy preventing him from doing it; yet he did not drop the activator that would have ended the nightmare he found himself in.

"You have an incredibly strong mind Gordon, but as I said, you are no match for me. Now drop it." He said this as he concentrated his mind power towards his adversary.

The activating device fell from Gordon's hand.

"Now, have the intravenous needles removed from my arm and free me from this bed."

Dr. Bradhurst was not yet ready to totally give in to the dizzying probe penetrating his mind. With every fiber in his being, he forced as much energy to his brain as he could in an effort to reject Michael Danvers' brain controlling technique and his herculean determination worked. Now he must try to convince his foe that he was under his control and bide his time until the opportunity presented itself to end this fiends' life. With his mind in a forced total blank and not letting any outside influence enter it, he entered the room and freed the patient from both the I.V.s and his bonds.

Once he was free from his restraints, Michael Danvers informed the three men who were now his submissive adherents, that they would all move to Dr. Bradhurst's office. Once there, speaking to Gordon Bradhurst he said. "You will implant Hanns' new cells that prolong life into me. Living much longer will suit me just fine. You will operate tomorrow morning and I will be awake throughout the procedure."

Hanns spoke up. "The age prolonging genetically altered genes have not been proven yet and…"

He was interrupted before he could add to his concerns about using untested cell structures. "I know all that, but in your mind, you believe the mathematics are sound and will work. That's good enough for me. All three of you will perform the operation and as I said, I will be alert enough to assure the operation goes well."

Gordon Bradhurst maintained the black nothingness in his brain throughout the operation, not letting his thoughts reveal that if he ever so slightly tried to sabotage the surgical procedure, Michael Danvers could easily kill him with a burst of energy from his mind. The operation went without a hitch. If Hanns' theory was correct, and Michael Danvers was certain it was, he would live to a much riper age than anyone in history.

Results of examinations of Michael Danvers mental capabilities were mind-boggling. There seemed no subject or topic related to anything in the world that he did not know. Every scientific issue presented to him was answered like it was child's play. His knowledge was so advanced that I.Q. tests would have been irrelevant.

Michael Danvers had taken over Gordon's office and summoned the man who had held him captive with plans to kill him. "I have come to several conclusions as how to proceed and some of them will involve you."

Gordon Bradhurst obediently nodded.

"I want six computers capable of hooking up to every corporate and governmental network in the word and I want them as fast as you can get them for me. I know these super-computers will be illegal to acquire but I believe someone with your worldly influences can do this."

Gordon nodded again. "It might take some time but I'm certain I can get them."

"Yes, I knew you could." Then in a most sarcastic voice he said. "You see Dr. Gordon Bradhurst, now that I am using you, (rather than you, using me) you are going to help me become the most influential and powerful man in the world. Your measly little agendas are nothing compared to what I have in mind."

Dr. Bradhurst forced his mind to once again project an idea that he hoped would be accepted as true. "Would it be advantageous for you to have your office located in the city? You would be closer to anything you may need."

With no hesitation Michael Danvers agreed. "Your L.A. office will suit me fine."

"Yes! I will have the computers in place as fast as I can have them delivered."

"Good! And Bradhurst, I will want a small team of computer experts, the most talented in the world. Shall we say six to begin with? Whatever it takes, have them report to me in my new office in five days with computers ready for them. Failure to do so is not an option for you."

"I will not fail." Gordon assured the mega-maniac he had created. But in reality, he could not wait to part with him, fearing that he could not hold up much longer against the telepathic probing that constantly penetrated his mind. As his chauffeur drove him to his office in downtown L.A. Gordon kept his mind focused on the task of ordering computers and finding experienced experts to operate them; this was part of his ruse to let Danvers believe he was completely under his spell just in case his powers reached out away from the hospital. But once he was seated in his office, he had to take the chance that he was well out of reach of the incredible power that his nemesis possessed. It only took him a minute to decide on the tactics he would use to rid himself of the creature he had created. Reaching for his unlisted phone he dialed a number that could not be traced back to him. After several rings he heard the familiar voice of Sid.

"I have a very urgent assignment for you. It will require the use of the best sniper you can locate. Money is no object."

"I have just the man for it." The gruff voice said.

"Secondly, a car might have to be destroyed."

"No problem."

"Thirdly, my office may have to go."

"Your office? You'll have to pay in advance if you intend to be in it." He snickered. "But that can happen."

Once the particulars were agreed to, Gordon sat back and relaxed. It felt good to feel he was in control again. When he ridded himself of this enemy, he would begin on the next leg of his carefully planned agenda.

To be on the safe side, he called his technology manage and discussed with him the computers he was interested in and their availability. Within an hour the manager called and informed the doctor that the equipment would arrive in four days. He emphasized the extreme cost involved which

Gordon waved off as inconsequential. In the meantime, he had got the ball rolling on locating computer geeks. If Danvers investigated, he would find that Gordon had followed his directions to-the-tee.

Two days later, at ten in the morning Sid informed him that all was ready. The snipper would be in place when the time was determined. He had a photo of the target so there would be no mix-up with identification. The company limo and his office were wired up and would be activated by remote controls if required. Good, Gordon mused. Three layers of offence in place! He was quite sure the sniper would do the job but if for any reason that did not work, the limo would be next in line. Losing a limo driver was of no concern to him. If the limo didn't rid him of his nemesis, his office would be destroyed when Michel Danvers was there. He was satisfied with his plans and called Michael Danvers. "Computers will arrive in two days as well as six of the best computer experts that I could locate. I have moved out of my office and it's ready for you. I suggest you move in tomorrow. That would give you a day before they arrive."

"Excellent. I have an aggressive plan laid out and will assign you to a few more tasks once I arrive."

"You can contact the limo driver. He can bring you here whenever you want." Gordon offered.

"Tomorrow morning as you suggested will suit me." Michael agreed.

The following morning, Michael Danvers called Russel Hieber into his office. "I will be moving into Dr. Bradhurst's office today and want you to accompany me."

"I have a surgery scheduled but I can have Hanns handle it for me." He replied.'

"Do that."

On a protruding ridge bare of trees some three thousand yards from the entrance to the Bradhurst Research Center, a man, made finite adjustments to the device before him. The apparatus was the creation of a gifted gunsmith but held no resemblance whatsoever to any known rifle in the world; yet it was a rifle, of sorts. It was controlled by a sophisticated computer that calculated distance, wind-drift, air density and humidity and projectile arc. It was accurate within an inch from the distance to the expected target. There was no trigger as such, the cartridge was discharge electronically, and the silencer at the end of the barrel almost completely deadened the muzzle blast. The sniper who manned this extraordinary firing device was a skilled marksman who contracted one million dollars for every setup.

Two men exited the door and stood on the steps of the Research Center as the limo approached. The sniper aligned the crosshairs of the powerful scope and activated the electronic trigger sending a .270 caliber bullet on its way. At a muzzle speed of four thousand feet per second, the bullet arched across three thousand yards of clear morning air and found its target, entering the left eye of Michael Danvers and blowing the back of his skull away. Death was instantaneous.

Having no idea what had happened, other than Michael Danvers' head being blown off, it took Russel, with blood and bits of brain splattered on him, a couple of seconds before he thought, 'rifle.' Not knowing if there would be more shooting, he screamed to the driver who was getting out of the long vehicle and they both ran for cover inside the entranceway of the Hospital's Research Center. Russel immediately instructed the driver to keep anyone from approaching the front door and called Gordon. "Danvers is dead!" He said in somewhat of a breathless state. "His head exploded not three feet from me."

"Good," Gordon interrupted. "Are you okay?"

"I don't know. Yes. It seems like a heavy load has been lifted from my mind. The hold he had on me is gone. What happened here?"

"Just something I had to take care of." Gordon replied. "Can you clean things up? I want this swept under the rug so keep it as quiet as you can."

"I'll do my best, but it happened on the steps by the front entrance and there's a lot of blood and gore. I'll get right on it and call you back later."

He called Hanns and two trusted orderlies who arrived straightaway. In less than fifteen minutes the body was removed to the crematory and the front entrance was cleaned; removing every trace of what had occurred there. Only five trustworthy men knew what had happened at the busy hospital! When the proper temperature in the oven was reached, the body of Gordon Bradhurst's brainchild was incinerated leaving no trace that he had ever been at the hospital.

When Russel reported to him that all was taken care of, Gordon treated himself to a noontime cognac. Contentment eased his mind for the first time since Michael Danvers clouded his head using his extrasensory powers in an attempt to brainwash him. And it did work for a short time. Only his strong will to withstand the tremendous force of his opponent's powers had saved him. "The damn fool," Gordon said to himself. "I gave him the power to destroy me with his mind, yet he procrastinated, thinking he had me in his control. He wanted to make me suffer before killing me." He sat and brooded for a spell, blaming himself for taking too many risks. He should have killed Danvers before the second operation but as it turned out, he learned what he needed to know. The brain was capable of accepting great numbers of clustered cells with no apparent adverse side-affects. It would be safe to infuse as many brain cells as he wanted in one single application. The time was rapidly approaching when he would have his team operate on him. He was getting anxious.

He called Sid, acknowledged his proficiency in executing his assignment, instructed him to remove the explosives from the limo and his office, and assured him that he would be adequately taken care of.

All was well!

As tied up with, and as important as the clustering program was to him, Gordon Bradhurst still had a very large organization to run. Shortly after the demise of Michael Danvers, he and his vice-president of finance spent a week in Europe on urgent business.

Upon his return he contacted Russel and Hanns via phone. Russel gave him an update on the many activities he was managing at the institute of which all seemed to be going very well. He would have missed Russel if they had to resort to phase-two in his plans to eliminate Michael Danvers. He hadn't planned on Danvers bringing his partner with him in the limo, but even so, he would not have aborted the plan even if he did know. As good as Russel was at his job, in Gordon Bradhurst's mind, no one was indispensable.

He had seen the powers that Michael Danvers possessed and envisioned himself reaching even higher levels. He smiled with the realization that the day was rapidly approaching when the operation would take place.

He was ready!

Fourteen
The First Indication

Frank Wallace had communicated with Carlene Linser on a regular basis since his first meeting with her, discussing issues related to the wolf program and the newly added grizzly bear dilemma. Through their many e-mails and telephone conversations, Frank and Carlene had become somewhat close and if friends can be made from afar, they had reached that threshold.

When she called at eight o'clock Monday morning (Frank's time) he could detect a slight change in her normal tone. "Sorry to call so early but I felt I had to talk to you."

As early as it was in California, Frank assumed she had discovered a breakthrough and had good news for him. "No problem, we just finished breakfast." He said as he pushed the speaker button on his phone so Sarah could listen in.

She got right to the point. "Something has come up and I was hoping you could come here to discuss it with me."

Frank had been up to his ears in problems for so long that he could hardly remember and had just returned to his ranch the previous day. Not only was he dealing with the nerve-racking wolf problems, but the gigantic bears had begun appearing in ever increasing numbers with reported sightings and deaths spreading far and wide. Consulting on the Canadian taskforce and now heavily involved in the U.S. program to address these disastrous problems had been keeping him extremely busy. He was exhausted and needed a few days of rest, but he detected an urgent plea in her request. "What is it, Carlene? It must be important for you to call this early."

"It is Frank. I probably shouldn't be involving you in this…" She paused and then added. "Something has occurred here that I am not ready or willing to report to the company yet because I don't have any concrete proof. The reason I'm calling you is because we have hit it off quite well and I know I can trust you. You represent the government and hopefully you can help me decide the best way to handle this. This is important enough that I don't want to discuss it over the phone…"

Frank knew that she was very concerned about something and not really wanting to travel to California, he pushed the issue. "Does it have anything to do with the programs you are working on with me? Have you discovered something important?"

"No, it doesn't, but it is related to the supercell program. I have discovered something very concerning that involved Hanns Korman and Michael Danvers. I shouldn't be burdening you with this and will understand if you can't come here."

"I've been busy lately and need a break. Sunny California might do me some good." Looking at Sarah with a questioning eye he added. "I might bring my wife. She's had a pretty rough time of it lately with me gone so often." Sarah nodded her approval.

"What do you make of that?" Frank asked his wife when he hung up the phone.

"Well, there's no doubt she's scared. The way she talked she must have discovered something quite serious. I'm surprised that whatever is bothering her isn't about the work she's doing for you. I can't imagine her requesting you to fly out there for any other reason."

"Neither can I. But I agree something quite unusual must have happened if she couldn't discuss it on the phone."

Late the following afternoon the Wallace's arrived in Los Angeles where they checked into the same hotel he had stayed at when he first visited Drechsler International. Carlene had made dinner arrangements and when they arrived at the restaurant, she introduced her husband and Frank presented his wife. Small talk prevailed throughout dinner where Frank learned that Howard Linser taught high-school history and also coached basketball and football. During their conversation Carlene, addressing both Frank and Sarah said, "You must think I'm mad the way I handled this by bringing you out here on the spur of the moment."

Sarah laughed. "Mad? Perhaps. Why else would you summon us to what Frank refers to as sunny California. This is the third time I've been to L.A., and I have yet to see the sun. The smog was so thick that the taxi driver lost his way from the airport to our hotel. And the traffic… well we won't mention the traffic. But I wouldn't think you were any madder than any other scientist." Then a grin appeared on her aging but still beautiful face. "If you want to know about being mad, let me tell you about Mad Frank Wallace. He retired to a ranch in Montana to raise cattle and ride horses and spend time with his beautiful and loving wife and no sooner had he settled down when he begins running around North America in a panic trying to rid the world of one menace after another. Now that's mad. And an even madder mad is the mad I experience by putting up with his madness."

This got a chuckle out of the others. "You will have to excuse her." Frank said. "She has a tendency to ramble at times."

"Ramble, now Frank you know I never ramble. I might roam, wander and even saunter on rare occasions but never ramble."

After dessert, the four retired to the lounge where they occupied comfortable cushy chairs. "Let me start at the beginning," Carlene said addressing Frank. "You know about Michael Danvers disappearance and that shortly after that Hanns Korman quit his job. One very disturbing and the other quite unexpected! Michael Danvers' disappearance is still a mystery. He just seems to have vanished from the face of the earth." She paused for a moment trying to decide how to best approach the next subject. "Hanns and I worked very close on our two areas of research. Just about every day we shared our thoughts and results and even aided each other on a couple of experiments we were somewhat secretly working on. I say secretly in that we had yet to notify Michael Danvers of our involvement in these areas. Through our close interactions we became good friends. So, you can see that it was puzzling when he quit without a word to me. I've told you that Hanns' wife died in an explosion at his home. Three mysteries in a very short period-of-time makes me wonder if they are all related."

Frank knew that more was coming but he had to agree. Too many coincidences never set well with him.

"I have tried to stay in touch since he left and that in part is why I asked you here. But I'm getting ahead of myself." She stopped to sip her cocktail and her husband patted her arm. "As you know, Michael Danvers was replaced by a man named Bernhardt Weber. He was transferred from another division of Drechsler. He hired Hanns' replacement, Dr. Chang Cheung. We call him CC. He's from China but speaks English quite well and from all appearances is well qualified for the position. In fact, I find him to be almost as good as Hanns was, and that's saying something because I thought Hanns was a genius."

"CC is very interested in the functions of the human brain just as Hanns is. He wants to address things like cognition and intellect, processing speeds of all interaction to brains; long and short-term memory, memory loss, logic and reasoning and a multitude of other areas related to neuroscience and the human brain. Hanns was involved with all of these areas and CC is following up where he left off. He wanted to see how far Hanns had progressed in a certain area of human intellect and upon finding little or no data, he reviewed the cell clusters in our repository related to that gene feature and found none there. This surprised him so he consulted with me. I knew that Hanns was involved with research in this area and that he did have many samples that were positively identified as human brain enhancing cell clusters related to this area. Not knowing what had happened with those specific samples or the records that should have recorded them, I pleaded ignorance to CC. He left it at that, assuming that Hanns did not get that far in his research. I was bewildered! I called Hanns, who is working at a private clinic in the area and told him we needed to talk. We did and he was very evasive. He told me to please forget about it. As I say, I think a lot of him, and I know he does of me."

More drinks were ordered all around. Frank was beginning to see the makings of what could turn into a dire situation, but he said nothing.

"I think he's dug himself into a very dangerous hole and I'm worried about him." She continued. "I tried to rationalize how the samples could have disappeared and the computer evidence of their existence erased. Hanns had access to the samples and Michael Danvers was in charge of all company computer records. Our system is considered infallible but the only way that I can foresee successfully stealing samples is to manipulate the computers. There are so many checks and counter checks and firewalls in place that it seems impossible, yet I think it was done. And if I'm right, what other samples might have been taken?" She let that sink in.

And it did. Frank's head was whirling. The first thing that came to mind was industrial espionage. Getting this science into the wrong hands could be disastrous. But before he could think any further, Colene continued.

"I have done a little detective work," she said as she looked at her husband.

"And I am very worried about it. God knows… if she is caught snooping around… I don't like this." Howard said in a worried tone.

"I know dear, but I am careful," she tried unsuccessfully to assure him. "I looked up the hospital where Hanns works, and the mystery grows even deeper. It's more of an institution for the mentally ill than a medical hospital. It's owned by Dr. Bradhurst. He's well known to anyone in the medical field. He's considered one of the leading brain surgeons in the country and is quite famous for research related to brain functions." She looked at Frank with a questioning eye. "He is also one of the wealthiest men in the country… I think you can guess where I'm going with this?"

Frank most certainly could. A brain specialist with enough money to buy whatever he desired could have approached both Michael Danvers and Hanns Korman with an offer they couldn't refuse. Were the two men capable of pulling off such a risky and dangerous undertaking, he asked himself. Yes! He believed that with knowledge and opportunity even the seemingly impossible was possible. Especially with strong enough incentive.

"I hope you can see why I cannot report this to the company. I have absolutely no proof whatsoever and don't want to create a fiasco if I am wrong about this. And there is also a little 'cyoa' involved. One of the experiments we were working on was somewhat under the table and if it comes-to-light with an investigation, I could suffer from repercussions. But honestly, I can see no other explanation. I know that the samples did exist, of that I am certain. I am not sure what to do and hoped that you might be able to help me though this."

The conversation continued for some time before the dinner party of four departed. Frank left his newly made friend and colleague with the promise that he would think about her worries and would discuss them further in the morning at her office.

He got little sleep that night. Countless scenarios troubled his mind, none of which were pleasant.

Despite being late for his scheduled morning meeting with Bernhardt Weber, Frank was greeted with a handshake and a cordial welcome. A somewhat warmer reception than he received from Michael Danvers.

"Sorry for being late," Frank apologized. "An accident on the thruway backed up traffic. Fortunately, the taxi driver was near an exit and wound his way through back roads or I might still be tied up in the mess."

"I've only been here a short time but it's not all that uncommon I hear. We have had some changes in personnel since your last visit, but I assure you we will support your needs to the best of our ability." After a short introduction related to each man's credentials and Franks involvement in the horrific mayhem caused by mutant wolves and bears, Dr. Weber turned his visitor over to Carlene Linser.

During the long day that he spent at Drechsler's Animal Research Center, Frank was introduced to Hanns Korman's replacement Dr. Chang Cheung and conversed with him for close to an hour about progress being made in the company's Human Research Center and hopeful future benefits anticipated from this new science.

By closing time late that afternoon, Frank, and Carlene Linser had meticulously gone through every issue related to the wolf and bear programs that Drechsler was working on. One of those issues was the deterioration in the strength of immune genes taken from dead wolves. When he first joined the Canadian committee, Frank had put in place an edict to have samples taken from as many wolves that were killed as possible. Since then, hundreds of wolves had been killed resulting in a growing number of samples being added to Carlene's reserve.

Now, as he reviewed the findings of the research team, he was able to see first-hand the enormity of the program they were involved in. A team of research specialists were assigned to the wolf and bear project and were uncovering significant data related to the biological makeup of this new strain of wolves. Approximately half of the younger wolves tested were showing more of a decline in the potency of their immune systems than previous generations. Data collected to date suggested to the scientists that the deterioration, (ever-so minor that it was), in the present years litter would likely accelerate even faster in each new generation. Certainly, the kind of information Frank had hoped to hear, but unfortunately, only half of the animals tested showed a weakening in their immune system, and they would have to wait until next years' litter to verify their conjectures. However, it did give some hope to cling to that something positive might come from health-related problems in the future. Only time would tell. But during that time, the animals would continue to raise havoc as they expanded their territory. Certainly not the quick fix that he had hoped for. Another issue that Frank had asked to be included in

Drechsler's list of evaluations was to keep track of female wolves' fertility capabilities and reproductive organs. Once again, he had been correct in his thinking. The team had discovered something in several of the youngest females; something unlike anything found in earlier generations. Hormone levels required for regulating egg fertilization in some of these animals were below that required for conception, rendering them infertile. In Frank's mind, even though the number of animals found to-date with this odd abnormality were few, it was promising. But would weakening immune systems eventually deteriorate enough to kill-off these creatures? The immune system and now the reproductive organs in the latest generation of wolves were starting to falter in some of the animals tested, as were several other biological organisms that Carlene's team had uncovered. Could nature eventually put an end to these man-made monsters as he once suggested might occur? Would their health eventually falter enough to kill them off? Possibly… But possibly not. Frank thought not. Nature had a way of fighting off diseases, infections and even plagues and pandemics. Why shouldn't she curb the weakening health of these creatures? Adding to his belief that biological breakdowns would not completely wipe out this new species of wolf, he was also quite certain that hunters would never kill them all either. They were already inhabiting much of the northern forests of North America. He felt they would eventually encompass the northern half of the world and even spread to the southern hemisphere as well.

To date, Carlene's team could find no weaknesses what-so-ever in the studies they were performing on the giant bears. Would similar findings to those discovered in wolves eventually be found in future generations of these gigantic bears? Drechsler scientists thought not. They found these mutant monsters to be the healthiest animals ever to walk the face of the earth.

Frank was deeply distraught as he envisaged the enormity of what these two monstrous creatures might have on mankind. He could only foresee doom and devastation.

He and Dr. Linser spent two hours during the day devising a plan of what Frank thought to be a logical approach to the issues related to missing samples. "I do agree with Howard," he said to Carlene. "You should not involve yourself with Dr. Bradhurst's hospital. Leave that to me. I know someone who might be able to help in that area. I fear there are likely more samples missing. Could you try to determine if more than one cell type was removed, and do it without drawing attention to yourself?"

She thought for a minute. "Yes, I think so. I'm developing a fairly close relationship with CC. I might be able to approach him with the idea of comparing computer lists of my research samples with a list of every sample he has in the human research program to see if we could benefit each other with our findings. I might learn something. It's worth a try."

"Good." Frank responded.

Frank left Carlene's office with mixed emotions. His scientific mind searched for reasons why, after several generations, the internal makeup of these animals would begin to weaken. He had always felt that mixing genes between wolf and bear, or any other species of animal, was a mistake and could result in adverse oppositional results. Many scenarios cluttered his mind, but all of his surmises were just that; suppositions, and only time would tell if eventually they would self-destruct because of biological reasons. He would report all findings to both Canadian and US officials but hold off relating his personal fears to them until more data was collected. One thing the two nations did not need right now was his dark thoughts.

As to Carlene's discovery of missing cell samples, that was quite another thing. From what he knew about Dr. Bradhurst and what Carlene had added; Frank feared the worst. Bradhurst was not only a gifted brain surgeon but also one of the world's leading researchers in neurology and the functions of the human brain. He cringed as thoughts entered his mind of what Bradhurst might do if he had access to cell clusters.

When they returned to the ranch, one of the first things Frank did was call an old friend who he had dealt with twice before when he was Director of the Fish and Game Department. Damon Courier operated a private detective and surveillance business in Washington DC. He developed that business through the years by providing exacting information to many people and organizations in the United States Government. His reputation of discretion was beyond repute. He was the man to call if information was required about anyone anywhere in the world.

Frank's call was answered by a receptionist who forwarded him to Damon Courier. "Frank," Damon opened with. "I heard you were chasing wolves again."

Frank laughed. "Yes, and we've added grizzly bears to the chase. We're in a hell-of-a mess."

"So, I've heard!"

After a short banter, Frank got to the point. "I need inside information on someone." He paused and then added. "I know I don't need to say that this is very confidential and must stay strictly between the two of us."

"Understood," Damon assured him. "Is it connected to the work you are doing with these monsters you're dealing with?"

"In a way," Frank replied.

"Okay, give me the details."

"His name is Dr. Gordon Bradhurst. He lives and works in Los Angeles. You may have heard of him. He is quite famous in the field of medicine."

"Yes, I know of him. If I am not mistaken, he is pretty well trenched-in with high level people here in the capitol and also worldwide." Damon replied.

"It's imperative that he does not find out he's being investigated. I want you to dig deep. What I hope to discover is likely buried far beneath the surface. Learn all you can about his hospital in San Bernardino. Who works there, what they specialize in; everything you can find. I suspect he has some involvement with Drechsler International. Check that out too. Remember that movie, 'Run Silent Run Deep'? That's what we need to do here. He must never suspect I am investigation him."

"Understood," Damon repeated himself. "We will as always be thorough, discrete and unobserved. When would you like me to report back to you?"

"I'm sure this is a standard reply to that question, but it is quite urgent. I'll leave it up to you when you feel you have enough information for me."

"It shouldn't take more than three or four days." Damon said. "I'll call you."

The remainder of that day Frank worked with his ranch manager, something that had become quite rare since the wolf problems exploded and even less once the mutant bears reared their beastly heads. That evening after dinner he was discussing the Bradhurst situation with Sarah when the phone rang. It was Erick Tuttle informing him that three bears had wandered into a small town and attacked several of its inhabitants resulting in seven deaths. One of the bears was killed and was being transported to his lab in Fairbanks. "You seem to have nothing but bad news Erick! One day I hope to hear something positive from you."

"The way things are going I wouldn't count on it anytime soon." Erick replied.

Damon Courier's call came three days later. "I was right about one thing," Damon said. "Dr. Bradhurst knows people in high places. He rubs shoulders with the elite and many government officials. He sits on the board of so many companies that it's hard to keep track of them all. I might also inform you that he is considered one of the most intelligent men in the world. He is a genius with an I.Q. in the top one percent. But that aside, I have some interesting information. I'll e-mail it to you. Once you browse through it give me a call so we can discuss the details."

"Thanks Damon. I appreciate the rush you put on this. I'll talk to you later."

The e-mail consisted of five written pages. Frank browsed through the data and then slowly read each entry carefully so as not to miss anything of importance. He made notes the third time he read the report. Damon had done his usual good job. How on earth he ever accumulated as much information as he did would always remain a mystery to those who were not familiar with the latest detection technological advancements. When he called Damon Courier, they talked for close to an hour reviewing every detail in the report.

'What to do next?' Frank thought about this for some time before he made up his mind. He called Carlene and was informed that she was unavailable. Would he like to leave a message? He did.

When Carlene Linser returned Franks call late that evening, it was obvious she was excited. "I spent the day with Dr. Cheung. We compared our two computer printouts listing every sample in both of our inventories. That includes those with known traits and function as well as unidentified ones. The lists are extensive. It was a tedious job but as it turned out, both of our departments will benefit from the exercise. Unbeknownst to CC, I kept a sharp eye out for Human samples that might be missing, and I found one. We were right, more than one sample is missing and those are only the ones I worked with Hanns on. Could there be more as you suspected? Probably! But now I am doubly sure that vials of clusters have been stolen."

"Not surprising," Frank said. "What was the missing sample?"

"Something Hanns called 'The Fountain of Longevity.' Shortly before he left, Hanns informed me that he had identified cells that he was almost certain governs the life span in humans. I assumed CC would follow up on this work but now I find no samples or records in the computer."

Frank had been thinking as Carlene updated him on this incredible news. Zoltan Proziver once told him that when the immune gene was perfected, he envisioned many other genetically defined features and characteristics related to both animals and human beings would follow. Now this had become a reality. He also said that someday his clustering science would include the human brain and all that it encompassed. And once again it appeared that his vison and prophecy was proving him right. In response to her latest shocking discovery, Frank related his deep concerns to her. "If you discovered two missing samples, many others could have been taken. It would make sense to only remove portion of the samples, leaving some behind to prevent anyone from suspecting the theft. If the computer records have been altered as thoroughly as we think they have been, we may never know what samples or how many were taken. I think you should keep this quiet for a time yet. I would like to come out there next week and visit with Dr. Korman. If you could set up a meeting between us, I would appreciate it. You could use the ploy that I want to discuss brain functions of hybrid wolfs and bears with mixed genetic cells with both him and you."

"I'll get in touch with him and let you know." Carlene said.

Fifteen
Too Late

It was a rare day in Los Angeles. The sun shone brightly with a slight breeze blowing off the ocean when Frank exited the airport and taxied to his hotel. Carlene had called to inform him that Hanns had agreed to see him, and arrangements were made for dinner.

The three scientists met in the lounge of the restaurant that Carlene had chosen for this meeting. As they shared a drink, Frank could see that Hanns Korman was visibly uneasy. Throughout dinner he said little. It was obvious that he and Carlene were not on the best of talking terms. She, being suspicious of his suspected larceny and him appearing somewhat embarrassed, like a boy caught with his hand in a cookie jar. What conversation there was; was directed by Frank Wallace. He talked mostly of the wolf and bear problems that were ravaging much of northern North America and how just recently, mutant wolves were being reported as far away as Siberia. What began as a major North American problem, was becoming a worldwide calamity!

Once dinner was over, Frank addressed Carlene. "I would like to have a private conversation with Hanns so I will say good evening to you."

Frank and Carlene had agreed that she would leave after dinner so Frank could deal with Hanns, one-on-one. She rose, said her goodbyes, and left.

Frank said nothing as the two men sat at the table. Finally, Hanns said. "Carlene said you wanted to discuss brain issues related to the mutant wolves and bears."

In a harsh and directing tone Frank responded to Hanns' statement with a somewhat harsh, "No. that is not why I wanted to talk to you."

Hanns was immediately taken back and looked somewhat bewildered at this man who had always been so calm and congenial.

Frank looked Dr. Hanns Korman in the eye and blurted out in the same stark voice, "I know what you have done."

Hanns was startled. "What do you mean? What are you talking about?"

"I know all about you and Michael Danvers!" Frank said this in a harsh accusing tone.

Dr. Hanns Korman became visibly shaken. Trying to regain his composure, he finally responded to what he thought was a threat from this man he had admired when they first met. "I…, I cannot imagine what you mean," he stuttered.

"Yes, you do Dr. Korman. But before we notified the FBI, I wanted to discuss it with you."

Hanns cringed at the thought. The FBI? Oh no, this can't be happening.

"We know about what you and Michael Danvers did. We don't know exactly how many samples you have taken but it's only a matter of time before we do." Frank was not sure about what he was about to say but the report that Damon Courier had given him about the darker side of Gordon Bradhurst's life gave him an idea. There was no doubt that the doctor was brilliant and was setting new milestones in his field and that he was also a very successful financier, accumulating what some thought to be several billion dollars. The report had a great deal more to say about this medical genius. In many circles he had established himself as a caring, charitable, and public-spirited humanitarian and was looked up to and was considered a pillar of the community. However, Courier had uncovered an entirely conflicting side of this renowned doctor and businessman. First-hand accounts from various people who worked for him or knew him in the medical and academic and business world painted quite another picture of the good doctor. By many he was considered a cruel and violent man who had ruined many people who stood in his way. There were strong rumors that deaths may have occurred resulting from unsavory operations held at his private hospital. He might be wrong about the idea that had crossed his mind, but he was going to act on it anyway. "As to the disappearance of Michael Danvers, I think you know what happened to him." He let this sink in and from the horrified expression that appeared on Hanns' face he knew he had been right. He continued in a much more serene tone. "Tell me Hanns, is Michael dead?"

The crest-fallen man sitting opposite him sadly shook his head as tears filled his eyes.

"I know that Dr. Bradhurst is behind all this so tell me about it."

"It was not supposed to happen like this," the choked-up man said. "I had no idea that Michael was even at the hospital until just recently. They were keeping him a prisoner in a locked room and were implanting clustered cells into his brain." Frank was startled at this revelation. He had no idea that the science had developed to the point that cell clusters could be used by direct infusion into a living organism. All experiments to date were performed on living animals by means of genetic pass-through to their offspring.

Frank held up his hand for Hanns to wait. "I think I would like you to start from the begging. Tell me everything that transpired since this first began."

Hanns seemed to gain some composure and began what became a long and involved oration. "Everything was going well at Drechsler. We were making slow but steady progress when DR. Bradhurst paid us a visit. He had just been appointed to Drechsler's Board of Directors and said he was visiting us just as a courtesy call. It turned out that was not true."

Damon's report to Frank had revealed that there were no openings in the Board until one of its membered mysteriously died. Dr. Bradhurst was immediately on the scene and because of his outstanding background, he was elected. Damon, a man who could read between the lines of just about any scenario suspected that fowl-play may have been involved.

"He took Michael and me to dinner," Hanns continued. "He offered each of us two million dollars to remove some samples from the company and I guess the money won us over."

Two million dollars, Frank gasped. My god! He must have wanted them desperately if he would pay that much.

"With me it wasn't so much the money as it was his offer to work for him. He's one of the top scientists in the country and had discovered a way to transfer human brain cells from one brain to another. A most incredible breakthrough in our field, and I wanted so much to be part of this new procedure. Anyway, we both accepted. Dr. Bradhurst reviewed a list of all of the samples we had amassed and chose the ones he wanted. My part was easy. All I had to do was remove them and walk out the door with them. Michael had to manipulate the computers so as not to show that any samples were missing. The timing was critical, but we pulled it off. Michael was a computer expert and was sure nothing would ever be discovered, and I thought that was the case until you discovered what we did. Shortly after Dr. Bradhurst was assured that he got what he paid for, and that consisted of hundreds of samples, Michael disappeared. I thought he took his money and ran. He had creditors and it seemed to me it was a way out of not paying them." Hanns continued to rattle on as a fear began to overtake Frank at what he was hearing. "Dr. Bradhurst thought it best if I didn't leave my position at Drechsler after Michael went missing so we waited for a time before I gave notice. Then a terrible accident happened. My home blew up and my wife was killed. Everything seemed to be happening all at once but as we all know, life goes on."

Frank thought too many things had happened too fast. It seemed to him that it was too timely that Hanns lost his wife just when he was ready to report to Bradhurst. Could there be a connection? He wondered…

"My work at the laboratory was most rewarding." Hanns continued. "It's really a mental hospital but my work, at least most of it, is done in one of the best equipped test facilities I have ever seen. Dr. Bradhurst was right, we were completely unrestricted in our work and our team of doctors, surgeons and research specialists made great progress. Not only on the many programs that were existing when I arrived there but also on the 'super-cell' program that I was put in charge of. I was happier than I had ever been. That is until I realized that some patients, most of them incurable and close to death, but others with at least some hope of recovery, were being operated on as though they were expendable. And in fact, they were to Dr. Bradhurst and Dr. Hieber. They only wanted results and losing patients during the numerous operations was inconsequential. People were dying on the operating table and that bothered me to no end. But I knew from conversations with both doctors that I was in too deep, and I worried for my life if I didn't stay loyal to their cause. I was caught in a dilemma; damned either way I went so I did my best to assure them that I was on their team. Things went fairly well until I heard about Michael. I informed them that I knew of his internment and tried to convince them that I had no ties with him and in fact despised him. And to some degree that was true, but I did not wish him harm. They believed me and told me they had operated on him. They had embedded his brain with many clusters of cells in an effort to improve the level of powers that the human brain possesses."

Hanns was becoming ever more nervous as he talked about Michael Danvers, indicating to Frank that something had happened that greatly disturbed him. "Shall I order you another whisky and soda?" He asked. "It might calm you."

"No," Hanns replied. "I want to get through this." Tears came to his eyes again as he went on with his story. "What I am about to tell you will be hard for you to believe but it's true. They created a monster, a monster that became a tyrannical madman." He paused and looking at Frank he said, "You cannot believe the powers that his mind possessed. He could read our thoughts. He not only knew what we were thinking but could delve into our minds and expose everything that was buried there. We couldn't keep anything from his probing brain. And even worse, he had some kind of control over us; a dominating influence that is hard to describe. He could command our every move. We were helplessly under the strong mental powers he possessed. Michael Danvers considered himself to be the Supreme Being and from his babblings it was apparent that he was planning to take over the world. We were helpless to do anything but obey his commands. That is except Dr. Bradhurst. His mind was stronger than ours, strong enough to resist at least some of the hold this devil we created had over us. Dr. Bradhurst somehow contracted a sniper who shot Michael ending our nightmare." Hanns had ended his incredible tale with a sigh of relief. It had felt good to get this heavy encumbrance out in the open and share his nightmare with someone.

Frank had had no idea what he would uncover when he met with Dr. Korman but certainly not the astonishing story he just listened to. A story that admitted to larceny, unethical and immoral medical practices, and even murder. Frank's mind reeled. What he had heard in the last few minutes was astounding. If it was all true, and he had no doubts that it wasn't, Dr. Gordon Bradhurst was a ruthless power-hungry psychopath with no qualms about sacrificing patients to gain the knowledge he wanted to reach his goals. Even committing murder to those who stood in his way! He had always feared what might occur if this scientific breakthrough that Zoltan had discovered got into the wrong hands. Now he knew, and it was terrifying. If Michael Danvers could possess the kind of powers that Hanns had just described, what would prevent others from doing the same? What other features, functions and characteristics of humans might be targeted and what results might incur? Frank feared that if this could not be controlled it would affect all of mankind. The human race as he knew it could be radically transformed into something that he did not want to think about. A foreboding horror spread through his being. He feared that proceedings in this scientific research had gone too far to be stopped and because of mankind's never-ending ability to circumvent even the tightest of controls, the process would invariably fall into other wrong hands, as it did with Gordon Bradhurst. He feared that it was too late to curb the disasters that he could foresee ahead. But he was going to try.

His thoughts were interrupted when Hanns added to his astonishment and fears. "There is something else. I recently discovered a means of creating continuous cell rejuvenation that can prolong life. All living cells age at different rates in animals and humans and that governs our longevity. All cells die and are replaced by new ones in a natural way but in the process living matter ages. The process I have formulated overrides natural cell production and replaces it with extremely strong regenerating super cells that slows cellular deterioration and replaces them with stronger ones that live longer. The process isn't perfected yet but every mathematical calculation I have made indicates that every living cell within the human body can replace aging ones with minimal breakdown of living tissue; and do so in a recycling of extremely strong cell structures. To what extent life can be prolonged remains to be determined but I believe the answer to that will be forth coming. If this develops as I am sure it will, humans will have the means to live a longer life. Possibly a very long life. Michael Danvers had these miraculous cell clusters implanted in him. We have no way of knowing what affect they had on him, but he was certain that his life span was increased dramatically.

"My god Hanns, what are you saying?"

"I know, it scares the hell out of me, but I am confident my calculations are accurate. And what scares me even more is that now that Michael is dead, Dr. Bradhurst is planning to infuse cell clusters in his own brain. I don't know when, but I think it will be soon. He has met with Dr. Hieber and me on what clusters he wants to use and their strengths. He plans to use stronger percentages of cells than those used on Michael, and he insists on using these fountain of youth cells when we operate. I urged him not to, but he's made up his mind. I have tried to convince myself that because his brain is advanced beyond that of most humans, he will handle whatever added strengths and powers he might gain appropriately and use them in a scientific and humanitarian manner. But I'm just fooling myself. Dr. Bradhurst is a strong headed unscrupulous Machiavellian and will do anything to dominate everyone around him."

Frank looked Hanns Korman directly in the eyes and said brusquely, "I'm finding all this hard to accept. Sure, we have always known the human brain is an incredible organ capable of amazing things but what you are describing is incomprehensible. Dominating and controlling everyone who comes in contact with him and using them as though they were nothing more than robots? I cannot even imagine where this might lead." Many unpleasant thoughts rushed through his mind. Another Hitler, or even worse! "I agree with you; his intensions are more than likely anything but ethical or moral. If this operation takes place, there might be no stopping him."

Hanns looked down and nodded his head. "I know! As I said, I've been trying to convince myself that this can all work out well, and good will come of it, but Dr. Bradhurst is Dr. Bradhurst and always will be." Hanns had said this with tears once again dampening his eyes. "Mr. Wallace, I am scared. I know if Dr. Bradhurst increases his mental capacities to levels as powerful as Michael Danvers' or even more-so as he is convinced will happen, he will read my mind and know all of my fears. I really think he has no reservations whatsoever of eliminating anyone who gets in his way. He only wants strong people around him and when he sees how weak I am he won't need me anymore."

"I think you are anything but weak."

Frank decided to change the subject and throw one more log on the fire. "Have you ever suspected that the explosion that took the life of your wife was not an accident?"

"My God, what are you saying?" Hanns seemed horrified by the thought.

"Can you think of any reason why Dr. Bradhurst might want your wife out of the picture?"

Hanns shook his head negatively. "We were having marital problems and I told Dr. Bradhurst that with the money he had given me for the samples, I planned to buy Margery off and get a divorce. I assumed it was an accidental gas explosion like the authorities said, but now that you mention it, he said he thought it would be a good idea to be rid of her and that I would be better off if she was completely out of my life. Do you really think he could have done this?"

"I don't know but I think it's possible."

He was pretty sure that if Hanns revealed his story to the authorities there wouldn't be enough evidence to convict Bradhurst of anything. The doctor was undoubtedly a very careful man and Frank envisioned him covering up any evidence that might connect him to anything illegal, or immoral. There would only be Hanns Korman's word against one of the most renowned physicians in the world. Frank knew that whatever approach he took in trying to expose this evil man, he would be facing a difficult, if not impossible task. He also had his own life to think about. How much digging could he get away with before he was caught up with? He needed help; more help than he could expect from Hanns Korman, however, Hanns Korman was all he had at the present and if Bradhurst was planning to inject power enhancing cells into his own brain that could possibly turn him into some sort of super-human being, he had to do something right away. He responded to Dr. Korman's fears with a plea for his help. "I need your help, Hanns. Without you I can see no way to put an end to this horrible nightmare. Are you willing to help?"

Hanns disconsolately agreed.

"At present you have a very valuable service to provide to the doctor and his agendas, so I think you should continue working as you have been. You must hold up as best you can and not let him know about any of this. Somehow, we must stop Bradhurst's operation." He paused as he considered possible options. "I have never met Dr. Bradhurst, but from what I have learned about him it won't be easy to deceive him; but I do have a couple of ideas that might work. You might be able to replace the chosen cell clusters with innocuous ones. Possibly re-label the specimens." Then another thought came to him. "Even better would be to sabotage the entire collection of these damn things."

"I don't know." Hanns said. "Dr. Bradhurst and Russel are very meticulous in everything they do. If they discover anything wrong, I believe that would be the end of me. They cover every possible track that might lead to anything negative of unsavory to them. There is no evidence that any of the clustered cells we have at the laboratory came from Drechsler. The only connection between Drechsler and Dr. Bradhurst is me. And as far as proving Michael Danvers was killed at the hospital, there are no records of him ever being there. The crematory oven was installed with a furnace hot enough to destroy any trace of human remains. As I said, they are very thorough."

"Yes, I'm sure they are, and I don't want to put you in anymore danger than necessary, but I don't see any other option. Right now, even though we know what's going on at the hospital, there is nothing that we can prove; yet we must do something to try and put an end to this madness."

"I work alone quite often. I suppose I could do something. But if I do succeed in hindering or preventing the operation, what happens if Dr. Bradhurst discovers that the operation failed because of me?"

"If you can do something to destroy the samples he intends to use, you should act and run. Get away as soon as you can. I will be able to keep you safe until we get proof of the unscrupulous goings on there."

"I'll do whatever I can."

"If, as you said, Bradhurst is planning to perform the operation soon, you should act right away."

"I'll try to do something tomorrow morning."

Even though Hanns had said this with little optimism in his voice, Frank, not knowing what else they could do said, "Good!" After exchanging phone numbers, he added. "Keep in contact with me Hanns. I want to know everything that happens. And please be careful."

"I will."

The following morning Hanns entered the experimental laboratory's dispensary where samples were stored. All research personnel were in the laboratory working on various programs they were assigned to, leaving the dispensary unoccupied. He had made up his mind; he would try to sabotage the experiment that if carried out, would likely change the maniacal Dr. Bradhurst into someone as horrifying as Michael Danvers had become; or even worse. He had introduced this science to the doctor, and he now felt that it was up to him to prevent it from doing any more harm than it already had.

Choosing one of the samples on Dr. Bradhurst's list, he contaminated the contents of the vial by combining it with another sample that was yet to be identified. His plan was to contaminate all of the samples that Dr. Bradhurst planned to use but he had no sooner finished the third specimen when his cell phone rang. Russel Hieber asked him to come to his office right away.

Russel pointed to a chair and indicated Hanns to sit. "Today is the big day." Russel informed his colleague. "Gordon has scheduled his operation for one o'clock."

Hanns tried to keep the stunned feeling that surged through him unnoticed and apparently did, because Russel continued without any apparent notice. "He should be here shortly and wants to see us as soon as he arrives."

No sooner had he said this when the phone rang. Gordon Bradhurst was ready to see them.

Hanns had prepped himself to act on the plan that he and Frank Wallace had plotted the previous night but had just begun when Dr. Bradhurst decided to perform the operation today. It was too late.

Gordon was riding on a high. It was obvious to his two associates that he was excited and even anxious for what was about to happen. This was something rare because Gordon Bradhurst seldom showed any kind of emotion. "Quick notice I know," he said. "But I think we can be ready by one can't we Russel?"

"Yes, I'll have everything ready. But Gordon, I don't like this. I think we are targeting too many different areas of the brain and the strength of some are far too strong. I really think you should reconsider and cut back some. If we are going to err, it should be on the light side. We can always operate again and add more cells if we need to but once we add cells it will be impossible to take them back."

"I respect you concern but I have evaluated every clustered cell I plan to use, and I am certain my calculations are correct." He turned to Hanns and asked. "What do you think?"

Hanns agreed with Russel, but he could see a possibility that if Dr. Bradhurst's brain was overburdened with a dozen different cell samples and some of them far exceeding what Michael Danvers was given, it might have adverse effects and that could possibly solve his problem. Looking at him he said. "I think you are the most brilliant brain specialist in the world, but I share Russel's concerns about proceeding too fast. But if you insist on doing this today, I am against using the life extending samples. Even though I have strong convictions that my calculations are quite sound, they are still unproven."

"I know your feelings, but I have studied your formulars and agree with your suppositions. I am as certain as you are that the rejuvenation process works; and besides, there were no apparent adverse side-affects with Danvers so we will go with my plans."

Dr. Bradhurst had been right in assuming the operation would take more than six hours. It was close to eight thirty when the patient was wheeled into the recovery room where two attendants would keep watch over him throughout the night. The two surgeons were exhausted when it was over and as they were cleaning up, Russell said, "That was one of the most intense operations I have ever been involved in, but it couldn't have been more successful. Think of it, Hanns, we just fused thirteen different brain enhancing cell clusters in Gordon's brain. We may have just made history by creating the most advanced human being the world has ever known. I'll keep him sedated until tomorrow afternoon before I bring him out of his induced coma. However, I don't want to rush his recovery so if he is in much pain, I'll put him under for another day." He grinned and added. "Whenever he does wake up, I'm sure he'll have a whopper of a headache."

Sixteen
Creation of a Horror

Even though he had failed to prevent the operation on Dr. Bradhurst, and only was able to contaminate three samples, he hoped that those samples would interact in a destructive manner and cause severe counterattacks against his biological and genetic makeup. Even better if the slight interference that he introduced into the cell structures actually killed him. Anyway, now it was over and only time would tell. As soon as he reached his office, he called Frank Wallace.

"Hanns, I have been waiting to hear from you. Are you okay?"

"Not really. Dr. Bradhurst scheduled his operation for this afternoon, and I only had time to alter three cell samples. The surgery went as he planned, using thirteen different biological samples and that includes the ones I altered. Russel plans to bring him out of his coma tomorrow or the next day and I don't want to be around when he wakes up."

"Damn," was Frank's first response! "It looks as though we were too late."

"Too late to stop the operation but we don't know what the outcome will be from the samples I contaminated. I can only hope they cause some setback in his plans of becoming what he's calling 'the supreme being', because God only knows what will happen if he succeeds. Then there's always the possibility that his brain will rebel the implanted cells. As I said, he crammed his head full of many different cell clusters and most were in large doses. We can only wait and see. I'm going to attempt to destroy all the samples we have here. I'll have to do it now because, as I said, if and when Dr. Bradhurst wakes, it will be too late."

In a pleading and concerned voice Frank said. "If it's too risky Hanns you should get out of there now."

"No. I'm the cause of this mess and I want to end it or at least delay any further experiments."

Frank urged him one last time to be careful. "I don't like this." Frank pleaded. "You may be signing your death warrant if you get caught."

"If I come through this, I'll call you." Hanns hung up the phone.

Frank felt helpless. He felt responsible for putting Hanns in danger and did not want anything to happen to him. He probably should notify the authorities but what would he say? 'I think Dr. Korman is in danger of being murdered by the renowned Dr. Bradhurst who has just been operated on and will become a super-human being with incredible powers capable of reading and controlling other people's minds?' A ludicrous story that no one would believe!

As soon as Hanns had hung up the phone he placed clinical gloves on his hands, went to the dispensary and unlocked the door. The laboratory closed at five every afternoon so there was no one around as he entered one of the most sterile cleanrooms in existence. The labeled 'super-cell' samples, like all other samples stored there were kept on large trays in temperature and humidity-controlled cabinets. As quickly as he could he began removing trays and upending them into a pile on the floor where many of the vials broke, spilling their content into a viscous mess. When he finished, he got another idea. He removed the content of several other cabinets that held various unrelated samples of micro-organisms and added them to the hundreds of samples mounded on the repository's floor. This would prevent anyone from thinking that super cells were the only target to be destroyed. He then retrieved four one-quart bottles of alcohol from a cabinet. After dousing the unbroken and broken vials, he set them on fire. Removing his gloves, he tossed them into the flames and retreated to his office where he immediately called Russel Hieber. "I'm glad I caught you." He said once Dr. Hieber answered. "I need to see you. I'll be right over."

He was able to control the tremor in his hands on his route from his office located in the laboratory section of the hospital to Russel's office in the executive area near the front of the building. In a somewhat excited voice, Hanns blurted out as soon as he entered the door, "Someone has been in my office."

"What?" Russel exclaimed.

"Someone has gone through my wallet and my desk. I keep my wallet in my desk draw during all surgeries and it's been tampered with. It happened while we were operating on Dr. Bradhurst. And things in and on my desk have been moved."

"My god, who could have done such a thing" Russel said in a surprised voice.

"I don't know but it pisses-me off." Hanns said in a harsh voice as he added to his story. "I don't think anything is missing from the wallet, but I'll take a better look." He paused ever-so shortly and then-added. "This might not have been the first time."

"What do you mean? Someone has been in your office before?"

"During every surgery we perform I leave my wallet and my keys in my desk draw just as I assume you do. I always keep my keys in the left front corner of the draw but several days ago I noticed the keys were on the right side of the draw when I returned to my office. I was pretty certain that I put them where I always do but thought maybe that time I didn't. Now, I wonder?"

"Is it possible someone made copies of your keys." Russel asked.

"I guess so, but why?" As he said this another idea came to him. "I haven't mentioned this before, but I think I am being followed."

"Followed? What are you talking about?"

Hanns was making his farce up as he went along and hoped he wasn't overdoing it. "Twice I have noticed a car following me home and this morning I think I saw it behind me on the way here. What's going on Russel?"

Before he could answer, the fire alarm blared. "What the hell?" Russel Hieber yelled as the phone on his desk rang. "He listened for only a moment before screaming, "Where?"

The two men ran down the hall as the alarm resounded through the building. Night attendants were already at hand, with more rushing from the hospital end of the building towards the smoke that was pouring out of the repository. Through the bedlam that followed, a dozen men with extinguishers were able to contain the flames before the fire department arrived.

It was after midnight when Hanns and Russel retired to the latter's office. By all appearances they were both devastated by the ruin of the specimens, but Hanns Korman was inwardly relieved that he put an end to the research being done at this dissolute institution. His entire life was spent trying to better the good of mankind, and when the opportunity arose at Drechsler to head up a team of researchers to do just that; discover ways to improve the well-being of others, he jumped at it. Here were possibilities of curing diseases and reducing pain. As he and his team identified more and more biological living cells and the bodily functions they controlled, the more he was sure that they were on the threshold of opening up the greatest medical discoveries ever made. His vision was to eliminate, cancer and Alzheimer's and Aids and countless other maladies that affected mankind. Now as he looked back, he could see that he had been too inpatient. He wanted fast results and Dr. Bradhurst had the means to give him those results. In the beginning he had unwittingly aided the brilliant doctor in using the science for what he thought to be ethical and moral purposes, but when he realized what the doctor's true intent was, he was deeply entrenched and held firmly in the mad man's grip. If only he could have been stronger, he might have been able to pull away, but his weakness and fear prevailed. Now, as Frank Wallace had urged, he was ready to flee. "It will take many months to rebuild the loss we have incurred," he said to Russel who was livid in both pallor and temper.

"I cannot even discuss the matter now." Russel Hieber was enraged. "I promise you that I will find out who did this, and heaven help him."

By two o'clock that night Hanns entered his apartment and despite the lateness of the hour, he placed a call to Frank Wallace. Waking from intermittent periods of sleep, Frank knew that the caller was Hanns. "It's done!" The caller said. "I destroyed everything and hopefully paved a way for the fire to be blamed elsewhere."

"Thank God you are okay. Are you ready to get away now?"

"Yes. But I still have a fear they will find me."

"I'll pick you up and we can decide what to do next."

Hanns hastily packed a few things in a large plastic bag. Just enough so when he was discovered missing, those looking for him would assume that none of his cloths were taken. He could only hope he was thinking of everything.

When Frank arrived at the apartment, he found Hanns in a state of anxiety. "I think I held up fairly well under the circumstances but now it seems to have all caught up with me." Within the next few minutes Hanns related everything that had transpired during the day.

Frank was somewhat astounded. "It was clever how you invented an intruder rifling your office. I hope you're right and they will think someone else destroyed the samples. And suggesting you were being followed, that will hopefully lead them to believe you were kidnapped. The way you deceived them was very shrewd. These ruses might throw them off the track. How are you set for money?"

"Not too good. Hanns replied. I seldom keep much cash on me."

"Credit cards are too easily traced so you won't be able to use them." Frank said. "It was good thinking when you planted the seed that someone went through your wallet. If you take money out of an AMT machine, they should think that one of your cards was stolen and the thief used it to empty the account. That's the first thing I think we should do so we'll look for an ATM on the way to my hotel. You will stay with me tonight and tomorrow I'll send you to a safe place to stay."

It had been a crazy day and Hanns was exhausted when he crawled between the sheets of one of the beds in Frank's hotel room.

The following morning as the two men sat drinking coffee, Frank said to the still somewhat bemused doctor. "You know that you will have to own up to what you've done and answer for it."

Hanns shook his head. "Yes. What a damn fool I was! I can only hope that if Dr. Bradhurst survives he will be exposed and pay for his crimes."

"Yes, he must!" Frank tried to agree, but deep down he feared that the doctor might be too clever and too entrenched with powerful people for justice to prevail. But he would do his best to expose him. He called an airline and purchased a ticket in his name to Bozeman, Montana. At the airport they destroyed Hanns' cell phone and purchase a disposable phone to replace it. Frank gave Hanns one of his credit cards and informed him that he would call ahead and reserve a rental car for him. "Remember, the car will be in my name. Use my credit card and there should be no trouble. You have the driving directions to the ranch and my wife will be expecting you. Stay there until you hear from me."

"Okay." Hanns said as he shook hands with the man who was going out of his way to help him. "Thank you... I cannot tell you how grateful I am to you."

Bill Thorp only worked at the Bradhurst Hospital for six months but as in his last job, he was making the most of what he called 'fringe benefits'. His maintenance position allowed him access to just about every area in the hospital and being the opportunist that he was, he always kept his eyes open. Shortly after hiring on, he saw his chance when he noticed Dr. Hieber drop his keys into the pocket of his lab robe prior to entering the surgical operating room. He had observed that operations usually took several hours, giving him ample time to remove the chain of keys and take them to the maintenance department where he had hidden in the bottom of his workbox the equipment to cut new keys. Thirty minutes after the removal of the keys from the white robe, they were back in place as though never leaving.

Bill was experienced in many areas when it came to building maintenance. There was little he couldn't handle, whether it be electrical, heating and air conditioning, plumbing or any other issue that might arise. He even helped resolve problems with electronic equipment. Yes, Bill was good at his job. But he had one problem, a problem that he successfully concealed from his fellow workers. He was into drugs. And what better place to work than in a hospital; that is if you had the know-all to dip into the vast supply of medications stored there. Of the five keys that he had copied, one he assumed fit the doctor's private office. He knew one was for the lab and another for the room that kept that department's supplies and biological samples. None of those areas held any interest for him, yet he still retained those keys because you just never knew when they might come in handy. There was only one key that really interested him and that one was for the door to the room that stored the hospital's medications. His job at times required him to work after-hours when some piece of equipment or other needed prepares. There was no one about at those times and that's when he used the key. Not wanting anyone to find large discrepancies in stock levels, he was careful not to take too much of any drug at any given time. Yes, Bill was good at his job.

The day after the fire destroyed the environmentally controlled room and most of its contents, Russel Hieber attempted to bring his patient out of his coma, but he could see he was racked with pain and put him back under. It was three days before Gordon Bradhurst finally awoke from his unconscious state. Even then Russel could see the extreme pain that contorted his face. The very first thing that Bradhurst said to his partner was, "do something about this pain."

His body was injected with powerful doses of pain killers, but nothing seemed to lessen the agony that the patient suffered. The following day, with no letup in the anguishing torture that plagued Gordon Bradhurst, he forced himself to talk with his partner. "I know that I have gone through a powerful transformation. My mind is full of astonishing things, but they are hidden behind this god-awful pain."

"I've given you more drugs than any man should ever take, but nothing seems to work. I'm not sure what else I can do." Russel said. "But at least you're talking."

"The pain is pulsating," Gordon said. "Ten or more seconds of unbearable pain, agh." he grimaced and shuddered in pain for a short time. "The pain is followed by a minute or two of relief; but even then, it's almost unbearable. It seems like my brain is trying to burst through my skull." He then went into another bout of discomfort so severe that he couldn't talk. The conversation went like this for some time. Gordon would have a pained discussion and then decline into a state of profound agony. When the broken conversation ended, Gordon Bradhurst passed into a deep sleep as his body tossed and heaved with agony. Three times the following day the same on-and-off conversation took place. Even if the pain did not ebb, Russel could perceive a slight improvement in his patient's ability to converse. He could only hope that in time the pain would diminish. The next morning Russel told Gordon about the fire and the loss of the entire stock of samples. He explained about Hanns' suspicions that his office was broken into and that his keys may have been copied. Hanns also believed he was being followed and now he had disappeared.

Bradhurst knew that if he confronted whoever had the key to the storeroom, he would be able to identify him by reading his thoughts. "Bring everyone who has access to the lab here. I'll see them one at a time." He got this message to Russel just before wincing with pain again.

There were quite a few men and women who had reason to be in the lab area from time to time, but no one other than Dr. Hieber and Hanns Korman had a key to the dispensary where samples were stored. As each person was presented to the heavily bandaged patient, Russel asked the same question. "Which one of you has the key to the storeroom?" When Bill Thorp heard the work keys, the stolen keys he copied jumped to his mind. Gordon pointed to him.

"What's this all about?" Bill asked. "I don't know anything about keys."

Through Gordon's ups and downs, he could read the fear in the man who could not get stolen keys out of his thoughts. Gordon was so furious that he directed an unknown force within him on the lying man standing before him. Countless nerve ends in Bill Thorp's brain exploded at the same instant creating a massive stroke. He was dead before his body hit the floor.

A fear rushed into Russel's head as he saw what had just happened. Even under the extreme pain that Gordon was experiencing, he had the power within him to kill a person with his mind. Russel reacted visibly by jumping back a step.

When the violent reaction to Bradhurst's next attack of excruciating pain had diminished and he was able to talk, he said. "Don't worry Russel. I know what you're thinking but you are safe with me. Your positive thoughts far outweigh your negative ones. Take care of him." He no sooner said this when he convulsed into pain again. "It's insufferable!" He wheezed when the pain ebbed again. "We have to find a way to end this unbearable agony."

Russel Hieber felt helpless. The x-rays and MRI's that he took twice daily showed the brain was slowly expanding in size. He deduced that at least some, if not all of the pain that Gordon Bradhurst was experiencing was caused by pressure build-up inside his skull from that growth. Everything the team of doctors tried failed to ease the pain or curb the growth. He knew that if they could not remedy this condition soon, Gordon would die.

Russel wished that Hanns Korman was with him to help resolve the problem with his mentor's expanding brain. But he had disappeared. There was a search going on for him but so far there was no sign of where he might be. Russel was sure that he had been kidnapped; but why and by whom he had no idea. Yesterday, in one of Gordon's good times, when the throbbing headache eased enough for him to talk, he gave Russel Sid's number. "If anyone can find him, Sid can." Gordon said.

The following morning Russel met with his team of specialists yet again. They were now desperate because Gordon's bouts with pain intensified during the night. All agreed that he was near death and the only solution to save his life was to remove the entire top portion of his skull and ease the pressure. Russel entered his patients' room with intent of notifying him of their plan but found him unconscious. He was rushed to the operating room where the team began the complex surgical procedure that would hopefully relieve the pressure that was killing the agony-stricken man.

The renowned genius and billionaire lay in a bed in the recovery room once again. This time with his skull plate removed, allowing space for his cramped brain to expand. It had been a messy operation performed under extreme time restraints. In fact, the patient died on the operating table only to be revived by the exceptional talents of the surgeons and medical specialists in attendance throughout the procedure. Gordon Bradhurst's head was a hideous thing to look at. His exposed brain bulged out of his skull in a grotesque mushrooming cauliflower-like protrusion. He remained in a comatose state for two days.

Seventeen
Unrestrained Power

After leaving Hanns Korman at the airport, Frank spent the afternoon at Drechsler where he met with Carlene Linser. He knew she was anxious to hear what had happened with Hanns, but he had something he wanted to do first. "I need to make a private call." He said to her. "Do you mind if I use your phone?"

"No, please do. I'll wait in the conference room across the hall."

Frank dialed Damon Courier in Washington, D.C. and got right to the point when the Private Detective got on the line. "I need more information and I was hoping you could help me again; or steer me to someone who can."

"I'll do whatever I can." Damon assured him.

"I want more information on the Bradhurst Hospital. I think something unusual is taking place there right now and want to know what it is."

"My associate in L.A. is still digging into Dr. Bradhurst's background. I'll check with him to see what he has. What specifically do you need?"

"I have reason to believe Dr. Bradhurst has undergone a brain operation. I want to know all I can about that and if possible, have updates on his condition. I also would like more information about what's been going on at his hospital; both recently and currently. Whatever you can come up with about his activities outside the hospital would also help."

When the two men ended their short telephone conversation, Damon Courier promised to get back to him as soon as he had any information.

Frank filled Carlene in on at least some of the less dramatic proceedings that took place with Hanns and his interactions with the Bradhurst hospital. He told her only what he thought was enough to satisfy at least some of her worries. "I haven't decided what to do yet, but I have the ball rolling. In a few days, I hope to have enough information to make some decisions. I can only ask you to hold off on reporting this theft until I do." She agreed.

Because of Hanns' involvements at the Bradhurst Hospital, Frank decided to remain in Los Angeles for several days and work in the Animal Research Department at Drechsler on the wolf and bear program.

To him it was almost like old times when he and his staff in Fairbanks involved themselves in oh' so many wildlife related programs. As he looked back on those days, he realized how much he missed them. But on the other hand, he loved his ranch and raising cattle and all the other pleasures found in ranch life. If only he could put the distractions that he was involved with behind him and return to normal.

The number of wolves that had been killed to date in Canada and the United States was staggering. Corporeal forensic samples and reports from authorized medical specialists who were examining the carcasses were being sent to Drechsler's Animal Research Department at an ever-increasing rate; building up a sizable backlog for Carlene and her team to examine. During the past week, while he was there, the team had examined hundreds of samples taken from wolves and of those hundreds, many were from young females. The latest results of the extensive lab work showed that close to six percent of the young female's examined were sterile. The growing number of cases was enough to give Frank a little more optimism than he previously had. He could only hope that the rate of this biological disorder would increase in future offspring of these demonic freaks of nature.

Damon called while he was working with one of the computer analysts. One of the software programs was designed to isolate and identify functions that cells governed, but even with the latest technologies, it was a very slow and tedious undertaking. More sophisticated software that would speed up the process was being developed but that was still months away. He took the call in one of the nearby offices. "I have a preliminary report for you." Damon informed him. We learned some interesting things."

"Thought you might."

"My man out there is still digging but here's what he has so far. There was a fire in the experimental laboratory that destroyed a great deal of valuable biological material. So much so that it will set the research center back for quite some time. At about the time of the fire, Dr. Bradhurst became seriously ill. All we could determine so far is that he is under constant observation. There is speculation that he might not pull through. We also discovered that one of his top scientists, a Dr. Korman has gone missing."

He didn't tell Damon that he knew most of what he was told. "I would like to be kept informed on Dr. Bradhurst's condition. And please keep digging. I want as much information as you can get for me."

"Will do. We are continuing with the investigation and hope to have more for you soon."

"Thank you, Damon! I appreciate your help."

"I'll be in touch."

As to Dr. Bradhurst's illness, he thought it possible that the doctor's infirmity could be the result of the three altered gene clusters that were administered into his brain; or the body's rebellion against the infusion of too many foreign cells as Hanns had suggested might occur. Even though Bradhurst had waived off Dr. Hieber's fear that too many brain enhancing cells (some possibly too potent) administered at one time could be risky, this certainly could be the cause of the illness. Or was it something altogether different? He would anxiously await Damon's next report.

It came two days later. "It's been difficult getting information from people working at the hospital. There seems to be a code of silence that is hard to break; possibly backed by fear! But we have found two men who were willing to talk. We haven't been able to determine why but several doctors, associates and research personnel have recently been let go. The two men who were willing to talk are still in contact with some of their colleagues. From what we hear, the doctor had a brain operation that went wrong. Severe swelling put so much pressure on his brain that much of his skull had to be removed. He might be dying. We'll let you know if we learn more."

"Dying?" When he had more-or-less forced Hanns to act against Dr. Bradhurst; his plan was to prevent the mad genius from administering strong power-enhancing cells into his brain, not kill him. However, the thought of Bradhurst (a psychopath who had no scruples about letting patients die on the operating table) turning into a more powerful monster than he already was, was appalling. He was one of the most brilliant men in the world but obviously wanted to become even more so. All in the name of science; a science that would be used to benefit himself by increasing his mental and intellectual capabilities! Michael Danvers had turned into a psychopath with depraved ambitions to rule the world. Might not Bradhurst, once he acquired similar powers react in a similar manner? Well,

Hanns had acted, and it appears that the actions he took may be the reason that Gordon Bradhurst lies near death. Frank had never wished anyone ill-will or harm of any kind, but in this case, he thought how all the dreadful scenarios that haunted his mind would go-away if the doctor did not survive.

Before leaving L.A., he wrote a comprehensive report detailing the findings on both the deteriorating reproductive organs in the wolf population and the weakening in their immune systems. He also touched on several other traits that Drechsler was studying that might or might not be showing signs of weakening. It was too early to know for sure but there was some hope that additional areas in the makeup of these wolves might aid in their demise. His report on the mutant bears was short. There was no evidence of biological breakdowns found as yet.

The Canadian task force had a scheduled meeting the following week, but he didn't want to hold back the important data until that meeting, so he placed a call to Bryce Mann and filled him in on the bitter-sweet news. When he finished talking with Bryce, he placed a second call to John Riggs. They were pleased to hear about the escalating breakdown in the youngest generation of wolves, but like Frank, they realized that no fast solution would come from these findings. He sent copies of his report to both men via his laptop.

He left Los Angeles the next morning.

Back in Montana, Frank, Sarah and Hanns sat in what the Wallace's called the family room; actually, a combination TV and trophy room with an open-hearth fireplace. They were enjoying cocktails after a dinner of chicken and rice. Sarah had gotten to know Hanns quite well during the time her husband spent in California. Their discussion this evening naturally centered around the astonishing happenings going on at the Bradhurst hospital.

As Hanns swirled the clear amber bourbon around the ice cubes in his glass, he said in a humbling voice, "It's hard to believe all that's happened in such a short time. I was just too anxious. We seemed to be getting nowhere and it appeared that Dr. Bradhurst had the answers; and to some degree he did. It's amazing how much progress we made. He is a genius you know! He has made more progress in learning about our brains and what they are capable of than all the research done before him. Unfortunately, much of that knowledge has come by illegal and immoral means. He runs his hospital like a mid-evil insane asylum with no qualms about sacrificing patients to satisfy his own ends. As I look back, I cannot even imagine how I became part of it all. I guess I was blinded by the prospect of discovering great things sooner than later. Zoltan Proziver's discovery of strengthening cells and benefiting from them by means of genetic transfer was certainly genius, but so is Dr' Bradhurst's ingenious method of introducing living cells directly into human beings and have them react almost instantly. At Drechsler we isolated and identified hundreds of cellular organisms and I've added many more during the time I've been at Bradhurst's. Our team there has learned enough to be convinced that every human feature, function, and trait can be influenced in some way or other. We have been concentrating our efforts on the brain and have, or I should say had, samples that match numerous mental traits. From the results that were achieved from Michael Danvers, I can assume that we can alter just about anything related to our human makeup; and that includes our mental psychological proficiencies. I truly believe that by properly using clustered cells, cures to many afflictions that plague mankind are just around the corner. I also believe that if he survives long enough, he will not only open up many incredible medical benefits related to the wellbeing of man but also many technological and humanitarian contributions related to this new science as well. What a shame that these are not his first priority."

Even though Frank knew that Hanns had stepped over the line in aiding and abetting Dr. Bradhurst, he still felt sorry for him because he believed that he was an honest and moral man. "It seems inevitable, doesn't it? when just about anything that we involve ourselves with gets in the wrong hands, it can result in grave consequences. I'm not sure what our next step should be. We have no concrete proof that he has done anything wrong. At least not enough to place charges against him. I have an investigator looking into the doctor and his operation but somehow, I doubt we will come up with anything relevant or substantial enough to matter. The latest word I have is that he is very ill and might not survive. We'll just have wait and see what happens."

"Would you like another drink?" Sarah asked.

"Thank you," Hanns replied. "I could use another. Talking about all this brings the enormity of it to reality."

Frank handed his glass to her and indicated that he too would have another.

There was a pause in conversation as Sarah prepared the drinks.

"I've had time to think about a lot of things lately," Hanns interjected. "Being a scientist, I have to believe in evolution, and I do. But when you think about each living creature and especially a human being, and the extreme intricacies and complexity of our bodies… Well, the more I think about it, the more I see what an incredible miracle we are just to exist and that our existence has to have come about by more than mere chance or accident. It seems to me that when God created man he did so with evolution in mind. Change has been the driving force behind mankind's existence since day one. We have constantly strived to make our world a better place to live in and the progress we've made is evident. As we look around us, we see countless advances we have made. Quite incredible advancements in every facet of our world. Think how far we have come in medicine and technologies… in just about every endeavor we involve ourselves in. We live in a world that our ancestors couldn't possibly comprehend. I credit our growth to our ever-evolving brains, brains that have developed to meet man's every need or desire. I think our brains have always been intended to grow or evolve. Why they range from feeble to genius is not known; but I believe Dr. Bradhurst was getting close to finding the answer to that and many more mysteries of the mind. And I have no doubt that with his advanced powers be will. That is if he survives. But even if he doesn't, I am certain that others will follow in his footsteps. This new science is here to stay and no matter how we try, we will not be able to completely control it."

"I have to agree," Frank said. "I think the process has developed too far to be stopped. It scares me to even think of where this might lead."

Hanns finished the last drop of whiskey and placed the glass on the end-table. "See if you agree with me on this, Frank. You know I believe our brains will never stop developing as long as we exist as a species. Through knowledge and education, we have already developed our minds to a level where we can alter the building blocks of life. It's true that we have not handled this incredible finding very well and have no assurance that we ever will. It's been proven that we can strengthen our brains capabilities to levels beyond any other living humans. We can get into peoples' minds and take command of their every action and can actually manipulate them to carry out any demand given to them. Zoltan Proziver and Gordon Bradhurst have opened up pandora's box but I'm afraid this is only the tip of the iceberg. I cannot believe that scientific discoveries like clustering cells that can alter living organisms, will end there. No! I think that clustering cells has only put us on the threshold of discovering what our human minds are capable of. I foresee even more incredible processes of expanding our minds, waiting to be discovered, and if Dr. Bradhurst lives, he could possibly discover them."

Frank's first though was incredulous about Hanns' statements. Surely it couldn't get any worse than it already was. But he never imagined that Zoltan's discovery could ever have led to where they were today. Then his scientific mind took over and he realized that progress never stopped, and he knew Hanns was right. Man had learned how to alter not only bodily features and functions but also the human brain and all it entailed. It was frightening!

The seriousness of Hanns' suppositions hung heavy over the three as they sat quietly contemplating the uncertain future that loomed ahead; all because of man's meddling with the laws of nature. It was terrifying!

Hanns Korman was moved from the ranch to a hotel in Bozeman the following day, where Frank insisted, he remain until more was known about Gordon Bradhurst's condition.

It had been some time since his last meeting with the Canadian taskforce. Everyone had been briefed on Frank's report, so he kept his discussion quite short as he filled the team in on the details of Drechsler's findings. For the first time since the taskforce had been assembled, a sense of hope, a thin hope at best, embraced the group.

As in all of the taskforce meetings, Bryce Mann ended the meeting with a brief summation.

"Even though we have some good news here, we must not get over-optimistic. As Frank indicated, there are issues we don't know or have answers too. The defects that effect the health of these animals have only been found in some of the wolves that have been examined. It is thought that these variances will increase in future generations; but there is no certainty of that. Finding close to six percent of the young female wolves being barren is certainly good news. This reduction in fertile females will reduce the number of future births and we can only hope that the trend continues. However, on the pessimistic side, most of the females tested have had no appreciable deterioration in their reproductive organs. We don't know if either of these anomalies will escalate or even occur in future generations. It does however give us a thread of hope to hold on to. It's quite ironic when I think that if these issues prove to be the downfall of this new species of animal, it will have less to do with all of our efforts to eradicate them but more with the interaction of Mother Nature."

"As we heard earlier, thousands of men continue to search-out these wolves and we have killed scores upon scores of them. Yet, with all this effort we have only succeeded in thinning out the horde of these savage beasts. But our efforts are not totally in vain. Attacks and sightings have slowed considerably. Yes, we are reducing the numbers of these beasts and killing the occasional mutant bear and will continue to hunt these animals down."

The wolf hunt aggressively continued as thousands of hunters relentlessly searched them out. The number of animals being killed dropped dramatically since the original onslaught when many hundreds were killed in a very short period of time. But even so, wolves continued to fall to hunter's rifles, however, despite the herculean efforts being employed, attacks continued to pile up and every attack left human bloodshed in its wake.

Adding to the misery caused by mutant wolves, another menacing beast had raised its ghastly head. Giant man-eating bears! Even though to date there were not many sightings or deaths attributed to these behemoth beasts, another fear was spreading across the land as it had with the mutant wolves. The media was playing this new menace up big, creating another uproar from the frightened public. The most horrifying beasts that existed since the days of dinosaurs was beginning to terrorize the world.

The day following his presentation to the Canadian taskforce, Frank flew from Edmonton to Washington. John Riggs thought Frank's findings with Drechsler were important enough to summon his taskforce to Washington for a first-hand account. The agenda he forwarded to each member included an update of the wolf situation in the northern tier states and the threat that the recently discovered bear-like monsters were creating in Alaska. Frank's presentation was quite similar to the one he gave in Edmonton and the excited reaction was about the same. His summation was short and direct. "Through hard work and determination, we have found two holes in the armor of what we all believed was an infallible new species of wolves. Over a period of time the melding of the building blocks of two distinctly different species is hopefully beginning to break down. So far, we have only identified weaknesses in the animals' immune systems and in their reproductive organs, however Drechsler scientists are actively looking into other areas in hopes of identifying additional biological malfunctions. We all share the hope that these findings are the beginning of what might develop into a complete breakdown of these creature's biological makeup, but once again, let's not get our hopes up too high."

"Thank you, Frank!" Rigg said. "Let's pray you're right and these animals will eventually eradicate themselves. Questions?"

Once questions were discussed and concluded, Riggs, addressing Frank Wallace's old friend, said: "Tom will update us on our efforts to destroys these wolves!"

Frank considered Tom Grimes the most knowledgeable wolf specialists in the world. He had been indispensable in locating and destroying mutant wolves in the Rocky Mountain west when this new breed of monstrous hybrid wolf first appeared. They thought they had killed every animal and rid the world of this menace, but they had been wrong. The ones that got away, proliferated into a scourge that now terrorized the world.

Tom Began. "I am rueful to report that even with the good results of our initial attack on these beasts and our subsequent efforts to destroy them, we are still faced with a very grave situation. We know of several groups that are spread from Minnesota to Washington State, and of course many more in Alaska. Unfortunately, they continue to migrate down from Canada and have spread into Wyoming, Utah and Colorado where this all began."

"Our dilemma is that they are multiplying almost as fast as we can destroy them. Unfortunately, more deaths continue to add up. We got a report last night that four more people were killed in the suburbs of Missoula. Three teams are there this morning and I have two helicopters and three airplanes in the air. Maybe we'll get lucky. I know we keep repeating ourselves, but it is by no means an easy task to track these animals down. Their ranges are far reaching in wild territory and the more they're hunted, the more elusive they become. So, what are we going to do about it? Frank and I agree as does Mr. Riggs, that we should add substantially to the already host of hunters we are using. I will put a plan together to add several hundred more hunters as soon as we can amass them."

When the discussion on wolves was completed, Tom addressed the small group, wearing another hat. "Finn Sorenstam was not able to make this meeting. He is bear hunting and asked me to fill you in on the problems they're encountering up there with mutant bears. From what he says, it's not a pretty picture and will certainly get worse. He has many teams of people hunting them down, but results are slow. I spent close to an hour last night talking with him and Erick Tuttle." What Tom was about to relate was not news to Frank who had also discussed the bear situation with his two Alaskan colleagues the previous day. "They think we are on the threshold of a statewide disaster every bit as bad, if not worse than the wolf mess we have. I've got a few maps and graphs that Erick forwarded to me." He displayed the first onto the screen. "This shows every reported sighting of large, huge, gigantic, enormous, colossal, monstrous, bear-like animals in the state. Many adjectives are being used when people described these animals. Forty sightings in all since Robbie Turner, who Erick calls the Fat Man, spotted the first one. They seem to have found homes in the remotest areas. There is no way of knowing how many of these god-awful bruins exist, but Erick believes that with as many as forty sighting spread over hundreds of thousands of square miles, there are likely quite a few. Mr. Riggs knows the reason why Finn is not here for this meeting. Would you like to fill the team in?"

"No. You are doing fine. Please continue."

"Two days ago, in the outskirts of a small town in the interior of Alaska there was a massacre. Nine residences were killed and two of them were partially eaten by a huge bear. Yes, a single animal did all this. Several people witnessed the attack and were horrified by not only the violent death of their neighbors but also by the size of the bear. One man shot at the animal three times with a rifle and was sure he hit it. The gigantic bear, showing signs of being wounded fled dinto the forest. Erick Tuttle has men on the ground and in the air. They found blood and tracked all day yesterday using a pack of hounds but haven't overtaken the animal yet. They're at it again today. That's all we know so far. Erick will keep Mr. Riggs informed as the hunt continues."

The committee was shocked by the horror of what had occurred. One man summed it up for all in attendance. "One rampaging bear massacring nine people, what in Gods' name have we got?"

When the room quieted down, the meeting continued. "Frank, do you have anything you would like to add?" John Riggs asked the tired looking man.

Frank had so many things on his mind that he wasn't sure he could handle them all. His involvement with the wolf problem alone was more than enough for him to manage. Adding monstrous grizzly bears to his burdens, beasts that were creating chaos and death every bit as devastating as the mutant wolfs to his worries was taxing him close to his limits. Possibly even worse than the atrocities created from Zoltan's genius, was Dr. Gordon Bradhurst. What calamities might lay ahead if he survived his battle with death. He shuddered just to think about it. Trying to pull himself together he replied to John Riggs' question. "Just a couple of things. You know we now have four bears in the Fairbanks' lab, and two more on the way there. The first one we killed is a young male cub, another a female about the same age. I know we all find it hard to believe that cubs in their first summer of life weigh as much as full-grown grizzlies, but even more astounding is that even though the two larger bears we have are not yet full grown, they weigh upwards of 3,500 pounds. All four of these bear-like monstrosities have a mixing of grizzly and wolf genes. I still cannot get used to the fact that genes from two totally separate species can be combined. But they have, and we have two totally new species of animals with new strains of DNA to prove it. I shouldn't say this, but now that I know they can be mixed, it scares me to think about this science getting into the wrong hands." He almost winced when he thought that it already had. Dr. Bradhurst had illicitly acquired living gene samples and perfected the process on humans with horrifying results. "Is it possible that many species of animals' genes can meld together and create even more devastating results? And what might happen if this science gets out-of-hand when dealing with humans? God help us." He reflected for a moment before continuing. "I'm sorry. I got off track there for a minute. Back to our bears! One thing of note is that they all have extremely strong immune systems. Much stronger than any ever recorded on any animal, including our wolves. This strong protection indicates they will likely be able to fight off disease and infection and any other malady with strong antibodies. It also might mean that wounds could heal much faster. There is no doubt that we are dealing with very healthy animals. Drechsler has examined samples sent to them by the Fairbanks lab and claim them to have the strongest immune resistance of any animal that ever lived. Another anomaly that was discovered is that these animals have enlarged endocrine glands and produce very high levels of hormones. This could indicate that they are quite fertile. We don't know what this means yet, but our research people are on it. You were all notified earlier that the first young bear possessed extremely high levels of peptide hormones that generate growth. Other animals that are undergoing complete autopsies have the same high level of these growth cells. This high concentration of hormones explains why a young bear in its first year of life can weigh as much as a full-grown grizzly. If the two larger bears, that we know are two years old, each weigh over three thousand pounds, we can only guess at this time what a full-grown male might weigh. If the hunt for the wounded bear is successful it might be a boar and give us that information. From what Tom told us the bear was reported to be gigantic. We have assigned Drechsler to put as much effort into understanding these beasts as they are doing with our wolves. Between them and the work being done in Fairbanks we hope to have a continuing flow of information that will be passed on to you."

John Riggs ended the meeting by repeating Frank's concern. "I think you said it all Frank, when you said, God help us."

Frank was glad to return to Sarah and the ranch. He was exhausted and needed rest and vowed to remain there as long as possible. If only he could stay at the ranch indefinitely and forget about his obligations with both the Canadian and U.S. committees he was on. Wishful thinking… He was committed to both and now he was deeply involved with Dr. Bradhurst… He could only pray that no crises would arise from the doctor's meddling with the laws of nature.

The following day he tried calling Hanns but got no response. Hann's newly acquired disposable phone was dead. He called the hotel and was informed that he had checked out the previous morning. Frank wondered what that could mean. He could only hope that Hanns would contact him.

Later that morning Erick phoned. He was in a panic. "Bad news Frank. Another disaster just took place in the outskirts of Fairbanks. Right in our back yard! One of the prehistoric-like monsters wandered into a strip-mall and raised all sorts of hell. It ended up killing more than a dozen shoppers and wounding a few more. Police arrived in time to fill the damn beast with a hail of lead but not before it killed three of them as well. I'm at the scene with a team of people and will have the bear's carcass taken to our lab. I can't even guess how much the boar weighs, but I'll have to move it with heavy equipment. Christ… There's panic everywhere. I won't even try to describe the gory mess. People are still crying and screaming, and the press is filming everything!" A few minutes later when the two old friends parted, Erick went back to his task at hand and Frank sank into a chair totally dismayed. Life continued to hit him with one nightmarish ordeal after another. He wondered how much more he could take.

Eighteen
Life or Death

Hanns sat in his hotel room contemplating what he should do. Dr. Bradhurst could be near death, and if he was, he would be vulnerable and powerless. Hanns thought that if he could go back and convince Russel Hieber that he had indeed been kidnapped and escaped his captors, he might find a way to help Dr. Bradhurst meet his maker, that is, if he didn't die on his own, which Hanns prayed would happen. But could he risk going back? If Dr. Bradhurst survived he would kill him for what he had done. After much thought he made up his mind to return to the Bradhurst Hospital and take his chances. He spent some time working out a scheme that he would present to Russel Hieber about his fictitious kidnapping before using his own credit card to book a flight to Los Angeles.

Sid had feelers out in many directions and one of those resources finally paid off. Hanns Korman, or someone using his credit card, had made the purchase of an airplane ticket. He was waiting at LAX airport when Hanns' flight landed. Hanns had no luggage other than a carry-on bag and when he exited the plane and entering the waiting area, he was greeted by a man he had never seen before. "How do you do Mr. Korman, I hope your trip from Bozeman was pleasant."

The first thought that entered his mind was 'how can this be? Who could possibly know I was on this plane and who is this man? "Who are you?" Hanns asked in a bewildered tone.

"I represent Dr. Bradhurst. He thought you had been kidnapped and was quite worried about you. He asked me to find you and as you can see, I have."

Hanns was stunned and didn't immediately know what to do. But he quickly pulled out of his stupor and addressed this strange man. "What an ordeal I've been through," he said in a quivering voice. He had prepared his story ahead of time but also made up lies as he went along. "First our lab was destroyed and then two men grabbed me when I got home late the night of the fire. They must have drugged me because I can't remember much of what happened to me. Of all places I ended up in Montana. They took my phone but thank God they didn't take my wallet. I can't explain any of it. I hit the man who was guarding me with a chair and got away and went right to the airport and got a flight home. I'm on my way back to the hospital; but how on earth did you know I would be on this flight?"

Sid waved this off and said, "I have a car; I'll drive you there."

Hanns rattled on about his 'ordeal' as the chauffeur drove the luxury car to the hospital. During the ride, Sid said nothing, but he did make a phone call to inform Russel Hieber that he had located Dr. Korman and would be arriving with him in less than an hour.

Russel was anxiously awaiting Hanns and showed surprise when they greeted each other. Because of the warm greeting, Hanns felt certain that he was not suspected of anything. Russel's surprise was based on his belief that Hanns was likely dead. He assumed that he had been kidnapped and his captors, after cleaning out his bank account had killed him. Sid, upon meeting his obligation of locating and delivering Hanns Korman, left with a bank balance somewhat greater than it had been before this lucrative assignment.

"What in hell has happened to you?" Russel asked.

Before Hanns got into his story, he demanded to know how Dr. Bradhurst had come through the operation.

"Not good!" Russel said. Something went wrong and his brain began to expand causing him excruciating pain. The pain became so severe that he was close to death. We had no choice but to remove a portion of his skull to give relief from the swelling brain. The best I can say is that he's still alive. The swelling abated enough for us to replace his skull pate. It isn't pretty to look at, in fact it's ugly. Because of the severity of his operations and the unbearable pain surging through his head we've kept him in an induced coma. Truthfully, I can't understand how he has survived after what he has gone through, but I'm feeling a little more optimistic if for no other reason than he's moaning less all the time; indicating the pain is likely abating. Anyway, I plan to bring him out of his comatose state tomorrow."

"My God!" Hanns said with as much sympathy in his voice as he could muster up, but his mind was spinning. He had to do something before Bradhurst was revived from his unconsciousness. The shark of Russel's next remark almost made him faint. "We discovered who destroyed the lab." Hanns shuddered thinking they knew it was him, but the fear that rushed through him faded when Russel added, "It was a maintenance man that was stealing drugs. Even though Gordon was in critical condition, he proved to me that he had gained some incredible powers. Before we had to operate on him, he was conscious enough between his bouts of agonizing pain to use those powers. He confronted everyone who had access to the lab that afternoon and immediately picked Bill Thorn out as the culprit. By just looking at him he burst every nerve-end in Thorn's brain, killing him instantly. Anyway, that's behind us; now tell me what happened to you."

Hanns relayed the story he had rehearsed, throwing in specific details about a kidnapping that never happened. "They were after my two million dollars, but I never gave in and didn't tell them the account number. I don't know how they even learned about the money. As far as I know only you and Gordon knew about it, and I never told a soul."

"Gordon or I haven't relayed it to anyone," Russel assured the seemingly upset man. "Gordon's bankers who transferred the funds also knew about it, but they are very reliable and trustworthy. I suppose someone in the financial institute could have learned of the money. If Gordon pulls through this ordeal, I'll talk to him about it. We were able to check your bank and discovered that all of the funds you had there were withdrawn from your checking and savings account."

Hanns felt good about the performance he gave relating the myriad of factitious events to Russel Hieber. But he was certain that if Gordon pulled through, he would surely see through all of his lies and the made-up farce that he fabricated. Hearing what he had done to the maintenance man, he was sure he would do the same to him. 'My only chance will be to act first before he even knows I am here.'

Russel interrupted his thoughts. "You will have to take precautions; the men who took you might try again. I'll contact Sid. If he can find the kidnappers, we can solve this puzzle and put a stop to them."

Hanns had never thought about this. If Sid had found him so easily, he might find Frank Wallace. Putting Frank in danger frightened him even more. He would call him as soon as he could to warn him about Sid. The more lies and the deeper he got in this appalling mess he found himself in, the un-easier he felt. Things were not working out as he had envisioned sitting in the hotel room in Bozeman and on his flight to California. He now realized that even if DR. Bradhurst died, he would eventually be found out. He had made a mistake in judgement and now felt he would pay for that mistake with his life. Russel would be bringing Dr. Bradhurst out of his coma tomorrow so he would have to act fast. He must somehow find a way to rid the world of the monster that he was convinced Gordon Bradhurst had become. A monster who could kill by using brainwaves. If Michael Danvers could control people around him as though they were nothing more than zombies, it was likely that Bradhurst could also. Hanns could not even fathom what other powers he might have. Then an idea came to him. "I would like to be there when he wakes up," he requested of Dr. Hieber.

"By all means; let's say ten in the morning."

As soon as he left Russel, Hanns went to his office and called Frank Wallace. He told him about his decision to return to the Bradhurst Hospital and try to put an end to Dr. Bradhurst. Once he informed Frank about Gordon Bradhurst's condition and what his plan was, he said in a choked-up voice. "I'm sorry Frank but I may have placed you in danger. They are hiring a man named Sid who must be some kind of private detective to find out who kidnapped me. He must be good because he was waiting for me when I got off the plane in Los. Angeles. I don't know if he can trace me to you but if he does, you should be careful."

Frank wanted to talk longer but Hanns ended the conversation.

Hanns obtained access to the dispensary and prepared a mixture consisting of toxic poisons and filled a small syringe with the solution. He knew the deadly solution would take effect almost immediately upon entering the bloodstream and the potency of the mix was strong enough to kill an elephant. He also knew that by injecting the serum into the doctor he would be giving up his own life, but he saw no other choice.

The following morning Hanns accompanied Dr. Hieber and two assistants to the room where Dr. Bradhurst was tended. He pushed his fear aside and walked up to the bedside of the seemingly sleeping man and quickly reached out to administer the injection before anyone realized what he was doing. The needle was no more than a foot from the intended arm that lay loosely on the bed when Hanns experienced what he could only describe as a blinding blow to his head. He staggered and fell to the floor screaming in pain. As he convulsed beside the bed that the semi-conscious patient laid in, he winced in agony. The attendant retrieved the syringe and Dr. Hieber rushed to the bed to make sure his friend and colleague was all right.

Soon after Hanns had been stricken down with excruciating pain, the pain subsided. But as he sat on the floor with his back against the wall with the attendant standing over him, he knew that something was wrong. He was paralyzed. He sat motionless unable to move his arms or his legs. He heard Dr. Bradhurst speaking to him, or was it just thoughts in his head? He couldn't be sure. "I'm sorry you strayed from my side Hanns. With your special talents I foresaw you assisting me in even greater things than we have already achieved. The first step in my quest for supremacy was to elevate my brain to levels beyond anything you could imagine. I owe you a thanks for helping me achieve that goal. My first thought when you approached me with intent to kill me, was to kill you. However, you are still the best scientist in this new field of genetic engineering, and it might be fitting if the man who destroyed my supply of living cells, is the man who replenishes them. What do you think Hanns? Would you like to live here at the hospital like Michael did and work on this project again? Yes, I think that would be fitting."

Russel Hieber was looking down at his patient who appeared to be under the influence of the sedative that slowly dripped into his vein from the surgical bag hanging from a tree next to his bed. Little did he know that Gordon Bradhurst was aware of everything taking place around him and in fact had been during his waking hours since the operation on his skull. He also had no idea that Gordon was communicating with Hanns Korman through telepathic thought transference. There was a great deal that Russel didn't know. He did not know that Gordon knew every thought that every person who entered his room (and even people directly outside his room) were thinking. Russel, who was in a furious temper was ready to kill Hanns for the treacherous act he tried to do, was startled when he heard Gordon's voice. "No," he said. "I know you want to kill him, but I want to keep him alive. I will control him so he will present no further problem to us."

"You're awake." Russel blurted out.

"Yes, but I need rest. We will talk later."

Russel was terrified! Gordon had turned Hanns into a submissive and obedient subservient incapable of having any control over his own actions.

This terrified him. Realizing Gordon knew his every deep dark secret, he feared that he too might be turned into a zombie-like servant with no will of his own, just as Michael Danvers had done to him.

Frank once again called Damon Courier. "I hate to keep pestering you." he said to the man on the other end of the line. "But something else has come up and I need your assistance. Have you ever heard of a man called Sid? He is most likely a private detective in the Los Angeles area."

"Sid," Damon mused. "Let me get with my contact out there. I'll let you know as soon as I hear anything."

Twenty minutes later Damon's contact in L.A. called Frank and Brad Cuttlebone introduced himself. "Damon said you only knew the name Sid. The only Sid I know in this area is Sid Ramone. He's a private detective who caters to the wealthy and from what we hear he is very successful in meeting his customer's needs. Rumor has it if the price is right, he will take on any assignment and that could go beyond normal private detective work. Nothing can be proven because he is careful but heinous crimes are not below him."

"It sounds like he's good at his job."

"Yes, he is considered one of the best."

Frank thanked him for the information and rang off.

Later that day Damon Courier contacted him to discuss Sid Ramone. Damon had discussed the unscrupulous private detective with Cuttlebone who shared more of his suspicions about the detective with him than he did with Frank. Hidden behind a cloak of shadows, it was suspected that Sid Ramone was 'a gun for hire' and if the price was right, any target was fair game. Damon related this information to Frank and informed him that a good private detective (and Brad claimed that Sid was a top-notch one) could likely trace Korman's travels to Boseman, especially if he had dates to work with. Damon assured Frank that if he himself was on the track, he would find a connection between Hanns and him and a trail leading to his ranch without too much difficulty.

"I'm not sure how you should handle this, Frank. Sid Ramone may, or may not, be looking in your direction, but just in case he is, I wouldn't take chances. My best advice would be to have someone looking over your shoulder. And I recommend doing it immediately."

Frank agreed; he didn't have only himself to worry about; If Sid found his way to the ranch, Sarah might be in danger also. "My ranch manager is always here. Between the two of us we should be able to handle whatever comes up."

"Good," Damon said.

"Take care. If this Sid fellow is as bad as Brad thinks he is, it would be a good idea to strap a six-shooter on your hip and play Matt Dillon."

Frank knew he had said this in jest but agreed that he would indeed be careful.

Nineteen
Death and Near-Death

Doctor Bradhurst had chosen extremely strong immune cell clusters to enhance his body's ability to not only fight off disease and infection but also aid in healing of wounds. In this case, once the pressure being put on his brain from its swelling was relieved by removing his skull plate, his recovery from the major operation was quite remarkable. Within just a few days after his skull was replaced, the seam was fusing together firmly, and the ugly looking scar was healing rapidly.

Four days following his near-death encounter from the hand of Hanns Korman, Dr. Bradhurst awoke feeling better than he had for some time. His mind was clear, and he knew that his newly acquired powers were incredibly acute. The pain he had suffered so severely was almost completely abated and he was not only feeling physically well but mentally exuberant.

His first action of the day was having Hanns brought to his room where he scanned his brain. Everything in Hanns' mind was revealed to him.

He was owing to Russel for saving his life but worried about his weakening constitution and his fears. He realized that every man alive had good, bad, and evil in their being. It was human nature. He wanted to assure Russel that as-long-as he stayed loyal, he would be safe, but that might not be easy. Putting pressure on a man to do one thing often caused them to react in another direction. He hoped he would not have to control his mind as Russel feared he might. He preferred him to remain a free-thinking man as he implemented his plans. Addressing his colleague, he said. "I just had a… discussion you might say, with DR. Korman and have him completely under my control. His mind, and his every thought, is open to me and I learned some disturbing things. He sabotaged some of the cell clusters used in my operation and it was he, not that miserable maintenance man who destroyed our supply of biological cell clusters. There never was a kidnapping; he and an accomplice were intent on putting a stop to my operation and then he tried to kill me. I'll get back to this later but first let me put your mind at ease."

Russel appeared somewhat uneasy as he sat across from the ingeniously recreated man that he previously knew as Gordon Bradhurst. Now, as he looked at him, he saw a completely new person; a man who could do unthinkable things by just willing them to happen. He believed, as Dr, Bradhurst did, that the human mind was like a super-computer and stored just about everything it had ever learned; however, mankind had not yet evolved to where it could tap into much of that data. The human mind was still weak and without the genus of Gordon, it would take many generations before all of the hidden information stored in this phenomenal organ could be revealed. He knew that Gordon's operation had advanced his mind to an incredible level and turned him into the most intelligent human that ever lived. He both feared and awed the astonishing powers his mentor had acquired. Powers that were difficult for him to fathom. He could peruse the mind of anyone who he came in close contact with, delving deeply into their memory and baring their every secret. These horrifying thoughts were interrupted by Dr. Bradhurst's voice.

"I know what you are thinking. Try to put those fears out of your mind. Russel, I want you to stand beside me as I build my new empire. Together we will march through the future making history as it has never been made before. To do that I want to give you many of the powers I now possess."

Russel's demeanor changed immediately. The fear that had haunted him so grimly suddenly vanished and was replaced with a feeling of excitement. From the very beginning he had wanted to join Gordon in this incredible brain enhancing program and now Gordon had agreed to fulfill his dream. He was more than elated.

Knowing Russel was overawed with a fervent surge of euphoria about gaining extrasensory and intellectual powers, and how anxious he was to acquire those powers, Gordon suggested, "I would like to schedule your surgery as soon as we can replace the cell-clusters I want for you. I imagine that should only take two or three weeks."

"Right now, I have an urgent matter to address. I want to find Frank Wallace; the man Hanns was plotting against me with." It was hard for him to believe that Hanns had betrayed him after all he had done for him. Then he smiled, thinking 'I wouldn't hesitate to betray anyone. Maybe Hanns is more like me than I thought.' He knew a little about the retired Director of Fish and Wildlife because of his involvement in the cell clustering program and his visit to Drechsler to discuss research being performed there on the wolf project. But now the retired wildlife scientist was working with Hanns with intents of destroying him and his work. He would have to take care of Frank Wallace before he could cause any further threats to him.

Dr. Bradhurst placed a call to the man he had always been able to rely on. "Sid," Gordon said when he reached him on his cell phone.

Sid recognized the voice. "Glad to hear you're up and about, and hopefully fit."

"Yes." The doctor said in response to Sid's inquiry about his well-being and got right to the point. "Where are you?"

"I'm on my way to a ranch in Montana. I discovered a connection between my original target and a man named Frank Wallace. I'm heading for his ranch now."

"Good. But there was never a kidnapping! This has been a plot to kill me. You know what to do when you find him."

"Yes," was all Sid said as he ended the call.

Frank was working in the stables with his ranch manager Billy Wendt when he heard a vehicle crunching gravel as it approached the gateway leading to his homestead. From where he was in the interior of the large structure, he could look out through the open door into the yard where he saw a car came to a stop in front of the house. When a man he did not know stepped out of the car Frank's first thought was "Sid." If this stranger was Sid, or someone he sent to do his dirty-work, Frank was going to take precautions. He summoned Billy and told him to back him up in case there was trouble. Billy retrieved the rifle that was kept with him or near to him since the potential threat to his boss arose. He stayed back out of sight but in full view of the car and the man standing just outside of it. He was as ready as he could be if the man threatened his boss.

Frank stepped out into the sunlight and took a few steps to one side so as not to be between Billy and the unknown stranger. He stood with his hand resting on the handle of the revolver strapped to his hip, just in case. "Can I help you?" He called out.

Sid smiled to himself as he studied the man who must have thought he was Wyatt Earp. He was big, wearing a dirty cowboy style hat, a blue and white checked shirt, jeans and of all things, shit-kicking boots. To Sid he looked ridiculous; right out of an old Louis Lamour western, ready to have a faceoff with the six-shooter so dominantly displayed at his side. But regardless of Sid's first impression, the man looked calm and capable. If this man was his target, and he was pretty certain it was, he would take no chances with him. Even if the cowboy knew how to handle the revolver, he doubted he would be accurate at the forty-yard distance between them. Even more-so, Sid knew that few men were faster with a handgun than he was. Certainly not this rancher who most likely was not a serious shooter. At most he probably only plinked at rabbits or coyotes and had never faced off against a man. Shooting humans was something altogether different than target practice of even hunting. For most men, the thought of firing a weapon at another person was repugnant and would invariably hesitate before pulling a trigger. But not so for Sid Ramone. He was a born killer and relished the memory of every person he had ever taken down. He was also a master marksman with every type of weapon. As he eyed the man standing near the barn door, he knew that he could easily take him out with his 9 mm Glock from where he stood. Once he was sure the man was who he was after, there would be no delay, just fast action, and complete surprise. He had already scanned the barn and surrounding area and was satisfied that they were alone. But even if there were others around, he would deal with them as soon as they appeared. "Are you Frank Wallace?" He asked.

"Yes," Frank replied and before he could react the man pulled a handgun and fired two rapid shots that sent him sprawling to the ground. So proficient was the gunman that even though Frank's hand was gripping the Colt revolver, the weapon never cleared the holster. Sid's two shots were spaced no more than a second apart but by the time the second 9 mm slug left the barrel of the assassin's handgun, Billy's shot rang out from inside the barn and sent a 30-caliber bullet into the man's shoulder, ripping through his scapula and exiting this back. The tremendous impact spun the surprised assassin around but did not knock him off his feet. His instinct was to locate the shooter and take him out but in that fleeting instant a second round from the 30-30 carbine smashed into his body. This bullet passed through the man's arm just above the elbow before penetrating his body and shattering his spine. Sid Ramone was dead before his body slumped to the ground. Sid, always a careful man had made a rare mistake and that mistake cost him his life.

As Billy rushed to Frank's side, Sarah came running across the front yard. She began screaming in panic when she saw her husband lying in a pool of blood.

Hanns Korman did not exist as Hanns Korman anymore. He existed in a dreamlike trance with no control over his life. He was assigned to work with a team of five other scientists, all specialists in various fields related to brain chemistry, biochemistry, genetics, and genome science and sequencing and all in the same mesmeric trance that controlled Hanns. Equipment damaged by the fire was repaired where possible or replaced. The zombie-like men were confined to the institution where they worked sixteen hours a day, ate decent meals and slept; only to repeat this regimen seven days a week. So strong was the doctor's hold over these men that the only thoughts that passed through their minds was to satisfy his every demand.

Hanns was not only programed to work on the clustering program with more intensity than he could ever have exerted in his normal life but was also encoded to delve into several other incredibly complex areas related to the human body and brain. Invaluable input from Dr. Bradhurst who could visualize the molecular makeup of cell structures, resulted in very fast gains in all of the work being performed. The stockpile of identified gene samples grew at such a fast rate that in a short time every cell within the human complex would be identified and available for Dr. Bradhurst to use as he saw fit. Advances in every project were opening up new horizons about the brain. The explorations into gnome science and sequencing, was developing rapidly. He would soon be able to manipulate DNA, and that opened up many more possibilities. In a very short time, the genius of Dr. Gordon Bradhurst had already performed what can only be described as miracles, but in the doctor's mind, this was only the beginning.

Dr. Bradhurst's mind was like a colossal-computer, housing incredible knowledge about every topic imaginable. His genius could look far beyond the present-day achievements of the scientific world. He could not only visualize unimaginable capabilities of the mind, but also determine paths to make his wildest visions become a reality. As advanced as his mind was, he planned to take his mental capacities and capabilities a step further. In his way of thinking, his present abilities were somewhat restricted. One thing that bothered him was that he had to be quite close to anyone he wished to manipulate. Having to travel around the world to achieve his objectives was frustrating and intolerable to him. Thought passage to a person or even a group of people over unlimited distances was one of the programs being worked on. There were many obstacles still ahead before this could occur, some seemingly insurmountable, but he was certain the problems could and would be resolved. It was vital to him to be able to control the people he was planning to recruit in the empire he was forming, from one location. When this, and several other important programs being worked on were resolved, he would schedule another operation. He was convinced that his fecund and procreant mind would soon be enhanced to the point where his powers would be infinite.

The day came when the nefarious Doctor, with Hanns Korman and two assistants at his side, performed surgery on Russel Hieber. Bradhurst carefully chose the cells, and the strengths of those cells, that he imbedded in Russel's brain. His partner would have many extraordinary powers, but none anywhere near as potent as his own. Gordon would have every advantage over his partner, but Russel would have none over him. Gordon was pleased. He had created a super-human being to aid him in his quest for greatness and he would create others as his plans progressed.

You might wonder how the newly acquired powers affected Dr. Hieber! He was fascinated with the knowledge that he could kill people with nothing more than a thought and began to practice this extraordinary power shortly after his operation. He first tried it on a patient in the research center. It only took a concentration of his mind to send brain waves that ended the man's life. He took this new ability to another level the following day when he killed three people simultaneously as they stood on the sidewalk outside his apartment building in downtown Los Angeles. He was overwhelmed with the power that Gordon had given him. The ability of killing people with nothing more than a thought not only fascinated him but when he actually used this astonishing ability to end human life, an indescribable ecstasy filled his senses.

When Russel Hieber recuperated sufficiently from surgery, Gordon summoned him to his office. "I have many plans to discuss with you," he informed his visibly excited partner.

Russel was in awe of his newly acquired mental powers and could not conceal his excitement as he sat across from his mentor. "I purposely waited all this time before launching my plans. I wanted to allow your operation to take place and reap the treasures that Hanns and his team are creating. Now I am ready and the first item to address is to have sole control of cell clustering techniques. We will dissuade Drechsler and every government agency in the world to disallow any further research on this program. We will convince the scientific community that the process is unstable and uncontrollable and far too dangerous to continue working on; that it delves into too many unknown areas that would upset the balance of nature. I am also ready to develop the world organization we have discussed. You and I have the power to induce anyone I wish into doing whatever I want them to do. We will recruit many key people in various positions and disciplines throughout the world to join our core group. You and I will visit chosen disciples and convince them to come to Los Angeles where we will operate and implant certain mental enhancing cells into their brains. Only a fraction of the mental capacities that you and I have, but sufficient to carry-out my orders and use their newly gained powers as we build my worldwide confederation. It will not be long now Russel before we rule the entire world."

Doctor Bradhurst wasted no time in putting his plan to end all research on the cell clustering program into action. He called emergency board meetings with six of the many company boards that he sat on. The first being Drechsler International! The eleven board members, (all quite curious about what vital information one of their directors insisted must be addressed immediately) met at the company's headquarters in Munich. The chairman, sitting at the head of the conference room table, turned the meeting over to their newest director. Dr. Gordon Bradhurst stood to address the assemblage. In an instant he had every man in the room under his incredible mental powers. He spent the next twenty minutes giving a solid and convincing oration on the devastating results already incurred with the cell splicing program that had become known as clustering, and the countless cataclysms that would spread across the world if they did not put an end to this iniquitous and immoral research. He placed such a strong hold on each man that they held him in awe and would do everything in their power to satisfy his every wish. Each of the other emergency meetings that he had arranged concluded with the same result, every person present falling under the powers of this charismatic man. He had a purpose for recruiting these powerful people other than just ending research on the clustering project. He foresaw some of them providing additional benefits to him as he built his empire.

Dr. Gordon Bradhurst had always aspired to greatness. Power was always at the forefront of his dreams. Over the years he had developed many eminent and influential contacts throughout the world. He had purposely targeted prominent and celebrated individuals in various fields of business, government, and academia; many of whom could possibly aid him in his plans to become the most powerful man in the world. He had used his charisma and his uncanny power of persuasion to gain the confidence of many who helped to escalate his position in the field of medicine and science to his present notable high-profile position.

He took another approach to those who did not support him in reaching his goals. Almost everyone, especially those wielding power in their positions in life, harbored some shady and even clandestine acts that they would not like aired to the public. Utilizing the services of various private inquiry services, Dr. Bradhurst had uncovered explicit information related to illicit, immoral, and sexual deviations hidden deep within the closets of oh-so-many seemingly respectable and righteous members of the upper echelons. Yes, Dr. Bradhurst had made it his business to have a hold over as many people as possible and over the years that list had become quite lengthy.

On occasions throughout his career, he requested favors from some of these individuals; making the steps in the ladder he climbed to reach his present status somewhat easier and faster. A small demand here, a little bigger one there and even intimidation and extortion when needed had almost always worked for him. Yes, he certainly owed a great deal to his colleagues and associates who, if at times somewhat reluctantly, aided him in his quest for power.

A few, who failed to sway to his way of thinking, or those he thought might cause him problems along his clime to greatness had been eliminated. His first attempts to rid those he thought to be threats, was to discredit them in hopes they would abandon their positions in life and fade away. But that was a tedious and often ineffective endeavor. He soon learned that there was only one sure way to eliminate his worst enemies and that was to permanently 'eliminate' them.

He found the solution to that problem when he met Sid Ramone. Sid was the most reliable and unfailing man he had ever met. He never questioned any assignment he was given; he just accomplished it with the utmost of proficiency and tact. A true professional in his field. Because of the ease in which Sid 'solved' his problems, Gordon Bradhurst created a small network of Sid-like 'eliminators' in various countries and to date several of them had earned their money. He smiled when he thought of how easy it was to purge the world of his enemies; all it took was money. Now he had much stronger means than money to deal with those who might threaten his ambitions. With his newly acquired powers, no one would ever stand in his way. if anyone hesitated or refused to submit to his bidding; by simply concentrating his will he could remedy that situation by inflicting a fatal brain hemorrhage. Russel Hieber was now also able to assist in eliminating undesirable and in fact was anxious to use his mental abilities to destroy human lives.

The eminent scientist's narcissistic self-centered visions of grandeur channeled his quest for supremacy. His advanced fertile brain devised a plan that would open the path to fulfilling his dreams. He would amass a legion of super-human beings (or rather semi-super beings) to entrench themselves in various world disciplines. Through these disciples, he would have control over every technical, scientific, and industrial enterprise, and governmental agency in the world. Under his guidance, the world would accomplish in a year what it would take a century to achieve at the present rate of progress. Technology on every front would escalate at rates faster than anyone could imagine. All this with him at the helm.

Gaining control of governments throughout the world would be his biggest endeavor. Infiltrating key positions with programmed advocates. He would begin to implement that part of his plan very soon. The same would apply to other targeted areas. Communications as we know it would advance beyond comprehension. Every industry in the world would escalate until it was operating at levels never before achieved. He would make the world healthier and better fed than ever before in history! His newly found powers would rid the earth of many diseases and pestilences. Under his sphere of supremacy people throughout the world would never go hungry again. Wars would seize to exist. There would be no need because every human on earth would fall under his control. He would create a perfect world led by the perfect human being. One leader ruling the entire world. There would be those who would not agree with his ideals, possibly millions throughout the world. For those who could not be converted and follow his leadership, they would be eliminated. There would be no place in his new world-order for insubordinates or misfits of any kind. A new world made up of only healthy and mentally stable people. He beamed at the idea.

Gordon targeted many world-ranging individuals; people he felt would fit in with his plans. Each was in powerful positions in government and industry, and he would soon have them doing his bidding. The most powerful coalition the world had ever known was about to be amassed.

He created a second list, a list much longer than the first, a list of people in many countries throughout the world, a list of people he thought unlikely candidates to join his team of followers, people who could be replaced with more desirable candidates to join the congregation of his world-leaders. Once they were eliminated and the shockwaves of their assassinations quieted down, he would replace them with his own candidates.

It was unfortunate that Sid was dead. But he knew others, possibly not up to the standards that Sid Ramone displayed, but non-the-less capable enough for his purposes. Although a trivial matter, he did not like loose-ends or unfinished business and that's what he felt about failing to eliminate Frank Wallace. It surprised him greatly that Sid had failed to complete his assignment to kill the man who had tried to destroy him. The fact that Frank Wallace was still alive (if only barely so) did not set well with him, so he took measures to remedy the situation. If Frank Wallace recovered from the coma that held him captive, a skilled assassin would see-to-it that the Doctor's wishes were carried out.

Within two weeks of establishing his list of 'undesirables', Gordon had lined up seven professional executioners. When he was satisfied that each assassin was sufficiently brainwashed and would never, under any circumstance, reveal anything that would point back to him, he provided each with capsules that would end their lives if they were captured. They were then given their assignments and sent to various locations around the globe.

During the next several days media from around the world were in reporting frenzies as more and more prominent people met their demise. And as each day passed and other dignitaries and business leaders were added to the growing list of murders, the world began to panic. Two assassins were killed, all after boldly affronting and killing their targets. Two others were taken alive upon assassinating prominent leaders in the middle east. Unfortunately, one swallowed cyanide before he could be questioned but the other was restrained before he could do the same. Authorities were not giving information to the media about the suspect. In fact, there was no information to report because the prisoner was totally mute. Not a single word could be pried from his sealed lips. A prominent psychologist determined that the man was under a strong hypnotic influence so strong that he was unable to break through.

Blame for the unprecedented killings was being pointed in many directions but the brunt of the accusations was directed to international terrorists. Uproars from several countries were echoed throughout the world as Gordon Bradhurst watched on with satisfaction. The first phase of his plan was working splendidly. Now it was time to launch the next step in his master plan.

There were reasons why Dr. Gordon Bradhurst chose Los Angeles as headquarters for his empire-building enterprise. LAX, being a major hub with daily flights connecting to most cities worldwide would be convenient for visitors he would be assembling during the months required to set up his newly formed coalition. Being one of the world's most highly rated technical, industrial, and medical centers also fit into his plans. The city teemed with gifted and brilliant individuals in many fields. He would surround himself with exceptional people and nurture them to carry out his mandates. Yes, Los Angeles would make an ideal location for the new world headquarters he was organizing. His present business office located in one of the city's largest and most prodigious buildings would be an ideal place to conduct business.

The list of people he wanted to employ in his new alliance consisted of leaders in their field of expertise. He and Russel began their travels to personally see these individually and convince them, using their powers of persuasion to join them in California. They would also be instrumental in replacing slain dignitaries with suitable replacements. Replacements that he would eventually bring under his wing.

Four weeks of almost non-stop travel to many countries resulted in assuring the brilliant Doctor, that no less than fifty-five highly ranked individuals representing government, military, and business, would relocate to Los Angeles and join his confederation. His new regime had begun.

During his travels he had time to contemplate and envision how he could further the extent of his new powers. One concept stood out in his mind. By analyzing the breakthrough his team had made in extending longevity of life, he knew that the formula only increased life expectancy by about twenty or thirty percent before cells begin to break down and age at normal rates from that point on. He taxed his incredible mind, and his advanced mental capabilities visualized the steps that would spawn an ever-ending regeneration of cells, possibly capable of prolonging life forever. He was certain the amalgamation of all bodily cells would soon give him what he wanted. Life eternal!

He put his team to work, giving them the strengths and order of integration of the elements required to prove his hypotheses. Hanns Korman and his team worked tirelessly following Dr. Bradhurst's directions. Hanns soon completed a computation and upon studying the results on the computer monitor, he knew he had just proven without any doubts that the formula for eternal life had become a reality. Every mathematical calculation indicated that all cell structures within the human body would constantly regenerate themselves thus extending life in an ever-ending cycle.

Gordon was not surprised. He had been certain that his theory was correct and now that Hanns had proven it so, he scheduled surgery for himself. The incredibly complex operation, performed by Russel and Hanns and a team of aids, took several hours. When Dr. Bradhurst awoke from his anesthetic sleep with no apparent difficulties., he experienced what he could only describe as wonderful sensations spreading through every fiber of his body. From his fingertips to his toes, from every inch, of his outer body, to every interior organ, a sense of ambiance flowed through him. When the idyllic, almost divine experience had passed, Gordon Bradhurst, genius doctor, surgeon, financier, scholar, and businessperson, smiled. He was the most powerful man alive and would live forever.

Frank Wallace did not die the day two bullets entered his body. The fast response of an emergency medical helicopter that flew him to the hospital in Bozeman saved his life. The bullets had done a great deal of damage and once the doctors stabilized him, he was flown to The University of Colorado Hospital in Aurora. A team of specialists operated on him three times in two days. It was their combined medical and surgical skills that pulled him through. He remained in intensive care for six weeks before he gained consciousness. Sarah had never left his side and cried when he woke from his long sleep.

When Frank came out of his coma, Sarah was beside herself with joy. For the first couple of days, he was dizzy and confused but the feeling of numbness finally passed, and he became at least somewhat lucid. She told him how so many of his friends and associates had sent their blessings and wished him a speedy recovery. Frank's mind was abuzz with questions, but Sarah insisted he rest. There would be plenty of time later to answer his questions.

His doctors finally allowed the authorities to visit him. They still had no idea why he had been targeted and wanted to know everything he could tell them about Sid Ramone, the man who shot him. Even though he had regained his memory, he told them little, feigning memory loss. He wanted to find out what had happened with Hanns and Dr. Bradhurst and the goings-on at the Bradhurst Hospital before he committed himself to anything.

Frank was feeling better the day Sarah informed him how Billy had shot and killed the assailant. The biggest news since he had been out-of-the picture was the assassinations taking place in many countries around the world. Apparently, no one knew who, or what groups were behind the wanton killings. As they were discussing this and how much of the world was in a panic over it, Erick Tuttle called from Fairbanks. In answer to Erick's question Sarah said, "He's doing fine but you know how he is, trying to milk all he can from these plush surroundings, fine food and lovely nurses. But seriously, he is straining at the bit and cannot wait to get home. I know he wants to talk to you so here he is."

"You scared the hell out of us, you old fart. You're too old for all this cloak and dagger business."

Frank's voice was still a little raspy from the lung damage that one of the bullets caused. "Good to hear from you, old friend. You're right, I'm getting too old to be playing with guns. Believe it or not, I had a Colt .45 strapped to my hip but was too slow on the draw. I never even made a move for it before he pulled his gun and fired. All I remember is hearing the blast of the gun. Since then, I've had a long peaceful sleep. I am doing rather good right now though. Doctors claim I should regain sixty to seventy percent of my lung capacity but other than that I should get back to normal."

In the background Erick could hear Sarah remark loud enough for him to hear, "Normal has never been that impressive, has it, Erick?"

"I see nothing has changed." Erick laughed.

"Anyway, I hope to be going home sometime next week. But that's enough about me. I want to know what's been happening since I've been playing Rip Van Winkle."

"A great deal and I'm afraid not much is good news. No matter how many people we put out there to these monsters, we are continuing to experience attacks from both wolves and bears. Lots of people dying and not much we seem to be able to do about it. I'm worried Frank. I have this daunting feeling that this is going to get worse. I've been keeping in touch with Bryce. He's pretty down-in-the-dumps too. For all the progress they made, and the tremendous efforts they are waging against these damnable beasts, their country is still overrun with them. You should give him a call when you can. You should give Riggs a call too, he still has problems in the lower states. I know he would like to hear from you."

"I will." Frank assured him.

"The wolves keep spreading across the world Frank. I think you knew they migrated into Siberia like we feared they would. That area is so big… You know how fast they breed. It seems hopeless. There are hundreds of small groups spread across Alaska and Canada and they continue to multiply into more and more animals. A never-ending propagation that we have to contend with. It seems our only hope is in the biological breakdown in their organisms that you discovered. But at best, that's long term and iffy. We have been keeping in touch with Dr. Linser. The percentage of defects they are finding in wolves continue to increase but unfortunately very slowly. No such luck with bears. They are healthy with no signs of weakness what-so-ever that we can find. The damn monsters are slaughtering dozens of people and all we seem to be able to do is show-up-after-the-fact. We send out hundreds of hunters and chase them from here to hell and back. As big as they are you would think we could find them easily but like our wolf hunts, it's hit and miss and more times than not it's miss."

Frank was not yet up to his full mental capacity and listening to Erick spreading gloom and doom put his mind in a muddle. The disastrous situation with wolves had not improved as he had hoped and the horror of it shook him greatly. And the escalating dilemma with bears added to his grief.

"We've had more than thirty bear attacks in Alaska and several in Canada since you last heard." Erick continued. "The latest monster was wounded after it killed several people. We were lucky to track it down and kill it. It traveled nearly fifty miles with several thirty caliber holes in it before the dogs caught up with it. Lost most of the dogs but fortunately no one was injured in that hunt. We send out teams of hunters to every reported attack and sighting, but like I said, the country is so vast that our results are disappointing. Our hunters have caught-up with about twenty animals but have only killed fourteen to-date. That might not sound too bad but in that time, we lost more than thirty hunters and the evil bastards have killed God knows how many other people. We found another very disturbing thing that I am sure will upset you even more. Two of the bears we killed are what we're calling hybrids of a hybrid."

Frank cut in on that statement. "What is a hybrid of a hybrid?"

"They're crossbreeds. We only have two samples so far, a female and a young male that were brought in not long ago, but we are certain mutant boars are mating with regular grizzlies. DNA prove these two bears are a mixture of both mutant bear and regular old-fashioned grizzly. Bad news when you think that if this is a normal process, there are more big bruins than we thought there might be and many more to come. We have determined that this new strain of bear's growth potential is somewhat less than that of a full-blooded mutant. So now we might have bears running small, medium, and large. Regular grizzlies, hybrid/hybrids, and mutant monsters! I guess to sum it up - just like with our wolves - we are faced with bears that are likely to haunt us for some time and more likely forever. Finn's best estimate is that there could be a few hundred of these demons running rampart through Alaska and some of the Canadian Provinces. It's a nightmare Frank."

Erick heard a disheartening groan before Frank said in somewhat of a distraught voice. "I cannot even tell you how I feel. We can only hope that the defects we found in wolves will eventually prove to be their downfall; but I doubt it. I can only repeat what I said once before, God help us."

"Amen to that Frank. God help us. You've heard about Drechsler I suppose?" Erick asked.

"No. What do you mean?" Frank asked inquisitively.

Erick paused before he answered. "You haven't heard?"

"Haven't heard what? I've only been conscious for a short time and Sarah's been keeping me in the dark on just about everything. She has apparently been trying to keep me calm by shielding me from the realities of the crazy messes going on in the world. You are the first person I've talked to."

"I'm sorry Frank, I should have known. The decision has been made to cancel all research on Zoltan's project. The government and regulatory agencies have agreed that the project is too unpredictable, uncontrollable, and too dangerous to continue with. You have always said that the program should never have been allowed to continue, even before the problems with mutant wolves. You were right and now others agree with you. Religious factions throughout the world are condemning the work as blasphemous and sullying God's creations. How right they seem to be. How this uprising against the program started is hard to say but it seemed to have happened almost overnight. People want to stop us playing with and trying to change the laws of nature. Drechsler is ending all work in this area, and I have been informed that no further research will be done here in Fairbanks other than related to our Big Bad Wolf and Bear problems. Drechsler will only be able to examine affected animals and use that data to aid us in finding ways to eliminate them, but that's it."

Frank was surprised that a hold had been placed on Zoltan's discovery. He had always been both awed by the potential good this new science could offer the world but at the same time a deep inner fear of the harm it might cause, terrified him. His fears became a reality when mutant wolves spread havoc throughout much of the northern hemisphere and now the emergence of malformed gigantic bears strengthened his trepidations. Then along comes Dr. Bradhurst with threats to the world that make wolves and bears seem trivial. The Doctor might try to create a super race of humans so evil hat he could not even think about it. A deep feeling of foreboding fell over him as he realized what a terrible mistake he had made when he learned about Dr. Bradhurst's involvement with super-cells and his sinister use of them. He took too much on himself; thinking he could get enough information against the mad Doctor to expose him. How wrong he had been. He had under-estimated Gordon Bradhurst and it had almost caused his death.

As Frank's mind ran rampart with questions, a fear spread through him. What had happened to Dr. Bradhurst? Was he alive? If so, how far had he advanced in his self-centered ambitions of turning himself into some kind of a super-human being? Learning that all work related to Zoltan's gene-splicing program had been halted pleased him. At last part of his dream of putting an end to the madness that was growing around this damnable genetic cell splicing procedure may finally be coming a reality. However, he knew that it did not apply to Bradhurst who would continue with his work at his isolated laboratory. And what had become of Hanns?

He and Erick's discussion lasted for some time. Both men were deeply concerned about the fear and trepidation caused by mutant, man-made monsters that they had both taken part in creating. "I'll give Drechsler a call," Frank said in parting.

Carlene Linser was glad to hear Frank's voice and learn that he was on-the-road to recovery. The first thing that Frank said to her was, "What about Hanns?"

"I don't know. I haven't heard a thing since I last talked with you. I was hoping you knew."

"No, but I'll try to find out. Erick Tuttle informed me that the supper-cell program has been put on hold. Can you fill me in on what's happening?"

"Somebody put the kibosh on any further work related to any and all aspects of the program. Millions of past research dollars came to a halt just like that, and no one seems to know why. I don't understand any of it because we were making such great strides in many areas. Our only involvement now is research on your wolf and bear program."

"Yes, I've been talking to Erick Tuttle about that. Can you fill me in on your latest progress?"

When he ended his conversation with Carlene, he called Damon Courier. After Damon related his concerns and best wishes for a full recovery, Frank learned that Dr. Bradhurst had survived but there was no word about Hanns Korman. All previous information that the L.A. private detectives were able to get had dried up. They couldn't get any word as to what was happening at the institution.

Twenty
Awakening

Early Wednesday afternoon, two days after Frank's conversation with Erick Tuttle, he and Sarah sat in his hospital room talking about going home. Frank had had enough of hospital life. His confinement to a bed in a sterile hospital room was making him restless. He craved the solitude and open space of his ranch. Sarah had moved the large soft chair close to his bed as she did most mornings so she could face him as they discussed his release that was tentatively scheduled for the following Friday. They were both excited and even a little giddy about leaving the hospital and returning home where he desperately wanted to start living his life again. Early winter had arrived since his close encounter with death, and he could visualize windblown snow streaked across the landscape, and the cold stinging his face as he tended the cattle and horses. Even the bleak backdrop of winter blurring the otherwise beautiful rolling hills surrounding his land stimulated his senses. Frank was overjoyed at the thought of going home to the ranch that he loved.

The private hospital room had two beds, one that Sarah had slept in during her husband's long stay. There were two visitor's chairs, one being a large plush recliner that she spent so much of her time in. A small stand sat against the wall at the foot of the bed next to the bathroom door where a vase of flowers (always refreshed with new blooms even in the dead of winter) filled the room with fragrance: a typical hospital room. Fortunately, a window looked over the hills to the west displaying a vista of western splendor.

Frank had called Bryce Mann and John Riggs who expressed their elation that he was awake and coherent and wished him a fast recovery. Despite Frank's urgings, neither shared their dire concerns about the mutant horrors that continued to plague the world. Regardless of his urgings to know everything going on, they thought there was no need in disturbing him with bad news until he had recovered from the ordeal he had suffered.

A woman came out of the nurse's locker room dressed in nurse's attire with appropriate shoes. She drew no attention to herself, acting as though she belonged, as though she had done it a thousand times before. She stopped at the desk to look at the roster, then casually strolled down the corridor heading for room 134. Just another nurse performing her daily duties.

Sarah excused herself, squeezed out of the chair and went into the bathroom. Upon drying her hands, she opened the door to see a nurse approaching Frank's bed; a nurse she had not seen before. But that was not unusual, hospital attendants had come and gone as they rotated throughout their stay. The woman couldn't approach close to the bed and the man lying there because of the chair between them, so she moved to the foot of the bed to give her an open view of the patient. She had no idea that Sarah stepped from behind the door and stood directly behind her. Before Sarah could say anything, the nurse reached under her apron and displayed a very small snub-nose handgun with a silencer attached to the end of the barrel. Sarah's yell and fast reactions surely saved her husband's life. In the second before the shooter raised the gun to fire, she was startled by a loud scream directly behind her and in that startled instant, Sarah grabbed the glass vase adorned with a beautiful bouquet of flowers and swung it with all the power she had in her. The blow missed the woman's head, glanced off her shoulder and hit the right arm that held the gun. The solid cracking blow shattered the assailant's forearm bones just above the wrist. Frank frantically pushed the emergency button as he struggled to free himself from the blankets, yelling as loud as he could for help. The assassin, screaming in pain from her shattered arm had fallen to her knees, but being the professional that she was, regardless of the severe pain she was suffering or the inevitable outcome that she knew would be her fate, she reached for the gun that lay only inches from her with her left hand. As her fingers touched the weapon, a second blow slammed into her head with a sickening sound. The woman's body sprawled flat, twitched for a moment, and then lay still. When orderlies and nurses rushed into the room, Frank was on his feet with his arms wrapped around his wife who was trembling with the glass vase still grasped in her hand. On the floor lay the woman with flowers and water spread around her.

Police arrived, the unconscious body removed to an operating room and cleaners picked up the flowers, wiped up the water that spilled from the vase and removed the blood that had pooled beneath the body.

If the police had been curious and probing for reasons why Frank Wallace had been targeted and shot by Sid Ramone, now that a second attempt had been made on his life, they were doubly concerned. Frank spent a grueling hour being grilled by detectives.

When the meeting ended, Detective Jim Nathan presented Frank with a two-page typed statement. "I think this pretty much covers the highlights of your statement. Please read it carefully and make any corrections or additions before you sign it."

In the report, Frank informed them that Dr. Gordon Bradhurst of Los Angeles, California must surely be behind these attempts on his life. The doctor was suspected of stealing vital biological samples from Drechsler International in Los Angeles and Frank surmised that he was trying to eliminate him as a threat. His failure to relate this information earlier was because, even though he suspected the doctor, he had no proof what-so-ever to substantiate his beliefs. Frank and detective Nathan went over Frank's assertions again, and before the detective left, he assigned a guard to be stationed outside his room. He also stated that because Dr. Bradhurst was from another state he was going to notify the FBI.

The following day Frank repeated everything he had told the local detectives to two FBI agents from the Denver office. He also added a great deal more than he reported to the local detectives. It was time to tell all he knew and hope that the FBI could somehow put an end to Dr. Bradhurst's mad plans, whatever they might entail. He left nothing out and at the end of more than two hours of briefing, when the two agents were preparing to leave, he said, "Almost everything I have told you is hearsay and I have little proof to substantiate any of it, but I am certain that Dr. Bradhurst is a major threat and must be stopped." When the agents left, with promises to follow-up on Frank's assertions, Frank realized how absurd the wild story he had told them must sound. 'They must think I'm a raving lunatic...'

Having an armed guard looking after them eased some of the fear that Frank and Sarah experienced, but still, they realized there was ways to get to anyone if someone was determined enough. Other than having the blinds drawn to prevent snipers from shooting through the window, all they could do was wait to hear from the FBI.

On Friday, Frank received a most unusual call. It was from Justin Simms, Secretary of the Interior. "I have just heard that the FBI is investigating another attempt on your life. I can only thank God that the attempt failed. I understand that your wife was a heroine. My blessing to her. Now, please fill me in on what the hell is going on." Frank did with as many details that he could.

When the FBI agents showed up Monday afternoon, Frank expected more of the same from them, but he was wrong. Agents Tom Grogan and Melisa Goodling met with the recovering gun-shot patient and his wife in a small meeting room across from the nurse's station.

The male half of the two-agent team began. "I would like to relay a communication we received from our Washington, DC office. We had no idea who you were when we met with you last week. Suffice to say we now do. Your credibility rolls down from the highest levels. The Director of the Federal Bureau of Investigation has been informed by the Secretary of the Interior that you're concerns about Dr. Bradhurst should, and must, be taken very seriously. And we intend to do just that."

Melisa Goodling opened a laptop, brought up a file and placed the computer between her and her partner. "When you first told us this story, and let's face it, it is a pretty far-out story, we found it difficult to accept. It's hard to fathom such a thing; someone capable of escalating their mental abilities to levels you are suggesting. Mass hypnosis, mind-reading beyond believability? Total control and dominance of anyone who gets near him? Scary stuff. But in lieu of another issue that has surfaced…" She paused and looked at her partner.

He continued where she left off. "When we reported your suspicions about Dr. Bradhurst being behind the attempts on your life to our superiors, it became a very serious matter to them. We learned that our people have the Doctor in their crosshairs so-to-speak on another issue that might fit in with your accusations against him. We are not at liberty to discuss this with you but want you to be rest-assured that everything possible will be done to protect you until the situation is resolved. We have not been able to find any connection between Sid Ramone and Gordon Bradhurst. If there is, they have been very careful to hide it. We have people digging deeper into that. The same applies to Eva Franks, the woman who tried to kill you. We haven't learned much about her yet other than she's from the United Kingdom. We will be questioning her when we finish here. We understand, that other than a bad headache and a cast on her arm, she will be fine. Sid Ramone on the other hand we do know a great deal about. He and his son have been operating a private detective agency out of L.A. for several years. Since his death we have investigated their business quite closely. Even though most of their dealings were legitimate, our team found many cases that were illegitimate. We have built up a sizable case against their agency. Ramone's son was arrested and will likely spend much of the rest of his life behind bars. As I said, we will continue with our efforts to look for a connection between them and Dr. Bradhurst."

Frank wondered about the issue they referred to but were unwilling to discuss. Could it have anything to do with the mass killings of prominent people around the world? He wondered… "I believe Hanns Korman, is your best lead in obtaining the information you require. You must try to locate him…that is if he's still alive. I told you that people who threaten Gordon Bradhurst have a way of disappearing or dying. I hate to sound like a broken record, but I feel certain Bradhurst has implanted very strong genetic sells into his own brain and very likely possesses mental powers beyond our comprehensions. I believed Hanns Korman when he said we are dealing with someone who can read minds and strongly influence anyone he gets near. How strong those abilities are I don't know, but if they are as strong, or even stronger, than what Hanns claims Michael Danvers possessed, we are looking at incredible powers of persuasion and mind manipulation. You cannot take these possibilities lightly."

Tom Grogan hesitated before he made the next statement. "I'm sorry Frank, but at this time all I can say is that the FBI is investigating Dr. Bradhurst, and we are indeed taking this seriously."

Realizing that was all the agents were going to say, he tried once more to distill in them the dangers involved when dealing with the Doctor. "If you haven't already, please pass on what I said; Hanns Korman was insistent that anyone who got near Michael Danvers was instantly under his control. He claimed that Dr. Bradhurst, Dr. Hieber and he himself were all put under Danvers' powers at the same time, and he had total control over them. How many people might Dr. Bradhurst influence? Possibly large groups! How many has he already under his wing?"

"Yes, that has been related to our superiors. And, yes, we will heed your concerns. If biological samples have been stolen from Drechsler we will find out about that also. I suggest you put all this out of your mind and recuperate from your injuries. Just leave it to us Mr. Wallace, we have people who can deal with Dr. Bradhurst, no matter what he's up to."

Frank wondered if anyone could 'deal with' Gordon Bradhurst. He brought up another issue that was worrying him. "Sarah and I have been discussing our safety." Tom Grogan broke in on him. "We will safeguard you in every way possible. You will have twenty-four-hour protection as-long-as you are here, and we will have your home guarded. Our aim is to keep you safe, and I assure you we will."

Ten o'clock Friday morning Frank Wallace was released from the hospital. He and Sarah were escorted from Denver to their ranch in Montana by two FBI agents who would be guarding them. The Bureau thought that two official vehicles with large FBI letters boldly displayed on the sides would keep anyone from approaching the ranch. Two vehicles would also suggest that several guards might be employed, further discouraging un-wanted visitors.

Two mornings later Elmer and Jody Horton arrived at the Wallace's home for breakfast. Frank enjoyed the first home breakfast he had in weeks and as they ate, he told his friends the horror stories about Dr. Bradhurst, the FBI's involvement and his suspicions that the Doctor was behind the attempts made to kill him. They had just finished eating when he received a call from Carlene. She was excited. "The FBI has been here for two days with hackers. I learned they were acting on information you gave them. They found out how Michael Danvers changed the computer programs when the samples were taken. Hundreds of samples were removed. Now they're looking for Hanns. They talked to me and CC already. We told them that we thought a sample or two may be missing but had no proof of it, only my strong belief that it happened. CC doesn't think we will be in trouble. I hope he's right." Frank knew the trail from Drechsler would lead to Dr. Bradhurst and was worried when he thought what might happen when the Doctor was confronted. He might kill every person who came near him. He thanked Carlene for letting him know and called Damon Courier. When he was on the line Frank apologized to the private inquiry investigator. "I'm sorry I was so brief and abrupt the other day. I was involved with several issues and had to cut our conversation short. It seems like all Hell has broken loose while I was hospitalized. The FBI is involved with Dr. Bradhurst for reasons other than my concerns; but I don't know why. I'm worried about Hanns Korman. Have you learned anything about him?"

"Nothing. No one knows where he is, but we will keep looking. The FBI knows about my connection with you and that I, and my colleague in L.A. have investigated Dr. Bradhurst and his hospital. We've been told to step aside. The FBI will not indulge any information to me. They stand to those old adages, 'loose lips sink ships' and 'need to know'. But you know how it is Frank, if you're in the circle so-to-speak, and I am to some degree, you hear things that slip through the cracks. It's strongly suspected that Dr. Bradhurst is connected to the assassinations taking place here and abroad and the mysterious deaths of many people dying of brain hemorrhages. He's been under tight surveillance for the past couple of weeks. It seems he has taken numerous trips and many of them coincide with these deaths. It seems he's hired many high-ranking people to work in his Los Angeles office. People in government, industry, commerce, military, and the scientific community. I've heard they have interviewed several prominent people that the Doctor has visited and think they may be under some kind of hypnotic trance. They have enough evidence against him to justify warrants to search his business office and his hospital. I don't know when the raids will take place, but I suspect quite soon."

Everything Damon had told him made sense. Gordon Bradhurst must have indeed elevated his powers to incredible levels. So much so that he could command mass murder against people anywhere in the world. Frank also feared he was brainwashing people on a large scale. Was he creating an army of people in prominent positions to aide him in what? Domination of the world? People under his powers and uncapable of self-control; destined to follow his commands? Frank was sure the Doctor was doing just that, and it terrified him.

It had started to snow during the night and was still coming down at eleven o'clock the following morning when the phone rang. It was Elmer Horton. Before Sarah cold say hello, he said. "Put on the news.

Some disaster has occurred at the Bradhurst Hospital and it's all over the news." Sarah handed the phone to her husband who followed her to the Den where she turned on the Television.

Breaking news flooded the airways. An explosion in San Bernardino, California destroyed a hospital, and it was suspected that more than two dozen people had perished in the disaster. Among the dead was the world-famous brain surgeon Dr. Gordon Bradhurst. Frank had a sudden start. He heard little of what the anchors from the networks were saying. Gordon Bradhurst dead! Hanns, what about Hanns? Two dozen dead and many injured! What could have happened? His mind cleared and he paid more attention to the news that showed the devastating fire that was consuming the large facility. The first cameras on the scene caught confusion and bedlam as terrified people fled the inferno. Patients on-foot, in wheelchairs and being carried on stretchers were being evacuated as the cameras caught the chaotic scenes.

As the day progressed, the news channels continued to cover the catastrophe with updates. As yet the cause of the explosion was unknown. Latest casualties had been listed at eleven, somewhat lower than the two dozen that was first reported. More than twenty injured, most not serious! A list of those known dead was being held until identifications could be confirmed and next of kin notified, but it was officially stated that Dr. Bradhurst and his immediate staff were in the building at the time of the explosion.

One week prior to the explosion:
Rebeca Hamilton hoped the friendly relationship she had developed with Hanns Korman would grow into something more than just friendship. Seeing the shyness in Hanns in anything related to any possible romance between them she realized that if something did develop it would have to be up to her to set things in motion. She had hoped to do so some time ago but so much had happened recently that she didn't have the chance. And now she was appalled at what Dr. Bradhurst had done to him. She had never liked the doctor because of his unethical and immoral treatment of patients. True, she was not a saint and had stepped beyond the line of righteousness from time to time but had never wished anyone ill-will or actually harmed anyone. Her sole purpose for any indignities she may have

caused others was solely for her personal gains and those slight injustices had paid off with advancements in her career. Now that she was aging, she became more amenable and looked at life in a more humanitarian way. Fortunately, Dr. Bradhurst took no interest in the hospital that she ran. He, and even Dr. Hieber, who she reported to, were only interested in the research department, and left the hospital operations to her. She made certain that no problem, no matter how serious it might be, ever reached out to the level of authority above hers. She found ways to deal with any and all issues related to what she considered her hospital and vowed that she always would. She successfully hid her anger and distress related to the unethical and heartless research that took place there. She knew a good deal more about the goings-on at the institution than anyone realized. A hospital and a segregated research center under one roof did not induce keeping secretes regardless of the tight grip that Dr. Bradhurst tried to maintain on security. Her position led her to know many things that transpired in Dr. Bradhurst's private 'chamber of horrors'. Even though there was a tight line drawn between the hospital and the research center that employed its own staff of personnel, selected doctors, nurses, and hospital support personnel who reported to her had interactions with the research center from time to time and information leaked back to her. People talked and because of her close relationship with her employees, word got back to her on just about everything going on 'up-stairs'. She made it her business to know everything.

Even though she knew little about the science of gene splicing, she knew about experiments taking place with patients and some of the incredible results achieved from numerous operations being performed. And as Hanns was so concerned about, she knew of deaths occurring resulting from these operations. She also knew that Michael Danvers, the mysterious patient on the third floor, was turned into a madman with uncanny abilities to overpower people who he came in contact with. And she had heard about his death and his cremation. She knew that Dr. Bradhurst used this brain changing procedure on himself and how it almost killed him. But he pulled through and was now using newly gained powers to his advantage. Now Dr. Hieber's brain was also heightened to greater levels with these gene cells. Two evil doctors with uncanny powers.

Dr. Bradhurst was turning some of his staff into zombie-like robots and one of them was Hanns and this infuriated her. So far, she had kept far enough away from the two doctors to hopefully prevent either from probing her mind as she was sure they could. She wondered how much longer she could remain out of their reach; it scared her to even think about it. She had no idea how, but she would try to free Hanns of the spell that Dr. Bradhurst held over him and together they would get away.

The two doctors had been away from the institute quite often lately and when she learned they would be traveling to several locations around the world for a couple of weeks, she decided to act. She contacted Hanns by phone and asked him to join her for lunch like they did so many times in the past. But he declined stating that he was too busy to leave his work. Even persisting as strongly as she could, he refused to leave his work. This made her mad. If he wouldn't come to her, she would go to him. She headed for the research center. Hanns was working in the computer center on one of the most sophisticated hi-tec computers in the world. There were three other scientists in the lab with him; all so intense with their work, they didn't see Rebeca enter the room. Hanns was evaluating genome data resulting from brain cell manipulations he and his team were experimenting on when Rebeca strode up to him, firmly grasped his arm, spun him around and said in suck a strong and demanding voice that it caused all in the room to take notice, "Hanns. You are taking a lunch break right now," and forcefully pulled him away from the computer. He resisted but to no avail, Rebeca was determined, and nothing was going to prevent her from getting him out of there. Seeing it was hopeless to resist the incredibly strong woman, he reluctantly consented and was escorted out and marched through several corridors and into the cafeteria.

It was obvious that her lunch companion was very uneasy and did not want to be there with her. He was not the Hanns Korman she knew; he was a man separated from his own psyche; a man disillusioned in a trance imbedded so deep in his subconscious it prevented him from even realizing who he was. When he said he must get back to work, she stopped him from getting up. "Tell me what you are working on?"

He thought for a moment. No, he could tell no one about his work. He didn't know why but he just couldn't and told her so.

"Wait," Rebeca said in her authoritative voice as she firmly grasped his hand. "I am acting for Dr. Bradhurst. He has instructed me to oversee the projects you're working on. You must tell me now."

"No, I can't do that…"

"Stop," She demanded. "He insists that you do as I say. Do you understand?"

Hanns' expression was that of total confusion. His brain was programed to work on the projects Dr. Bradhurst had assigned him to and tell no one about them. He was unable to get that out of his head.

"Listen to me Hanns. You know I am your friend and would never lie to you. You must obey me! You will be coming home with me. We will be leaving right away. Is that clear?"

The befuddled Hanns Korman resisted, stressing the need to return to his work but was forcibly led by the stern and persuasive woman out of the building to her car in the parking lot. Thirty-five minutes later they arrived at her home. Try as she might she failed in her efforts to break him out of the influence that Dr. Bradhurst held on her friend. He continued to insist that he must return to his work. If persuasion failed to work, she would have to try something else. Shock? pain? or both? She went to the kitchen and returned with a fork and stabbed the back of Hanns' hand with enough force that blood spurted from the wound. He leaped back and screamed. "What are you doing?"

"I'm trying to bring some sense into your scrambled head. I've got to get rid of the hold Dr. Bradhurst has on you and wake you up from this terrible nightmare. I've got to save your life Hanns."

Hanns knew something was different, something was wrong. He struggled to think straight but the nagging thought in his brain to return to work persisted. However, Rebeca detected the change in him and decided to try once again to shock him out of his torpor. After bandaging the wound in his hand that bled profusely, she returned to the kitchen. She took the knife sharpening steel from the rack, turned on the burner and heated the long thin metal rod. This time, the pain was so severe that he burst from his chair screaming in agony. The hot iron burned into his forearm leaving a blistering welt. If ever she was going to rid her friend of the incredible hold that Dr. Bradhurst held over him, it had to be now. The longer she pleaded with him to listen to her; the more he became aware of what had happened to him.

It took some time for the spell that Gordon Bradhurst had on him to wear off but when it did and he finally came to his full senses, they discussed everything they knew about Dr. Bradhurst and his sinister plot to dominate everyone he came in contact with. Before his falling out with the doctor, Hanns had been close enough to him to know at least some of his mad plans. The narcissistic megalomaniac madman had delusions of using his new powers to propel him in position of becoming a world leader.

Hanns had been in a bubble and knew nothing of what was transpiring in the world outside his small sphere of research at the Bradhurst Institute and was surprised when Rebeca told him about Drechsler ending all work on the clustering program. She related to him how the doctor and Russel Hieber had been spending a great deal of time visiting Senators and businesses in California and Washington D.C. and several other states, as well as influential people in other countries.

"Look at me!" Hanns said as he held out his arm. "Covered with wounds. I'm lucky the burn worked. No telling what you would have done to me if it hadn't". Rebeca got up and hugged him. "I'm sorry but I didn't know what else to do. I prayed that pain would work and thank God it did." Hanns smiled but then his features became serious. "I can envisage Dr. Bradhurst brain-washing people in high places so he can use them in his quest for dominance in the world. It terrorizes me to think of him becoming the world's tyrannical leader.

In a serious tone he said. "This is all my fault Rebeca. I don't know what I can do but I have to try to stop him."

Rebeca couldn't say that he wasn't to blame, at least to some degree. "Not the time to point blame," she said. "I agree, we have to do something, and we must do it right away. When he returns, he will know his spell on you is no longer in place and will either put you in another trance or possibly even kill you. And he'll find out about me as well. I think we should run far enough away that he will never find us."

"No, he'll find us if he wants to. I'm going to face this myself. I don't want you involved."

At that moment, Hanns learned that Rebeca Hamilton was not a woman to argue with. "Don't even go there." She said in a voice so commanding that Hanns was set back. "I'm here with you because I want to be and that is the end of the conversation. I mean it Hanns. Do you understand?"

Before Hanns could respond she continued. "You're probably right. Running with him on our trail wouldn't work. Even if it did, we would be looking over our shoulders forever. We'll just have to put an end to him."

"I have an idea." He paused for a few moments before continuing. "I'm almost certain that he had someone kill my wife by blowing up our house. Maybe I can find someone to blow up the lab when he's in there. I don't know if I can find someone to do it or how much it would cost but I have two million dollars."

"Mm," Rebeca mused. "I might be able to find someone to help us."

Epilog
One Year Later

Rebeca's long-stemmed glass of red wine twinkled in the candlelight and Ice clinked in the glass of rum and coke the waiter placed on the table in front of Hanns. A warm evening breeze drifted from the darkening blue ocean as the sun began to set on the Caribbean Island of Martinique; a perfect setting for the two middle aged lovebirds. They felt safe with their new identities. How easy it was to become someone else; it only took money and they had plenty of that. Hanns still had a great deal left from his savings and the money Gordon Bradhurst had given him, and Rebeca had accumulated close to half a million during her life. They owned a quaint island-style cottage on the coast and neither of them had ever been happier in their lives.

Rebeca had found the person they were looking for. Hanns thought the cost of a quarter million dollars to get the job done was outrageous, but now, as he looked back, it had been worth it because they were rid of a tyrant. Rebeca had hand carried two small valise-size cases into the hospital and placed them in closets next to Dr, Bradhurst's and Dr. Hieber's offices. It could not have been easier or worked better. As soon as the Doctor and Russel Hieber returned and entered their offices, she called Hanns who pushed a button on a remote hand-held device and their nightmare was over.

Hanns nor Rebeca had no way of knowing that two men accompanied Dr. Bradhurst and Dr. Hieber to the institution that infamous morning. One a United Nations dignitary, the other a high-ranking officer from the Pentagon. The first of many scheduled for brain surgery. They assumed that only a few doctors and zombie-like followers would be in the laboratory and hopefully out of the impact area when the detonator was activated. It was unfortunate that others were killed and injured but getting rid of Dr. Death and his partner would never have happened if they were not sacrificed. Other than the two dignitaries who had arrived with the doctors, Hanns was not overly distressed by the deaths of those who were part of Dr. Bradhurst's inner circle; unprincipled and immoral people who had taken part in unscrupulous operations performed in the West Wing. The explosives were much stronger than intended resulting in an enormous explosion that blew the laboratory and surrounding rooms to kingdom come. It rocked the entire hospital complex and created a fire that quickly spread through the large facility. Rebeca organized a successful evacuation that resulted in only a few patients and assistants incurring slight injuries. The only casualties and serious injuries were from the research center. When all were safely out of harms' way, Rebeca and Hanns watched the Bradhurst Hospital burn to the ground destroying every genetic cell cluster with it, ending a mad scientist's nightmarish dreams.

Hanns had a contented look on his face as he sipped the after-dinner rum with the love of his life smiling at him. He had helped create a monster, and in part had become one himself, but in the end, he had slayed the dragon and now all was well. Looking at the beautiful woman across the table he asked. "What would you say to us taking a world tour? There are so many places I would like to see."

She reached out and touched his hand and answered with a tantalizing smile. "That would be wonderful."

Frank Wallace recovered better than could be expected from his near-death experience. As his wife said, 'It would take more than a couple of bullets to put an ornery old bull like him down.' He ended all involvements with both the Canadian and U.S. taskforces. Whatever happened in the future would have to fall into the hands of others. He would spend the rest of his time on this earth living the quiet life of a rancher. The documentary series that he and his team filmed was well received by the viewing public and considered a success by the National Geographic Society. He was sitting a horse again but would never be the rider he once was. He and Elmer Horton added fifty more cattle to his heard and calving had gone well. His herd consisted of almost three hundred animals, the maximum his ranch could maintain. Life on the ranch was good, but he would never rid himself of the nagging blame that hung over him. He would forever be tormented by the fact that he, at least in-part, was responsible for the terror and devastation the wolves and bears continued to spread throughout the northern hemisphere. He had tried to convince the Secretary of the Interior to hold off on Zoltan Proziver's discovery, but Will Hogan over-ruled him, and the results were devastating. If only he had stood stronger and somehow convinced the Secretary to take more cautions. If he had, the horrors the world was now faced with may have been averted. His one solace was that Zoltan Proziver's scientific breakthrough in genetic engineering had been put on hold. Albeit in his thinking it would only be a temporary reprieve because he was certain it would only be a matter of time before the program reopened. The benefits to the health and well-being of mankind were enormous and could not be ignored for long. He could visualize stronger regulations put in place to control the processes involved but there were always ways of getting around the tightest of security systems. Gordon Bradhurst had proven that. He feared someone like Dr. Bradhurst would eventually gain access to the process again and cause more chaos in the world.

As Frank mused about his concerns, he didn't realize that his fears were already becoming a reality. The government was discussing the feasibility of re-opening the program. Several high-level meetings had already been held and it seemed likely that an agreement was imminent. Over the past several years many scientists and research specialists had been involved with the science of clustering and a number of them had the knowledge and ability to duplicate the gene-splicing process. Unbeknownst to the world, a couple of small ignoble companies were already in the early stages of perfecting the process. Would there be more unauthorized enterprises to follow? Certainly! On the positive side, it would only be a matter of time before this new science would provide significant benefits to mankind. But if this new science could not be controlled, incredibly bad detriments to the human race might plague the earth. Only God knows how man's interference with the laws of nature will affect the future of the world.

Frank received a hand-written letter, post-marked, 'Paris, France'. It read: *"Dr. Wallace. Thank you for saving my life. As you must have guessed, I finished the job you and I planned. The monster no-longer exists. Changed my name and enjoying a tour through Europe. God be with you. HK.*

Frank smiled as he said. "Hanns…."